HIDE LITTLE WOLF

Annette van Geloof

Title: Hide Little Wolf
Author: Annette van Geloof
Copyright © 2024 Butterdragons® Publishing
All Rights Reserved

Published by Butterdragons® Publishing
https://butterdragons.com

ISBN: 9789493287549 (ebook)
ISBN: 9789493287556 (paperback)
ISBN: 9789493287563 (audio book)

Cover Design by: Dazed Designs

Audio book narrated by Martha Webb

To my grandmother in heaven

Thank you for the love of stories you passed on

He sees a maiden in distress
She sees an obstacle in her path
Yet, their friendship is inevitable
But not everything is as it seems

Their differences divide them
Their secrets keep them apart
But their shared troubles bring them closer
Will it be enough?

As evil emerges
And the peace is at stake
They must come together
And put their differences aside

by Helle Gade

Chapter One

I had my arms wide open and enjoyed the cold wind touching my warm, naked skin. The dawning sun was giving the forest a special glow and I still couldn't believe that the rest of my family preferred staying at home over being here, over being outside, over being free.

For everyone else in town, these woods would be dangerous. Especially right before the nightfall, when human eyes couldn't see much. Everyone knew about the wolves, howling to the moon even if the moon wasn't visible. Everyone knew about the highwaymen waiting for their next victim, even if that victim had less than a penny to spend.

I wasn't afraid of the wolves. I wasn't afraid of the highwaymen. I wasn't afraid of anything but that one sentence my father had whispered in my ear before he died.

"No one can find out that you're a wolf, too!" He tightened his grip around my wrist while he said it. He stared at me with wide open eyes, even though he could barely see anything anymore. "They need to believe I was the only one."

He had closed his eyes and within a second, his heart had stopped beating and his lungs had stopped breathing.

I had begged my mother to ask for an autopsy, but she had told me that we didn't have the money to pay for one, let alone an honest one.

Since the day my father died, my family mostly locked themselves within the four walls of our small cottage. They were afraid to be seen by prying and fearing eyes. They were afraid to suffer the same fate as my father had suffered.

They only left the house for work, and only let their wolves out when they really couldn't fight them any longer. We even discarded my father's last name and started using my mother's instead.

I've tried to be like them. I've tried to deny myself the pleasure of running as fast as the wind. I've tried to deny myself the wonder of the elements not being able to harm me. I've tried to fight the urge to use my sharp eyes to see things my human sight would never discover. And I failed hopelessly.

My family has tried to stop me and lock me in. They've tried to keep me from giving in to all those longings that consumed my brain, heart, body, and soul. And they failed as hopelessly as I had.

No four walls could ever contain me. No stones could ever lock me in. No cottage could ever be the place where I felt safe. Only the forest could ever be my home.

I felt safe when I was surrounded by trees and animals. I felt safe when I was freed from the clothes that irritated me every second of the day. I felt safe when there was nothing but air surrounding me.

"Whoever reaches the castle last needs to help Cookie with dinner!"

I looked up and cursed. The footsteps of their horses were three maybe only two kilometres away, and I quickly grabbed my apple green dress and pulled it over my head.

A bright white horse ran past me. A young man

with dark blond hair held the mains, but he didn't seem to notice me.

I assumed helping Cookie with dinner, whoever Cookie might be, was not something he looked forward to.

"Seriously, Philippe…" a handsome looking man cursed on top of his spotless brown horse.

His dark brown curls were glued to his forehead and, thanks to the fading sunlight, he had little lights dancing in his piercing blue eyes. "You will get a little brother, they said. It will be fun, they said. You will love him, they said." He didn't seem to attempt to force his horse to walk any faster. He even stopped when his eyes fell on me.

I shifted my weight from one leg to the other. Even though I didn't even notice the cold, I acted like I was shivering and wrapped my arms around my own chest. Just like I had once learned from my father.

The young man, clearly much wealthier than I would ever be, came down from his horse and I saw his eyes wandering over my unusual posture.

I didn't need a mirror to know what I looked like. My bare feet were covered in dirt. My long black hair had at least a million tangles and the sleeves of my dress barely covered my tender shoulders. A few years ago, the dress had fitted me perfectly, but now it was a few sizes too big because of the ongoing lack of food my family was suffering from.

"Is everything alright, my lady?" The rider bent his head slightly and I swallowed a few times.

Everything was fine until a few minutes ago. Everything was fine until he and his brother interrupted the silence. Everything was fine until the fear of being discovered had forced me to pull this uncomfortable dress over my head.

"I know, I shouldn't be here after dark, sir." I tried to sound lighter than I normally would and licked my lips, like I had seen a lot of nervous girls doing. "I was looking for the perfect flowers to give to my mother. It's her birthday today. I'm afraid I forgot the time and the way home."

"It's easy to get lost in these woods, isn't it?" His lips curled up into a smile. "But I promise that I have no indecent intentions and mean no harm." He didn't seem to realise that saying something like that automatically made him less reliable. An honourable man wouldn't see the need to defend himself.

"All those trees look scarily alike, indeed." I wasn't good at this kind of small talk. I had never been.

I just wanted the man to climb on his horse again and ride away. I wanted him to leave me alone. I was fine on my own. I was more than fine on my own.

"Do you live in one of the villages?" He held the reins firmly and he had his other hand folded behind his back. He was barely a few years older than me, but he seemed to wear more confidence than normal boys my age.

"Yes, I live in Waterfield." I had to make sure I didn't accidentally nod into the right direction.

Even if I wouldn't know where I was, I could easily track my own scent until I reached my home.

But that was something he didn't need to know. That was something no one needed to know.

"Where are your shoes?" He pointed at my bare feet and I shrugged my shoulders.

"I must have lost them along the way." Over the years, I had become terribly good at lying, especially since I kept on using the same excuses. I had to. I had to lie if I didn't want to lock myself up like the rest of my family.

"I can bring you to Waterfield, if you want?" The young man cocked his head, and I raised my eyebrows slightly.

He had already generated some distrust by telling me that he was totally decent and meant no harm. By offering me a ride home, he was not making himself more believable.

"My mother always told me that I shouldn't accept a ride home from strangers."

Not only my mother had told me. My father had said it, too. My grandparents, when they were still alive, had repeated it over and over again, and every time I left the house, someone reminded me of it, in case I had forgotten.

"A stranger?" The young man frowned his eyebrows as if he couldn't believe that I didn't recognise him. "Of course, where are my manners?" His lips curled up into a slight smile and he walked towards me, his horse closely following him. "My name is Nick."

"Nick what?" I cocked my head slightly and crossed my arms over my chest.

"Nick…" He hesitated for a moment and with his free hand he scratched the back of his neck. "Nick Edwards." He straightened his back and he gently grabbed my hand so he could kiss my knuckles.

He didn't seem to notice that they were as dirty as my feet. He probably simply lacked the eyes to do so due to the dimming light.

"I've never heard of that name before." I wondered at what point I could turn around.

The last time I had been caught in the woods I was

with my father and he had assured the stranger that he would get me home safely. This time, I looked like a damsel in distress.

Nick seemed to be trying to become my knight in shining armour.

Like I needed one.

"I have not been in Waterfield that often, I admit." He dropped my hand and stepped back. "I can't leave you here in the woods on your own, though."

"If you know which way I should walk to get back home, I will find it myself." I sighed once more.

I appreciated his kindness and I hoped that one day he would meet a girl who would actually need it, but I wasn't that girl.

"I insist on getting you home safely. What was your name again?"

For a moment, I doubted if I would come up with another lie. "Emily." I eventually gave him at least one thing that was true. "Emily Rivers."

Even though we have been using my mother's name ever since my father's dead, it still felt strange not to call myself Emily Parker.

"It's my pleasure to meet you, Emily." He bowed slightly and then he held out his hand again. "Allow me to help you on my horse."

As if I wasn't hopeless enough already. "No, thank you. I know how to get on a horse."

Even though most girls would believe that the back of his horse was quite comfortable, I only thought about how much faster I would have been if he had just passed me like his brother had done. Just like I wasn't too happy about his chest pressed to my back.

"You are lucky that I have been the one to find you." He made sure to speak loudly, probably because he was used to the wind blowing away his words.

I could tell him that even if he whispered, I would still hear him loud and clear but, combined with my too thin and oversized dress and my bare feet, I would give away a few hints too many if I did so.

"I couldn't have been luckier." I tried to sound like all those pretty girls I had seen playing in the meadow while I had been trying to gather what little money I could get. Deep down, I was far from amused that I managed to run into the only nobleman in the entire kingdom with a heart.

If he had been a little less decent, he wouldn't have offered me a ride home.

I would have been home already.

"I hope you have an extra set of warm clothing and a pair of comfortable shoes at home?"

I had to bite my lip to prevent myself from laughing.

He had clearly never been talking to commoners before. He would have known that we didn't own more than one pair of shoes and more than one set of clothes.

We already had enough trouble saving enough money to replace something that was beyond repair.

I was in the lucky position that I didn't depend on those clothes to keep me warm and that I preferred being barefoot anyway. "I think I'm already lucky if we have enough wood to keep the fire burning tonight."

For a couple of very long minutes, he didn't say anything. Maybe he really wasn't aware of what the normal people in this kingdom were going through, those who weren't born with a golden spoon in their mouth. His brain clearly needed an insane amount of time to let my words sink in.

Eventually, after what seemed to be an eternity, I saw the lights of Waterfield in the distance. I had lived in Waterfield my entire life, but I never got used to how small the houses were and how many people lived in them.

"Can you tell me which one of those houses is yours?" Nick made his horse slow down a little. "I assume it's one where the lights are still off?"

I raised my eyebrows and looked over my shoulder. I didn't exactly see his eyes, but I frowned anyway. "I do hope that my family didn't leave the lights off. That would mean we didn't have any money to buy wood and candles today."

"You have to share your house with your entire family?" Even though I had already told him that I would be happy with enough money to keep the fire burning tonight, he did seem to be surprised that I was not in the position to have one of those places for myself. "How many people are living in such a house?"

I gave him directions and ignored his question until we stood still in front of my home. "I have two sisters, a brother, a mother, and two uncles."

My uncle Calvin, my mother's brother, had once dreamed of moving out with his husband, uncle Aaron, to start their own family. But, even if they could have afforded it, they refused to leave us behind ever since my father was killed.

"And they all live in this small house?" Nick stared at the stone walls. "Why would anyone want to live with so many people inside such a small place?"

"We don't really have a choice." I shrugged my shoulders. "With so few available jobs, we wouldn't be able to earn the resources needed to live separately." I sighed.

When I was younger, the house didn't feel as crammed. I liked playing games with Nora and Charlotte, both younger than me and not half as independent as me.

The fear of being discovered was not as bad as the horrible thought of never having a moment to myself. "By now, I'm probably too late to claim one of the beds for the night." I wanted to add that it was thanks to him, but I assumed he wouldn't understand me. I hoped he wouldn't understand me.

"You are not serious, are you?" He stepped off his horse and like a true gentleman he held out his hand in case I would need it to come down, too.

"Do I look like I'm joking?" I ignored his hand and sighed in relief when my bare feet touched the cold ground again. I wanted to enjoy the dirt between my toes for a little longer, but those last few seconds before I would disappear inside would have to do.

"But…but…" He stared at the house and at me again. "If I offered you a job, would you be able to get your own house?"

I crossed my arms over my chest and wanted to come up with a thousand reasons why he shouldn't be giving me a job, but I had to admit that my own house would be nice.

"That depends on the job. I'm not sure if you have a job available that would make me earn enough to furnish it and buy wood."

"I can give you however much I want." He awkwardly folded his hands behind his back and avoided my glance. "My father won't notice. I don't think he knows who works for us and who doesn't."

I wouldn't notice either if I didn't have to worry about the money. "What kind of a job do you have to offer?" I cocked my head. I was wary of his intentions, even though he had returned me home safely.

"I don't know…." He swallowed and he shifted his weight from one leg to the other. "I will give you a decent reward daily and I will simply let you know whatever I need you to do."

I lifted my chin a little and straightened my back. "I hope you were not planning on using my yes for any indecent purposes?"

His cheeks coloured and he probably felt protected by the dark. He didn't know that my wolf eyes weren't exactly worse during the night than during the day. "Of course not."

"I don't want a daily reward if I don't have anything to do." I swallowed. "You pay me for every task I complete. I have the right to refuse whatever you ask me to do."

"You don't seem to be in the position to refuse my offer."

"I'm not refusing your offer. I'm just protecting myself. Just because I can use every penny, it doesn't mean I need to allow anyone to take advantage of my situation."

"I wouldn't dare to take advantage of you, my lady." Nick bent his head slightly again. "I will send someone with the first task tomorrow."

I curled up my lips, even though I didn't like being in debt with this young man for the rest of my life, I curtsied. I grabbed my dress to lift it a little, while it didn't even reach the floor. I bent my knees slightly and stared at my own bare feet.

"Aren't you freezing by now, my lady?"

I looked up again and raised my eyebrows.

He had his chest pressed to my back the entire ride

and now he's asking if I'm freezing? He should have noticed, even if he was the least perceptive person in the entire world, that my skin had been warm despite the cold.

"I have always been very warm blooded, sir." I didn't dare to look at my front door.

Even though I was not looking forward to having to explain to my family how I ended up as the employee of a nobleman, I wasn't exactly looking forward to having to answer more of these questions, which was certainly going to happen if I kept standing here. "But I do have to admit that the air is quite chilly tonight."

Maybe now, he would let me leave.

I hoped he would let me leave.

"I hope you can get a good night of sleep tonight and I hope you can look forward to tomorrow." He smiled once more, but he didn't seem to hurry to get on his horse and leave.

"Goodnight, sir, and thank you once again for bringing me home safely." I hoped this was the right moment to turn around and walk away from him.

With trembling hands, I opened the front door and once I was inside, I made sure to keep on listening until I heard his horse galloping away.

"Where have you been, Emily?" My mother had her arms crossed over her chest. Due to spending most of her days inside, her skin was pale white, and her dark eyes looked terrifying in the dim light.

"Two men were riding through the woods." I bent my head and avoided her glance.

"Did they see your wolf?" My mother, with her impressive posture despite the lack of food, walked towards me and almost forced my back against the wall.

"No, they didn't see my wolf." I shook my head. "They only saw a lost and helpless girl in an old, torn dress and bare feet." I swallowed. "One of them brought me home."

"Those adventures of yours will kill us all one day." She opened the door to the overcrowded living room, and I already saw the judgement in the eyes of my entire family. "You better have a very good explanation, young lady."

I didn't have one. But I would give it a try.

Chapter Two

All the seats in the living room were taken. My younger sisters, Nora and Charlotte were sharing one of the chairs with each other and my little brother, Benjamin, sat on my uncle Aaron's knee.

"Tell us exactly what happened and who that young man was." My mother leaned against one of the walls and crossed her arms again. Even though she was not tall, she had the ability to make an impression.

Nick was lucky that it wasn't her he found in the woods. His only chance for survival would have been the fact that my mother was against drawing attention to us by leaving a dead body behind.

"I promise that what happened will not put our family in danger." I shook my head and I licked my lips.

I shifted my weight from one leg to the other and I wrapped my arms around my body. I wasn't in need of comfort, but I felt the need to protect myself, even though I trusted those people with my life.

"What happened and who was that young man?" My mother repeated her question and I bent my head.

Dirt covered my toes and I made a mental note to make sure to wash them before the messenger arrived in the morning with my first task.

"I was just enjoying the last few seconds of letting my wolf free…" I emphasized the last word with a slight bit of bitterness. "Then I heard horses coming my way." I swallowed. "I wanted to hide, but one of the young men had already seen me and the second one decided to stop to help me." I rolled my eyes. "He believed I was a damsel in distress and didn't allow me to convince him that I would get home safely by myself."

"Does he suspect anything about your wolf?" My mother lifted her chin.

Her eyes narrowed and I held my breath while my glance met hers. Even when my father was still alive, she had been our leader and it wasn't hard to understand why.

"No, I told him it was my mother's birthday and that I was simply gathering some flowers. I explained that I got lost and that somewhere along the way I lost my shoes, too." I monitored the expressions on the faces of my family members. "He believed every word I said, but he insisted on bringing me home, which took a lot more time than walking home would have taken."

"This was the last time you went out by yourself to let your wolf free." My mother put the emphasis on the last word, but added a mocking undertone. "I lost your father already because people discovered that he wasn't entirely human and I don't want to lose any of you, too." She took a deep breath. "If anyone discovers that you have inherited his wolf genes, they will surely examine our entire family and we all know how that ends."

We would all die. Or we would get executed. Or we would get poisoned, just like my father. Only because humans had no idea that we were far from dangerous and that we were in full control of our wolves. If only there were a way to prove them that we didn't mean any harm, that we could even protect them if they agreed.

But even though my mother was right, I was not planning on giving up the little bit of freedom I had left. I enjoyed running through the woods and awakening my senses. I enjoyed the wind touching my naked skin. I enjoyed the dirt and grass between my toes. I needed all those things to survive. My longing for freedom could get us all killed, but locking myself up like the rest of my family preferred would eventually kill me.

"Tomorrow, you will go and find a new job to keep you occupied." My mother stared at me, and I licked my lips.

She made us switch workplaces all the time. I just quit my last job a couple of days ago, after having worked there for three full weeks.

"I already have one, actually." I swallowed. I wanted to keep that part of the story a secret. I wanted her to find out tomorrow, when I would probably be able to buy my entire family enough food to fill their stomachs for the first time in months.

"How?" My mother narrowed her eyes once more and a shiver rolled down my spine. My mother was not only my mother, she was, firstly, my leader, which meant that her love for me would never outweigh the importance of our survival.

"The nobleman who found me and brought me home offered me a job." I tried to read her face once more, but her expression didn't change. "He will send a messenger tomorrow with my first task and he will pay whenever I have completed it."

"You are certain this is not a trap?" My mother raised her eyebrows, but I shook my head.

"I know it's hard to believe, but this nobleman seemed to possess a heart. He was shocked by my living circumstances and wanted to do something to change them.”

By only changing my fate, he would do nothing more than saving one drop of water from being swallowed by the sea. However, I wasn’t exactly in the position to say no to such an offer. I didn’t believe he was going to offer the same thing to another random stranger anyway.

“If there are any signs that he knows more about you than you believe him to know now, you’ll have to quit.” My mother stared at me and if looks could kill I would have died right there and then. She didn’t even think about all the indecent intentions he could have had. She could only think about the possible danger he could present for me and the entire family.

“I will be careful, Mother.” I wanted to turn around and leave the room, but my mother cleared her throat.

“We have saved you a slice of bread, if you want.” She nodded at a plate on the table.

My great-grandmother had gotten the plate, which was part of an entire set, when she married my great-grandfather. Even though they were both long dead already, our family was still using them.

We couldn’t afford to buy anything new.

“I have already eaten something in the woods. You should give it to Benjamin. He still needs it to grow.” I lied. Even though I was tempted to go after one of the bunnies or even one of the bigger deer, I was afraid to leave any traces behind. I did however know that Benjamin was way too small for his age and needed the food a lot more than I did. Even if I hated everything about the task I got tomorrow, I would still complete it for his benefit.

“That’s not your decision to make, Emily,” my mother spoke with her deep voice, and all my muscles tensed.

"You gave the food to me. It became mine the moment you did so. I give it to Benjamin." I walked towards the table and shoved the plate towards my brother.

He had no colour in his face. Mostly because he had barely seen the sun since he was born. There was no fat between his skin and his bones and with his dark brown eyes, he looked a little bit like a ghost. If he ever left the house during the day, I was certain he would scare the neighbours.

"Benjamin? Eat." I ordered and Benjamin looked at me, at our mother, and back at me. "I promise I will do whatever I can to make sure there is enough food for everyone tomorrow," I assured him and reluctantly, he took the slice of bread.

Once he took the first bite, however, he couldn't control himself any longer. Within seconds, it seemed as if the slice of bread never even existed.

"You can't undermine my leadership, Emily. It's too dangerous." My mother hissed between her teeth.

One day, I would be able to challenge her. One day she would no longer be the leader of this family. She was, however, afraid that if I became our leader too soon, I would destroy the facade of false safety she had created.

"I'm not undermining you, Mother." I shook my head and walked towards the door. I couldn't see her anymore, but I felt her eyes burning my back. "I did the only right thing." I opened the door of the living room and walked out. I could claim one of the few beds upstairs if I wanted to, but I decided to lay down on the ripped rug on the kitchen floor instead. I didn't want Benjamin to be the one to end up without a bed, because I decided to give him my slice of bread.

"She's getting stronger, Maria," Uncle Calvin whispered, but my perfect hearing understood his words anyway. "Maybe you should stop trying to contain her."

"I know she's getting stronger, but if I don't contain her, I have no idea how long she, and we all, will survive."

"Maybe a lot longer than you think."

Chapter Three

I opened my eyes before the first rays of sunshine could burn them. I could barely move my arms and legs and my back felt like a carriage with six horses ran over it. I only had myself to blame for my sore muscles and painful body. I had been the one picking the rug in the small kitchen instead of one of the comfortable beds in one of the bedrooms.

The floor in the kitchen was empty. No one wanted to be anywhere near me for the night or when I woke up.

I couldn't blame them. I pushed myself up and walked to the sink. We had to be careful with our water, but I hoped that even mother would see my first day working for a nobleman as a special occasion. I tried to make no sound while I filled one small iron bucket. At first, I cleaned my dress as much as possible with cold water and no soap. Then I took a small cloth and washed myself.

"Emily?" My mother was the first to walk into the kitchen. "We need that water for our food tonight."

"I wouldn't use this water if I were you." I showed her the dirty cloth and the black water. "A nobleman has asked me to work for him. I can't show up covered in dirt."

"You wouldn't have been covered in dirt had you not been wandering barefoot through the woods." My mother raised her eyebrows, but I shrugged my shoulders and emptied the bucket in the sink.

"If I had not been in the woods yesterday, I wouldn't have gotten this job." I passed my mother on my way to the front door and let the wind blow my dress until it was almost dry. I pulled the dress over my head and used my fingers to comb my hair before I braided it.

My mother's eyes followed me through the house, but she didn't say anything anymore. Maybe she realised that I heard my uncle Calvin's words yesterday. Maybe she was simply surprised that I seemed to understand that this job was somehow important.

I used a shoelace as a ribbon and lifted my chin while my glance met my mother's. "How do I look?" I cocked my head a little and, for a moment, I thought I saw the lips of my mother trembling, as if she was trying to stop them from curling up into a smile.

"If you get the impression he's trying to expose that you're a wolf, you return home immediately." Her lips formed a straight line again and a deep frown covered her forehead.

If she didn't worry every second of the day, she would probably be considered beautiful. Maybe she would even stand a chance to find a second husband to bring in some extra means.

She didn't, however, trust anyone in this small village. She preferred being alone, struggling to feed all the mouths that had to be fed, over having to share her deepest secret with an ordinary human who might end up killing us all in our sleep.

Sometimes, I dared to wonder if being killed in my sleep wasn't a much better option than being alive in a world where we had to lock ourselves up constantly.

"If you believe he knows what you are, you make

sure to report it to me." She stared at me, and I swallowed.

She used to stare at me in a different way and, even though she had not done so since my father died, I still couldn't get used to the cold and distant look she displayed.

"Do you really think I would get us all killed?" I interrupted her, staring at her.

I still loved her. Maybe I had never been as close with her as my sisters had been, most of all because I took way too much after my father, but I did long for that time she held me and kissed my tears away when I had a nightmare.

"Not on purpose." My mother shook her head.

There had been times I considered calling her Maria. But I never wanted to give up hope that my mother was still in there somewhere, hidden behind countless of masks and facades, waiting until the world felt safe enough again to show her true colours and nature once more.

I always liked her true colours and nature. I had admired them. And even though I had my father's soul and heart, I had tried to adopt my mother's strength, courage and wisdom.

"It could only be one small little mistake." My mother stared at me for a few more seconds and then she disappeared into the living room.

At the moment, she was in between jobs. We all were, and often. We never dared to stay with someone for too long. Mother was afraid that someone would pick up on something. Our heightened senses. Our increased strength. Our eternal warmth. And we never grew tired. She was afraid someone would pick up on one little mistake any one of us could make.

I understood her concern. I was the first one to notice that it was impossible that father died because of a natural cause.

We didn't get ill. We didn't get heart attacks or brain damage. Even the endless hunger and endless cold couldn't kill us. Poison could. Silver bullets could. Chopping our heads off could. But, we never found a shot wound and his head had still been attached to his torso.

I've tried for years to find out how they did it, but I never found anything. I didn't even discover who in Waterfield learned about his wolf and decided to get rid of him.

"Emily?"

I looked up when Benjamin, dressed in nothing but his underwear, walked into the kitchen.

He wrapped his tiny arms around my body, and I pressed him to my chest. "Thank you for the slice of bread yesterday," he whispered.

I heard his stomach growl from hunger again.

A child his age needed more than a few slices of dry bread a day.

"You're welcome, Benjamin." I rubbed his back and leaned down to press a soft kiss on his black hair.

Benjamin didn't know how much he looked like father. After all, to him, father was no one but a stranger we all told stories about. To him, father was no one but the one who had helped create him, but had not been there when he was born.

Sometimes, I wondered if Benjamin would have been the same shy and almost broken boy, he was these days, if father had been there to take him out of the house once in a while. More than once, I wanted to promise him to leave the house, to explore the upside of being a wolf with him, to show him the perks of being part of this extraordinary family. However, my mother would personally kill me without even feeling remorse about it if I would do so.

Benjamin had never experienced the cold wind touching his naked skin. He wasn't aware of the top speed he could reach if he used all his four feet to run. He had never been overwhelmed by the smell of blooming grass and flourishing flowers. He had never been outside the house for long. He had always been surrounded by those same four walls and the same people who claimed they only wanted the best for him.

I believed my mother, but I didn't share her definition of the best. "I will try everything I can to make sure you'll have a full stomach tonight, too." I placed my hand on his head and tossed his hair.

He didn't say anything, but he looked up with a smile on his face. He had never known the freedom I already missed, even though I had last experienced it yesterday. Maybe he didn't know he missed it in the first place.

I looked up when someone knocked on the front door. I reluctantly let the tiny boy in my arms go, but he didn't protest.

He only stepped back from me and gave me the space I needed to open the door.

"I am looking for miss Emily Rivers." A messenger, dressed in a uniform covered in so much gold that it would be worth more than the food Benjamin would need for the rest of his life, cleared his throat when he saw me. "I have a message from pr…" He stopped in the middle of his word and coughed a few times. "I have a message from Sir Nick Edwards." He narrowed his eyes slightly while he read the name out loud, as if he had no idea who this person actually was.

"I'm Emily, it's nice to meet you." I held out my hand, but the messenger barely looked at it and only slightly bent his knees and head. "Your first task will be signing this contract." He gave me a piece of brownish paper and I read the words.

I, Emily Rivers, hereby declare that Sir Nick Edwards has hired me as his personal helper. At any time, I have the right to decline a task. At any time, I have the right to breach this contract. I will however not refuse any reward for any completed tasks.

I lifted my eyebrows and looked at the messenger. "Are you sure this is the entire contract?"

The messenger nodded and I stared at the paper again.

"Emily?" Benjamin was still standing behind me and I took a deep breath.

I was not accepting this job for me. I was accepting this job for Benjamin. For the rest of my family. My finger trembled while I pressed it to the ink pad and then to the paper.

"Lord Edwards will be pleased to see this." The messenger smiled as he folded the contract carefully, before he handed me a basket filled with food and candles. "Your reward for signing the contract."

"Oh, but you can't pay me for..." I couldn't finish my sentence.

"You have just agreed to accept any reward for any completed task. I have communicated that this was a task. You have chosen to complete it. You can't refuse the payment."

I took the basket from him and stared at it once more. "Benjamin?" I turned around and looked at my younger brother. "Enjoy your meal."

His eyes widened when he noticed the sandwiches with ham and cheese, something he had never even tasted before.

"You don't need to share, if you don't want to." I whispered.

"Miss Rivers?" The messenger cleared his throat again. "I have another assignment for you, if you please?"

I turned towards the door again and nodded. "Of course."

When I walked outside, I noticed the carriage, covered in even more gold, looking hopelessly out of place on the dark cobbles. "Do I have to travel in that?" I raised my eyebrows, and the messenger nodded at me.

"Lord Edwards has planned a few appointments in the capital, and he wants you to accompany him." The man held the door of the carriage open for me and my eyes almost fell out of their sockets when I saw the soft and expensive red fabric covering the seats.

"Aren't people going to think it's weird when they see Lord Edwards accompanied by a commoner from Waterfield?" I hesitated for a moment, but the messenger curled his lips up into a smile.

"That is not something you should worry about, miss." He held out his hand and helped me get into the carriage.

The seat had already looked beautiful, but they were also comfortable, and I enjoyed the softness of the material touching my skin.

"If there is anything wrong or if you need anything, there is a small bell above your head to call for me." The messenger waited until I glanced up before he closed the door.

I had already noticed yesterday that Lord Edwards had quite some money to spend, but I was surprised with the greatness of his riches.

I had always thought that only our king and queen and their family had carriages like these, but now it seemed I had been wrong about that.

In a way, that also made me angry. If the lords and ladies of this kingdom also possessed carriages covered in gold, there was an even greater disparity between rich and poor than I imagined.

I saw children like Benjamin, nothing but skin and bones, daily on the streets.

They were holding out their hands for every little bit of money or food they could gather, but no one who ever passed them had anything they could afford to give them. Those children eventually disappeared, and it was not hard to guess what happened to them in the end.

I screamed slightly when the carriage moved all of a sudden. "Sorry…" I murmured.

I wasn't sure if the messenger heard me, but I didn't want him to think there was anything wrong. I just needed some time to get used to the rocking movements of the carriage. Eventually, I leaned back and enjoyed the comfort.

Even though running to the capital would have been much faster, I had to admit that I could get used to traveling this way, even though I had no idea how long I would have to sit in this carriage. The lack of sleep, however, bothered me and I closed my eyes, slowly drifting off into a dreamless slumber.

"Miss Rivers?" The messenger placed a firm hand on my shoulder, and I shook, all too aware that I had been asleep. "We have arrived at our first destination for today." He smiled at me.

If he was judging me for not enjoying the view and the comfort of the carriage, he tried his very best not to show it.

I straightened the skirt of my forest green dress and took a deep breath before I placed my hand in his and stepped out of the carriage.

"Welcome to the capital." The messenger allowed me some time to look around, but my eyes had no idea on what to focus first.

The capital was overwhelmingly big. All the buildings were at least twice as high as the houses in Waterfield. Not one building seemed to be made of wood and even the cobbles beneath my feet were clean and almost white. The windows and doorframes were painted in the most beautiful colours and in places, the glass was replaced by works of art. It was hard to believe that human hands had created this.

"You have never been in the capital before, miss?" The messenger was still smiling while he followed my glance as if he was trying to see the city through my eyes.

"No…" I lifted my chin and all of a sudden, I felt incredibly small and unimportant in this world. "But I think I understand why the royals are not that keen on leaving this place." If I would have lived in a house like these, surrounded by beauty like this, I wouldn't have wanted to visit dirty, colourless villages either.

"Even the prettiest houses cannot buy happiness, though." The messenger licked his lips, and I saw a glimmer of sadness in his eyes. It only lasted for a few seconds and then it was gone.

"I do believe it helps, though." I turned around slowly.

The sunlight made the golden ornaments even brighter than they were. I believed, the capital would still look pretty in the pouring rain, but I was glad the weather was on my side at the moment.

I was also aware how out of place I looked and felt. Even though, I was wearing my simple and comfortable shoes, I still felt like a barefoot girl.

Around me, heels were ticking for every step and the dresses the ladies wore were puffy and moving along with their hips. The sapphires and rubies decorating all the silk and cashmere were worth more than our entire house.

Although, I couldn't deny the beauty of it, a small sting pierced my heart.

The silk, the cashmere, the sapphires and rubies could save the lives of thousands, if not more. They were used as decoration, as jewellery, and other luxury items, while they could be traded for food and clothing for the poor.

"I've never felt this much out of please before…" I eventually let out a sigh and the messenger placed a comforting hand on my back.

I didn't know how much he got paid for his services. I didn't know if he had a wife and children or other mouths to feed. But I assumed that he still knew less about hunger than I did. And I was in the lucky position to be able to survive on the free treats the forest had to offer.

Something most people in our village couldn't because they lacked the tools, skills and time to do so

"I am certain that Lord Edwards is planning on helping you with that." The messenger seemed slightly amused with my discomfort, as if he were aware of any unwanted surprises the lord would have in store for me.

"I guess the basket filled with all kinds of food, I have not seen in years, was only the beginning?" I was not expecting the messenger to answer, but he did curl his lips up once more and nodded slightly. "I would have heavily protested against being a charity project had I not had a younger brother who is too small for his age due to the lack of food." I sighed.

"I am certain that lord Edwards is not just seeing you as a charity case, miss." The messenger locked his glance with mine and I raised my eyebrows.

"He finds a girl in the woods, dressed in a ripped dress and without shoes. Then he discovers she lives with her entire family in a small house and decides to offer her a job and a stable income." I shook my head. "I believe that's the definition of being a charity case, but I am not in the position to refuse the opportunity to bring some food home." I lifted my chin and straightened my back. "As long as he doesn't demand anything indecent, I am willing to complete whatever task he offers me."

Chapter Four

"I'm glad to hear that, my lady." Lord Edwards all of a sudden came out of a yellow-coloured door.

He bent his head slightly when he reached me and I made sure to bow to him, like I had learned a long time ago in case any of our royals would decide to visit Waterfield one day.

That day had not come yet, but it seemed it was a useful skill after all.

"Your first task is to help me decide on what uniform to wear to the royal ball in three weeks." He smiled and offered me his arm. "And I ask you to call me Nick, please."

"Of course, whatever you want, my l..." I swallowed and forced myself to smile. "Whatever you want, Nick."

I felt slightly uncomfortable while I linked my arm with his. Even though it wasn't his intention to make me feel like this, I felt even more like a charity case than before. "What is so difficult about choosing a uniform?" I cocked my head while Nick pushed the door of the shop open.

As soon as I stepped inside my eyes widened and my jaw dropped.

Colourful dresses, made of materials I had never seen in my life, covered two walls, while uniforms, decorated with ornaments, covered the third wall.

"This is why I need your help." Nick curled up his lips into a charming smile and in the dimmed light his blue eyes seemed to sparkle.

"And why do you think that I can be of help?" I raised my eyebrows and took a few deep breaths.

I've had several dresses during my life, but only because I had outgrown them after some time. On top of that, I couldn't remember ever having a say in the clothes I was wearing. "I have never even seen anything like this," I hesitated and wondered when would it be appropriate to unlink my arm, but didn't dare to ask.

"You can determine whether you like something or not, can you?" Nick grinned and leaned a little towards me. "Each and every piece of clothing in this shop is made with love and care." He shrugged his shoulders. "And all of them are of the same great quality. I only need to know which option you prefer."

"I must have made quite some impression if you let me decide for you what to wear to a royal ball." I raised my eyebrows slightly and Nick lead me to a comfortable couch, which looked better than any piece of furniture I had ever seen in our village.

I wondered if most of our, so called, rare new items were secretly already used in the capital before they even reached us. Maybe I would find the courage to ask the question one day.

"I need a pair of fresh eyes." Nick waited until I sat down and made myself as comfortable as I dared to.

I was afraid that if I found the most pleasant position, I would fall asleep again and waking up in an embarrassing way once, was more than enough for today.

"I will show you four different outfits. You can comment on them as much as you like and as harsh as you like." He smiled once more before he turned around to greet, who I assumed, was the owner of the shop.

She was probably only a few years older than I, and her beautiful blond hair was glowing despite the lack of sunlight. "How can I help you, your r…" she couldn't finish her sentence.

"I would like to fit the four different uniforms we have discussed last week." Nick leaned on the counter and after one more look at me I realised that maybe he was not that comfortable with me trying to overhear his conversations.

Not overhearing them, however, would be a lot harder than he could possibly imagine.

"Of course, y…"

"You did reserve them all on the name Lord Edwards, didn't you?" Nick cleared his throat and looked over his shoulder once more, while I acted like I was drowning in the riches and beauty surrounding me.

"I did, my lord." The young woman slightly bent her head and then, disappeared through a hidden door behind the small counter.

"There are so many titles these days." Nick smiled at me and shrugged his shoulders. "I can't blame people for mixing them up and using the wrong one once in a while."

I forced myself to smile at him and moved a little uncomfortably into another position. Surrounded by all those dresses, I was even more aware of the sorry state of mine.

"Here are the outfits we have spoken about, y…my lord." The young lady returned with four bundles of clothes in different shades of blue draped over her underarm.

"I see you've at least already decided on the colour?" I stretched my neck to have a better look at the uniforms, but they were folded in such a way that I could barely see any details.

"The colours are determined by the royal court." Nick followed the young lady towards one of the giant dressing rooms. "But I promise that there is more than enough to still decide on." He disappeared behind the wooden door and the young lady's eyes wandered over my body.

"You are wearing quite an interesting dress."

I was not sure if she meant it as a compliment, maybe my dress was not as bad as she had expected from someone from the villages, or if it was an insult, which was the more likely option, in my opinion. "It's an old one from my mother." I licked my lips and took a deep breath.

"What do you think?" Eventually, Nick opened the wooden door and I held my breath. The blue of his uniform was matching the colour of his eyes and beautiful golden linings decorated the entire uniform.

"It looks beautiful."

I discovered more details. The golden linings were forming patterns.

Eventually, I discovered a lion, a deer and, I assume, a dragon-like creature on his back. "I don't even know if you have to fit the other outfits." I exhaled and Nick curled up his lips into a smile.

"Of course, I have to." He winked and a strange kind of warmth spread through my body. "You can't compare an outfit with itself."

He disappeared into the dressing room and even though, the young shop owner did attempt having another conversation with me, I only replied with brief answers.

The less she knew about me the better. The less anyone knew about me the better.

I was certain that Nick was secretly eavesdropping, even though his hearing wouldn't be able to compete with mine.

"How do you like this one?" Nick appeared in the second uniform.

The shade of blue was slightly darker than the previous one and all of sudden, his eyes seemed to darken a little, too. The silver ornaments on his shoulders immediately caught my attention and even though this outfit seemed to highlight the different shades of brown in his hair, I wasn't as fascinated as I was with the embroidered animals on the previous uniform.

"I liked the other one better." I swallowed while the lady next to me stared at me with wide eyes, as if she wondered where I found the courage to speak about any of her creations like that. "I don't mean to say that this outfit doesn't look good on you, it does." I hurried to add. "I however preferred the animals on the other uniform." I licked my dry lips and Nick turned around to have a closer look at the jacket he had just taken off.

"My father and brother enjoy hunting." His fingertip followed the golden lines and his eyes drifted off, while his lips curled up into a slight smile. "I prefer looking at the animals. More than once, I have been accused of being the cause of one of their pray getting away."

I cocked my head slightly while I stared at him. I had known about the famous hunting parties organised by the royals and all the other lords and ladies. I just hadn't allowed myself to picture Nick with a gun in his hand, with his eyes on one of the poor animals who had no idea they were being shot for fun.

"They say there are more than enough animals in the woods and one more or less won't matter." Nick looked at me again and I bit my lip. "But even animals are mothers or fathers, brothers or sisters, or sons and daughters."

His eyes locked with mine and I wondered if he was more aware of what I was than I had thought and hoped, or if he was really just this kind-hearted person he pretended to be.

"I don't understand the fun of killing a poor animal without a good reason." I sighed and I turned my head away from him. "I do have to admit that I've killed to make sure I had at least something in my stomach. And I might have given my brother flesh without explaining its origins to him." I bent my head and stared at my shoes.

Spending time with Nick was a bad idea from the start.

He was rich and could buy and get anything he wished with barely a snap of his fingers. I was poor and had done the questionable things to survive.

"Maybe next time I can convince my family to donate their catches to the villages instead of using their heads to decorate our houses." Nick coughed, clearing his throat. "I assume you don't need to see the other two outfits?"

I shook my head. "Unless they also have those animal patterns."

"They don't." Nick stared at the owner of the shop next to me. "Do you have anything for her to wear during her working hours with me?"

"Oh, no!" I stood from my chair and shook my

head. "You don't need to do that!"

"I do." He nodded at me and smirked. "It's your payment for helping me choose my own uniform and you have signed a contract stating you can't refuse that."

Somehow, I got the impression that signing that contract would become one of those things I would regret some day. Not because I didn't enjoy assisting the lord and being paid for tasks I couldn't even afford, but more because he seemed to use it as an excuse to spoil me rotten.

No matter how many amazing dresses he gave me, I wouldn't be able to wear them in Waterfield. He might notice how out of place they would look if he took the time to wander around the village for more than a few minutes after dark.

"Please, I can't explain to my family that I've gotten a wonderful dress, but didn't earn any money to buy them wood, food, or herbs for tea." I almost begged Nick, but he cocked his head and raised his eyebrows meaningfully.

"Who says that this has been your last task for today?" He turned towards the young lady of the shop once more and repeated his question. "Do you have any dresses for her to wear while she's accompanying me?"

The young lady nodded and hurried towards the colourful dresses covering the walls. She looked over her shoulders once in a while to look at me. "Slightly pale skin." She shook her head while passing a yellow dress with a slightly puffy bottom. "Dark eyes…" She walked past the darker shades and eventually she selected a few different colours and styles.

"Why don't you try the red one first?" Nick held the dress and my eyes widened when I noticed the corset that would compress my chest.

"I don't know if I have the slightest idea of how to put that dress on…" I stumbled. I had never worn a corset before, but I had seen rich ladies almost fainting because of the lack of air.

If wearing a corset already did that to a human body, it would probably feel even worse for me.

I didn't necessarily need as much oxygen as the average human. I was simply oversensitive to everything touching my skin.

"I will help you." The young lady walked towards me and grabbed my shoulder, almost pushing me into the dressing room, leaving me next to no choice.

I would never be able to explain why I couldn't wear a dress like this without giving away too much about the wolf inside me.

Although my family had managed to hide away for a while, we were certain that the rumours about our kind haven't disappeared into the shadows.

Someone poisoned my father because he was a wolf. And one day, someone might realise that he wasn't the only wolf in our family.

Villagers never visited the woods at night, because they feared the wolves. But so far, people have never shown any hostility towards us, so they didn't seem to suspect us, and we preferred keeping it that way.

Before I could protest, the young lady lifted my dress and I was ashamed of the undergarment I was wearing, which was even more ripped and damaged than the dress itself. But she acted as if she didn't notice or as if she seemed to be fully focussed on putting the red dress on me.

She impatiently waited until I held my arms up and, right when I decided that maybe I should take a few extra breaths, she slipped the red dress over my head.

As I had already expected, I felt locked up the moment she pulled the strings, tightening the corset. Even though the silk was softer than anything I had ever touched in my life, my skin seemed to be on fire, and I had to close my eyes and bite my lip to control the overwhelming pain consuming my mind.

"Are you okay, miss?"

I wasn't. I was far from okay. I wasn't made to wear tight dresses like this one. I wasn't created to look like a porcelain doll. I wasn't built to enjoy wearing pretty clothes. I was born to be naked. I was born to walk around like nature meant for us to be. I was born to not be ashamed of anything that made me, me.

"I won't pull them too tight, so you have time to get used to it." She smiled at me, but I couldn't bring myself to smile in return.

I felt locked up before. I knew what it was to feel like there was only a way in and no way out. I had never thought I would experience that feeling while fitting new clothes.

"You do look wonderful." She turned me around so she could look at me and, for a short moment, her eyes met mine. "And I will discretely help you with the undergarment, too." She whispered and I sighed. She had indeed acted like she had not noticed. At least, she was kind enough to not embarrass me in front of the lord, even though I hoped he was aware that my dress was probably the best outfit I owned.

"Thank you." I tried to be polite, but stiffened when she opened the wooden door to show me to Nick. "Please tell me that I look ridiculous, because I'm not sure if I can still breathe."

Nick grinned, but he didn't answer immediately. Instead, his eyes wandered over my body and a soft blush brightened his cheeks. "I would never force you to wear something, but from a solely viewing point, this dress would be an excellent choice." He kept on looking at me as if I had, all of a sudden, become a different girl.

I couldn't fight my curiosity any longer, so I turned towards the mirror on the outside of the dressing room.

While I stared at my own reflection I held my breath. If I ignored my braided, unwashed hair, I would actually dare to call myself pretty. I still remembered the last time someone called me that.

My father had been out of breath after an entire day of running and hunting in the woods as wolf. We had lain next to each other in the grass and stared at the leaves of the trees above our heads and enjoyed the soft wind caressing our blushing cheeks.

"If you had been born in the capital…" he had sighed. Father had always regretted that he had not been able to give us a better life, that he had not found a way to climb the social ladder, that he was still living in a small wooden house in a poor village.

He had been the only one to think that, but no matter how often we had assured him that we didn't blame him, he didn't seem to be able to shake the guilt completely. "If you were born in the capital, you would stand a chance to marry a prince one day."

I had smiled and then laughed. I had not been able to imagine myself next to a prince. I was still not able to imagine myself next to a prince, not even in this dress. But at the time, I had loved my father for saying it, even though he had spoken without hope and without expectations.

"What if I would ask you to wear this dress for the rest of the day?" Nick stood behind me as he spoke. He hesitantly started to place his hands on my almost bare shoulders, but decided against it the very last moment. "You can tell me at any time that you want to take it off and I will bring you here to do so." He swallowed. "I do hope, however, that in a way, you might get used to it and might consider keeping it."

Even though my skin still burned, I had to admit that his soft voice and calming smile had a certain effect on me. I was clearly still breathing and I even inhaled enough air to make sure I wouldn't faint. Maybe I would even be able to learn how to deal with the pain the soft fabric still caused.

While standing behind me, he kept his eyes locked with mine in the mirror and waited for my answer. The light in his eyes made clear that he was hoping for a "yes," even though every wolf part of my body screamed to deny his request, to ask him if there was something more comfortable I could wear.

"Please?" he whispered and, this time, one hand touched my shoulder for a brief second before he realised that he was touching me and pulled his hand back.

"We can return at any time to take the dress off if I'm uncomfortable?" I cocked my head and Nick nodded. "No matter what we are doing or where we are?"

"No matter what we are doing or where we are, I promise."

I took a deep breath and shrugged. "I will give it a try then." I already regretted the answer before I had finished the sentence, but the smile on Nick's face at least made up for it a little.

Chapter Five

I had trouble keeping my eyes open on the way home, even though I hadn't done half as much as most people in my village had done. I sighed and I stared at my green dress, cleaned and stitched by the charming lady owning the clothing store. I had not asked her to do so and Nick had assured me that he had not asked her to do so either, so I couldn't count it as any form of payment.

Nick had also told me that I could keep and wear the red dress if I wanted to. After all, he had said, I had worked for it.

I just couldn't step out of a golden carriage while wearing an expensive dress. Not in Waterfield.

People in Waterfield had to work hard to get very little. The hands of most women were damaged beyond repair, because they could never take a short break from sewing. All the men had damaged backs from working in the field for far too many years. Once in a while, a child died because of infected wounds caused by tools they couldn't handle yet.

Every month the crown seemed to ask for more, while giving less in return. At least, that's what the chiefs of the lands told us.

I had barely done anything of significance today. I had surely not done anything that would explain the payments I've received. Apart from the dress I had gotten after helping him pick his outfit for the royal ball in a few weeks, I had gotten one month of food for simply accompanying him for a long afternoon stroll through the park.

And if that had not been enough already, he had paid me one month of wood for feeding a few fat and clearly already overfed ducklings.

I had only been able to think about Benjamin, who had been seeing sandwiches with ham and cheese for the very first time in his life this morning.

Nick didn't notice any of my discomfort. He was clearly not aware that my circumstances weren't abnormal and that there were hundreds of girls and boys like me, maybe some of them even in worse conditions than I would ever be.

While he had paid me by promising new clothing for my entire family for simply playing a few games with a group of children, I had almost gotten angry with him. He had turned everything into a task and this whole contract was clearly nothing but some false excuse to give me everything I didn't ask for.

I just didn't know what else to do. I couldn't simply tell him that it was a fun day, but that it was not for me.

In a month, we would be out of food and wood again. In a few years, all our clothes would be ripped and dirty again. Benjamin would never grow up to be the young and proud man he could be. Maybe he wouldn't even survive his teenage years.

My lips curled up into a smile when I allowed myself to imagine him healthy, fierce, and strong. I saw how he would resemble father more and more each day. Maybe I would even be able to show him what freedom and happiness really looked like. Maybe I could show him the perks of being what he was, the perks no one wanted to show him right now.

I smiled even broader when I thought about my sisters. Nina would probably marry the son of the carpenter she has been talking about for months now. Charlotte could finally start her own gallery to expose the lifelike drawings she made when she couldn't sleep.

Nick had asked me a couple of questions about my family, but I tried to be as vague as possible. He wasn't telling me much about his family either, so at least, there was no need to feel guilty about it. The less he knew about my family, the better.

I signed a contract and I would do whatever I could to give my brother a brighter future, but I would never become part of his world and he would never fit into mine.

The smile on my face faded again. I didn't know why he did all of this for me, and I didn't dare to ask him about it. I was too afraid of his answer.

He was rich and he was handsome. He probably didn't even notice, but every girl in the park was staring at him as if they were halfway in love with him.

I couldn't blame them. If I had grown up in the capital, if I had become that girl my father had once dreamed of, maybe I would have been standing there with them, staring at the handsome nobleman strolling around with a girl who wasn't even comfortable in a corset and washed her hair in creeks.

He really seemed to think that he was making a difference. He seemed to think that he was saving me from life. He seemed to believe that his payments and his little tasks would change my life for the better. But his tasks and payments wouldn't all of a sudden make me one of them. And would he still try to save me if he knew who we really were, what we really were?

I took a deep breath. I was pretty certain he wouldn't. I hated having to hide my wolf. I hated being forced to sneak out of the house into the woods and back. I hated having to be on my guard all the time. But I also knew my mother was not keeping me chained because she enjoyed doing so.

She kept me chained, because she knew all too well what would happen if she didn't.

I knew all too well what would happen if she didn't.

"Excuse me, miss?" The messenger, who was actually a coachman, opened the door of the coach and tapped my shoulder. "We have arrived." He smiled at me and I forced myself to smile in return.

I had no idea how I would ever explain the overload of food and wood I earned today. I had no idea how my mother would react to my earnings, but I already imagined that she would have her own thoughts about what I had done for it.

The coachman held out his hand and I stepped out carefully.

My dirty shoes matched the pavement again and even though I was happy to be home, I also realised that maybe I could get used to the capital, its cleanliness and its greatness.

I shook my head as I couldn't help but cursing myself for thinking like that. I was a simple girl from a simple village. I would be delusional if I allowed myself to believe in the slightest chance of living there. I didn't belong and I never would.

"I received the order to pick you up again in three days." The coachman bent his head and I bent my knees slightly, too.

"Thank you so much and I'm already looking

forward to it." I wasn't sure if I meant those last words, but I decided it was better to fake a little politeness. I turned around and squeezed my eyes when I stared at the small house in front of me.

Even though all houses in the village looked scarily alike, this house was clearly not my house. Not only did it miss the characteristic smell that always surrounded our home, it had also quite a few more decorations than we could afford.

I turned around and cocked my head slightly. "I think there has been made a mistake. This is not my home."

The coachman smiled and nodded once again. "This is your home now. You have not been paid for picking that wonderful flower bouquet that will brighten my lord's room tonight." He climbed on the carriage again and greeted me while he ordered the horses to find their way back to the capital.

I felt sorry for the horses. Not only were they forced to pull a carriage made of gold, they probably experienced next to no freedom, just like me. I watched until they were out of sight and then I turned back to the house. My house. I didn't have to share one with my family anymore. I had my own bed and I wouldn't have any prying eyes following my every move. I had the entire house for myself, but I wasn't sure how I felt about it.

When I pushed the wooden door, of the very first house of my own, open, I sighed in relief when it squeaked, just like the one at my parents' home did. I didn't even know why I liked it, why I was relieved about it. Maybe because it was one familiar thing.

It would take time before my house smelled familiar. Just like it would take time for me to feel at home in a house I had never thought I would have.

I walked towards the living room. I was used to people greeting me when I walked in, or at least people staring at me with judging eyes, depending on where I had been. Now, I found the living room with a comfortable couch, a wooden table and four chairs, but no people.

The fire was already burning, but the warmth was unfamiliar, even slightly strange. The first thought that crossed my mind was how long the fire had already been burning and how much wood had been wasted while there was no-one here to enjoy its purpose.

I didn't have to think like that, but it was a habit I could not easily shake. Maybe if Nick kept on giving me more food and wood than I actually needed, I could give some of it away to people who needed it more. A small, slightly bitter voice in the back of my mind wondered why Nick had not bought me a house in the capital, but I corrected that voice by adding that he probably knew just as well as I did, that I wouldn't be happy there, that I didn't belong there, that it was too far away from my family.

A strange smell, coming from the kitchen, filled my nose. A huge bowl of soup, filled with vegetables I couldn't even name, boiled on the fire. Fresh baked bread waited for me in the oven.

I didn't even dare to open any of the closets. I already suspected what I would find, and I was certain I wasn't ready for it. I wasn't ready to have more than I needed.

Nick had probably given my family the exact same thing. They had probably gathered in the living room with filled plates and growling stomachs, while they discussed what I had done to earn it.

I wished I was there to see the look on Benjamin's face. He had already been happy with a couple of sandwiches this morning and I imagined the glimmer and wonder in his eyes when he saw this. I hoped they realised that I earned them enough food for the rest of the month and they didn't have to be careful with the portions. I hoped they would fill Benjamin's plate two times, even three times if he wanted, so he would experience a full stomach for the first time in his entire life.

He would probably gain weight during the next couple of weeks. He would grow and maybe he would eventually manage to catch up with the healthy children in the capital. He would probably also notice the desire and longing, so far numbed by the lack of food and warmth, for the outside world.

My mother would take care of him. Even though she would never take him into the woods and wouldn't teach him how to give in to the longing and hunger and urges, she would teach him how to control it, how to enjoy the benefits without being bothered by the downsides. She would tell him the stories about father and why she kept our entire family within the four walls of our home as much as she could.

As long as we didn't know who poisoned my father and how they did it, we had to make sure no one suspected us being more than the mere humans we tried to appear to be.

I eventually had to open one of the closets and found a full set of plates and bowls, clearly brand new and out of place in a house for a girl like me. I filled one of the small bowls with the soup and broke off a huge piece of the bread before I headed back to the living room.

The house lacked cosiness. It missed voices, whispering of people. It lacked life and it seemed too big for only me, even if it wasn't big enough for an entire family.

I wished I could have Benjamin living here with me, maybe my sisters too, but my mother would never allow that. Not only would she be afraid of me teaching them all kinds of manners I had been taught by father, but she would also feel challenged in her position as our leader. I've already been close to challenging her position several times.

My father had always known that one day I would be the one taking control of our family. He had been preparing me for it. He had taught me how to determine whether I wanted something for myself or whether I wanted something because it was best for everyone. He had taught me how to recognise danger and how to respond to it. Instead of locking me up, like my mother had done after he died, he had helped me develop my senses and talents so I could use them to our advantage. In a way, he would have been proud of me at this moment, even though he might have admitted that I wasn't supposed to rise this fast and this soon.

My mother was still healthy, especially compared to human women her age. I should allow her to lead us for another few years at least.

I sighed once more and tried to stop thinking while emptying my bowl and eating my bread in absolute silence. The full stomach combined with the tiring day took their toll and before the sun had set completely, I climbed the stairs to the first floor.

A huge double bed stood in a big bedroom, with two huge pillows, thicker and softer than any pillow I had ever seen in my life. The sheets were whiter and brighter than I had ever imagined sheets to be, and the bed was covered in more blankets than my family had ever owned.

Nick had tried to give me a house from the capital. Even though the exterior fitted into Waterfield perfectly, the interior didn't. No one in Waterfield owned anything this new or this luxurious. I was now certain that everything we gathered came from rich families who didn't want it anymore.

I pulled my dress over my head and took off my briefs. The smile on my face brightened while I lay down on top of the blankets and my head rested on one of the pillows. I closed my eyes waiting for sleep to overcome me.

But sleep didn't come. Over the last few years, my body had gotten used to sharing a bed with at least two others and how to find the most comfortable position on the wooden floor. The severe circumstances had become my habitat and it seemed that not even soft pillows and a tower of blankets changed that.

I turned from my right side on my back and stared at the ceiling above. Yesterday, I was a girl enjoying the woods and the company of animals to the fullest. Today, I owned a house, a bed, and more furniture than I ever expected to have. I should be happy.

My life had changed for the better after running into Nick. He had given me more than I ever wished for, but there were so many others deserving his help far more than I did.

As a wolf, I had the means to take care of myself. Most of our neighbours really had only what the chiefs gave them for their work.

I turned to my left side and folded my hands under my head. Even though I was tired and kept my eyes closed, my heart raced in my chest. I haven't seen my family today, after I left in a golden carriage to work for a man I had met in the woods in the middle of the night.

Maybe I should have gone to their house to check on them. Maybe I should have assured myself that they had indeed gotten everything Nick had promised to give them. Maybe I should have passed by to give them an explanation.

A part of me knew that just like me, they couldn't be as happy with all those things as they should be. It made them stand out. The very thing we tried not to do.

Chapter Six

"Emily!"

Without thinking, I hid my naked body under the blankets and placed one of the pillows over my head.

"Emily! Where are you?" My mother clearly attempted to be everything but silent.

She climbed the stairs with hammering steps, and I took a deep breath while refusing to open my eyes.

"Emily!" My mother threw the bedroom door open and I didn't have to look to know what kind of expression she wore on her face. "I demand an explanation!" She grabbed the blankets and uncovered me without warning.

I threw the pillow on the floor and my muscles tensed, triggered by my instinctual response to fight when feeling threatened, even though in this case, the threat was simply my own mother yelling at me.

"Who is that boy you're working for? What kind of work have you done and how is it possible that you have earned all of this in only one day?"

I sighed and refused to even push myself up to face her. I didn't remember if I had fallen asleep before the sun had risen again, but the little sleep I had gotten wasn't enough to make up for all the energy I used up to survive the previous day or the energy I needed to wear that dress for an entire afternoon.

"Emily!" My mother grabbed my shoulders and my eyes flashed open.

My heart beat rapidly in my chest and I took a few

deep breaths to control the adrenaline racing through my veins. "Mother..." I eventually managed to whisper. "I would have visited you and the rest of the family later today, there was no need to march into my house." I quickly searched for my clothes and put them on without being bothered by my mother's judgemental stare.

"I expected you yesterday with a good explanation." She had her arms crossed over her chest and I noticed her muscles were as tensed as mine. "We do appreciate the food and the wood, but we do not appreciate you simply disappearing without having the decency to tell us in person that you are moving out."

I rolled my eyes and crossed my arms over my chest, too. I wasn't sure if it was to close myself off or if it was more to protect my mother from whatever was boiling inside of me. "I'm sorry that the carriage dropped me off at my own house and that I was too tired to find out how to get from my place to yours." I tried to keep my voice calm, but I heard the slight trembling and realised that my body was already prepared for where this conversation would eventually lead.

"You still haven't given me an explanation, young lady." My mother spoke twice as loud as I did and the veins in her neck were visibly beating. "Do I need to make it an official order for you to talk to me?"

"No, you don't." I shook my head, lifted my chin, and straightened my back. "I just don't understand what other explanation I could give you, since I've already told you the entire story right after I was brought home by Lord Edwards."

"You told me that he offered you a job, not that his payments would be this extraordinary, which makes me question the nature of the work he makes you do.”

“You are worried that I have allowed him to take advantage of my body in exchange for food, wood, clothes and an entire house?” I raised my eyebrows and after a few more deep breaths I wondered what I had done to make my own mother think this of me. I had expected the entire village to gossip about our sudden living improvements. I had not expected my own family to do the same.

“Are you really demanding a report of my entire day?” I swallowed and she nodded sternly. “Fine,” I sighed. “At first, he made me sign a contract that seemed to be to his disadvantage.”

“What did the contract say?” There was no doubt my mother demanded a detailed report.

“It stated how I have the right to refuse each and every task and that I can decide not to continue with the agreement at any moment.” I kept my eyes locked with my mother’s and saw my own initial confusion mirrored in her glance. “It also stated that I was not allowed to refuse any payment.”

“Why would someone phrase a contract like that?” My mother raised her eyebrows and I did the same.

“For some reason, he seems to have decided to save me from poverty and misery. He’s clearly making up useless tasks to have an excuse to spoil me with payments I can’t refuse.”

“Are you sure he’s not setting a trap?” My mother cocked her head.

I wasn’t sure if he was not setting a trap, although I got the impression that he really did all of this because he simply had a heart that big beating in his chest. “I don’t think he’s aware of what I am, or what my father was.”

"You don't think so, but you are not sure?" My mother furrowed her eyebrows this time and once more, I saw her tensing her muscles. "If you can't be sure about his intentions and knowledge, you have to quit this job."

"I won't do that." I narrowed my eyes a little and stood up from my bed. I was slightly taller than my mother, but I leaned on the tips of my toes to tower over her. "I understand that this is all overwhelming and questionable, but I know that yesterday I fell asleep with a full stomach for the first time in years. I didn't need to fight for a mattress, blankets or a pillow. I didn't need to worry about Benjamin possibly not waking up because of starvation."

"The entire family could end up in huge danger, because you believe food, mattresses, blankets and pillows are more important than our safety."

"I believe that you and I no longer share our definition of safety, mother."

A certain kind of warmth was feeding my muscles and brain with a strength I already sensed within me, but kept it hidden. "I do realise that we have to protect our lives." My voice was remarkably calm now and the true damage had already been done. "I do not believe that denying ourselves our basic needs supports that claim."

My mother wanted to interrupt me, but I lifted my hand and shook my head. "I know that there are people in the outside world who are terrified of our kind and who will do anything they can to erase our existence if they ever discover that we are wolves." I took a deep breath. "It will be my responsibility to make sure they don't find out that we have more in common with father than a couple of genes." I looked at my mother, who seemed to become smaller and smaller by the second. "I am also responsible for giving my sisters and Benjamin a chance at better future."

"I order you to let Lord Edwards know that you will no longer work for him," my mother's voice trembled and no matter how much she tried, I was no longer compelled to follow her orders.

"His carriage will pick me up again in two days and I will not allow it leave empty." I took a deep breath. "I order you to tell the rest of our family that they are welcome to my house at any time." I saw how my mother opened her mouth to reply, but realised that what she wanted to say was stuck in her throat.

"I do hope you realise that if any member of our family dies now or in our near future, it will be on you and no longer on me." My mother dropped her arms and for the first time, the fear she had always spoken about reached her eyes.

"I allow the rest of my family to make their own choices for a while. We have followed strict rules and unreasonable measures for far too long. Everyone is free to decide what they think is good for the pack." I paused for a moment. "If anyone feels the need to see me or to talk to me, my house will always be open." I licked my lips. "And if Benjamin is ready to explore the limits of his powers, you can send him to me. I will be his teacher, just like father has been mine."

"You can't do this, Emily."

"I already did, Mother."

She turned around and rushed down the stairs. On her way out, she slammed the door and I dropped on the bed with my face buried in my hands.

What have I done?

Chapter Seven

Three days later, I entered the golden carriage with trembling knees and a racing heart. I had spoken to each of my family members to tell them myself that I wouldn't give them any orders, that they were free to roam the woods if they wanted to.

I trusted them with putting the safety of our family first, just like I had always done. But no one had dared to use the new-found freedom so far. Not even my uncles who must remember how it felt.

Even though my mother was no longer capable of giving orders, her firm hold on the family was still there and probably wouldn't disappear over night. Especially since I was living in my own house, away from them.

I had a certain responsibility, though. I had to protect Benjamin, Charlotte, Nora, and the others, but I wasn't ready for it. I wasn't ready to think for the entire family instead of just me. I wasn't ready to organise an official meeting to set out the course for the future, until someone else would be strong enough to take my place.

"Welcome back to the capital, my lady." Nick bent his head slightly, while he held up his hand to help me out of the carriage.

He offered me his arm as soon as I got out, and without a word, he lead me into the clothing store where my dress was still waiting.

"Did you enjoy your time in your own home?" He

smiled a bright smile.

He probably waited to see my reaction ever since I returned to Waterfield three days ago.

I curled my lips up into a smile, too. Even though I had once hoped that the noblemen of this kingdom would have more eyes and ears for the problems of the common people, I saw the beauty in his naivety.

I let the young lady of the clothing store help me into my dress and I didn't even complain when she tied the corset a little tighter than she had done last time. She was still gentle with me and I couldn't help but think that I would have had to endure a lot worse had I been born here instead of Waterfield.

"I hope you don't mind me saying this, since I barely know you, but you somehow look different." Nick made sure to lock his glance with mine, as if he wanted to prove that he was not talking about the dress I was wearing.

"I feel different, too." I replied absentmindedly and bent my head to avoid his staring glance.

I couldn't shake the thought that when my father had talked about what my future would have looked like in the capital, he had talked about someone like Nick. "My mother actually tried to forbid me from coming back today." I looked up slightly, observing his reaction.

"She didn't appreciate the food and logs I delivered to her house?" Nick raised his eyebrows slightly and I noticed the honest disbelief in his eyes.

It seemed that he really couldn't imagine that my mother had any reason to complain about my wages. He couldn't imagine the kind of thoughts that had crossed her mind when she heard about all I had earned and he couldn't come up with any reason to not accept his gifts, which, in his eyes, probably didn't seem that big.

"She was worried about my safety here in the capital." I cocked my head slightly while I made sure to not look as confident as I really felt.

I noticed a certain increase in my vigour and that was not just because I started having three healthy meals a day. "And she is worried about our safety in the village when other people find out about our sudden riches." I licked my lips and once more I bent my head. I didn't have the illusion that I could explain the possible dangers to him.

"My mother is always worried about everything, too." Nick gave his boyish grin and I saw dancing lights in his beautiful blue eyes. "If there is anything I can do to assure your mother that you are safe here in the capital and that we are willing to do everything we can to guarantee your safety in the village, I would love to do so."

How could my mother even think that this young man, was aware of my family being wolves, and the reason behind my father's demise? How could she believe that Nick had ever heard of the name we carried before we took my mother's name? How could she think that there were any bad intentions and hidden motives behind his offerings apart from pure goodness?

"I will ask her if there is something you can do to reassure her, and I will tell you when we meet next time." I looked at him again and I noticed how the smile on his face brightened as if that one statement made him happier than he already was.

"Does this mean that you are not going to listen to your mother and are planning to continue working for me?" He shifted his weight from one leg to the other and scratched the back of his neck.

"I have to admit that there is a certain guilt eating me at night. I know that there are little children in my village forced to do work long hours in the scorching sun for much less than I have earned with simply signing a contract." I paused for a short moment.

I had no idea what kind of position Nick had, how important he really was and how much influence his family had, but if I wouldn't take this opportunity to tell him what the people in Waterfield endured, I would have even more reason to feel guilty and lie awake at night.

"The children in Waterfield are working?" Nick's eyes widened and I fought the urge to stretch out my hand to touch his cheek.

He had, without a doubt, grown up thinking that every child in this kingdom was born with the same luck.

I was sorry for disturbing his wonderful image of a perfect world, but sooner or later, he would have to face the truth anyway. "Most of them don't have a choice. Our families are big and it's impossible for the parents to earn enough to feed all those hungry mouths." I cleared my throat and, in a way, I was glad that Benjamin, even though he had never had an easy life, had not spent his life like those other children.

"What kind of work are those children doing?" Nick spoke softly as if he was still processing my words and what they implied.

"The same work as the adults." I swallowed.

Even though I had to shatter his image of the kingdom, I wanted to do so gently.

"The crown asks for more and more goods to be

transported to the capital. Since we only get very little in return, even children are forced to plough, weed, and harvest." I paused for a moment. "Not every child survives the wounds and dehydration."

"Children are dying?" Nick's eyes widened even more, and I nodded, even though I wished I could undo the tearing in his beautiful eyes.

"The children and families in Waterfield, and I assume most other villages, don't have much of a choice." I spoke softly. "Either they die because there is nothing to eat, or they take the risk of possibly dying while earning what little they can by doing work no one else wants to do."

"I…" Nick opened his mouth to say something, but all his words seemed stuck in his throat.

He had probably never visited the villages before he met me and even though the older noblemen in this capital had to know what kind of life we endured, they didn't seem to see the need for telling their children about our circumstances.

"I know it's not your fault that we are forced to live like this." I looked at the young man in front of me and noticed his blushing cheeks, as if a certain form of shame consumed him. "I believe you didn't even know we lived like that."

"No…" Nick bent his head and this time he was the one to avoid my glance. "I have never been taken to the villages and I had always thought that the villages were just like the capital but only smaller."

"It's okay. It's up to our king to do something about it, not up to you." I grabbed his hands without even thinking about it and squeezed them gently. "I assume you had plans for today?"

"Yes…" He cleared his throat and his cheeks

turned even redder as if, all of a sudden, he understood that each and every one of these tasks felt like fun to me. "The king has asked me to find the best cake in town for the royal ball and I wondered if you wanted to help me taste them all?"

I couldn't help but smile. "I'd love to."

Chapter Eight

"We hope that you'll enjoy our strawberry chocolate cake, pr…" a pretty server with a big smile didn't get the chance to finish her sentence.

"The real question is not whether I enjoy it, but whether she does," Nick nodded towards me, and I raised my eyebrows.

I knew nothing about cake and how it was supposed to taste. I was almost certain that I had never eaten cake before. Of course, I've heard people talking about it, but my mother had never earned enough to get luxury goods. I wasn't even sure if she had ever learned how to make something like it.

"If there is anything you don't like, feel free to let us know." The server turned her face towards me, and I smiled at her.

I was certain that I wouldn't even notice if there was something wrong with the cake, but I appreciated her gesture. "So…" I exhaled when she turned around and walked away. "How do we eat this, before I make a complete fool of myself?"

Nick lifted his eyebrows and a playful smile brightened his features. He was surely charming in his own special way and, for a moment, my lips curled up before I realised that I was staring.

"I'm sorry, but I'm not joking, Nick." I swallowed. "I really have no idea how to eat this." I bent my head and stared at the small plate with a little fork in front of me.

"You have no idea how to eat cake?" Nick shook his head and folded his hands on the table. "Are you implying that you've never eaten cake before?"

"We barely have enough for bread. I don't know which ingredients are essential and which aren't, but I'm sure they are out of reach and have always been." I bent my head and avoided his glance, but there was no judgement in his eyes.

He was surprised about certain things, but he didn't laugh or judge, and he didn't seem to believe I was stupid because I had no idea how to do some things.

"Does this also mean that you have never celebrated your birthday?"

I didn't know what birthdays and cake had to do with each other, but I shrugged my shoulders. "My family congratulates me for surviving another year and sometimes they are kind enough to grant us a place on one of the beds for the night, but that's all the celebration we can afford."

"How many birthdays have you celebrated like that?" Nick reached for my hand over the table.

He probably didn't notice that there was a certain intimacy in that. It also felt out of place, considering I was working for him. But he most likely also forgot about that most of the time.

"Twenty-three," I replied while avoiding his glance.

I had to admit that I never asked my parents how we used to celebrate my birthdays when I was a small child, but I assumed it wasn't that different. Probably it had only been considered a miracle that I had survived another year. I remembered trying to sing for my siblings on their birthdays when I was younger.

"Then we have to make up for twenty-tree missed opportunities to have cake." Nick smiled and I stared at the enormous cake in front of us.

I didn't know how many different cakes we were supposed to try, but I was sure that I wouldn't even be able to finish this one, and I was sure my panic was visible on my face.

"There is no need to panic. They made this entire cake to show us the design. We will only taste one small piece, then we will politely tell them how lovely it was, and that we will let them know if the royal family wants to order a replica of this cake for the ball in a couple of weeks."

I nodded, even though my muscles tensed and my heart rate increased steadily. I understood that the design of the cake was as important as its taste, but the thought that most of it was going to be wasted while the people in the villages went to bed hungry, started to feed my guilt, which was already eating me anyway.

"Is everything alright?" Nick leaned a little towards me and I took a deep breath.

"Do you realise how many people you could please by giving them this cake after we've tasted just one slice?" I looked at him and observed the frown on his forehead growing deeper and deeper. "And I don't know how many more cakes you were planning on tasting, but maybe you can feed everyone in Waterfield. Probably everyone in a few other villages, too."

"Do you really think giving them the leftovers of our small tasting session would make them happy?" Nick raised his eyebrows, but the frown on his forehead disappeared slightly.

"Of course, it would!" I raised my voice and

realised that we were not alone in the cosy restaurant. "Even though this is probably not as healthy as bread or meat or milk, it's still better than having to go to bed with an empty stomach," I spoke softly this time, as I stared at the cake.

The cake had at least three layers. They were all decorated with flowers and animals, and a sweet smell of sugar filled my nose.

"I will see if I can cut the cake with as little damage as possible, so they won't see immediately that people have already eaten from it." He grabbed the sharp knife next to his plate and carefully cut two small slices, each from another layer. He placed the bigger piece on my plate and put the other on his. "If you prefer eating the cake without a fork, I promise I won't comment on it." Nick winked while he grabbed the tiny fork and started to take small bites. "Actually, I can imagine why someone would prefer not using the fork that forces you to eat small bites."

I grinned, but I grabbed the fork and copied his movements. Carefully, I took a small bite, but I moaned softly when the unfamiliar tastes mixed in my mouth.

I had eaten strawberries before. My father had taken me to one of the fields during the night and we had eaten fruit until we both got sick. We never told my mother or the rest of the family about our little adventure and if someone even noticed the missing strawberries, they never found out that we had been the cause of it.

"I assume this is meant as a compliment for the cake?" Nick grinned and I opened my eyes while my cheeks heated.

"I've heard the stories about chocolate, but I've

never gotten a chance to taste it and I have to admit that it didn't disappoint." I stared at the slice on my plate and quickly took another bite, and another bite, until the plate was empty.

Had I been at home, I would have licked the plate clean, so I wouldn't have wasted any of the deliciousness, but I was fairly certain that no one in the capital felt the need to do so.

"At least, we now have a standard measure for the other cakes we are about to taste." Nick smiled. "If they manage to make you sound like that, they are perfect candidates. If they fail, they are not good enough for the occasion."

But they would still be good enough for the people in the villages, just like I was certain they would still be good enough for me.

"That's what happens if you're asking someone who has never tasted a cake before to pick the cake for such an important occasion." I cocked my head and stared at the young man in front of me.

An unfamiliar warmth spread through my veins and I forced myself to look away from him until the feeling passed.

"You seem to think that your lack of experience is a disadvantage, but you would be surprised how biased some of the royals can be."

"If you were implying that not all people have the luxury of being biased when it comes to food, you are right." I swallowed and the sweet taste in my mouth turned slightly bitter.

"I didn't mean it like that." Nick shook his head, and I saw the slight panic in his eyes.

"I know." I paused for a short moment and took a deep breath. "I'm glad you're thinking about bringing the rest of the cake to the villages." I tried giving the conversation a more positive turn. "You have a big heart, Nick."

"So have you."

"Giving love to others is free and something everyone can afford."

"Sometimes, the things that are free are the rarest and most valuable."

I've never been sick in my life. I was gifted with an abnormally fast recovery. I was however not immune to too much food, and especially too much cake, in my stomach.

"And which cake should be served at the royal ball?" Nick leaned back in his chair and folded his hands on his stomach. Even though he was not used to an empty stomach like I was, he seemed to feel a bit heavier, too.

At least, that was something we had in common.

"I really enjoyed the cherries, but there is nothing that can top chocolate." As I already expected, I liked every cake we tasted, and I wasn't sure whether I was simply picking the chocolate cake because it was the first cake I've ever tasted.

"I will let the baker know that he can make the chocolate cake ten times as big as the one we tried. I'm certain he'll be pleased to hear that." Nick paused for a moment and then he stared at my hand before he gently grabbed it.

Even though my skin was naturally warm, his touch didn't feel as cold as I had expected it to be. His hand felt slightly sweaty while his fingers tenderly rubbed my knuckles.

It was an unusual feeling. I wasn't used to being touched at all, not even by the members of my own family, apart from Benjamin, and I was especially not used to being touched with so much kindness.

"And I will demand the bakers to bring their remaining cakes to the nearby villages, as you've requested." He nodded his head slightly and then let go of my hand, as if he was, all of a sudden, aware of how intimate the gesture was and how unfitting it seemed.

"Do you think the king will agree to that?" I looked up and smiled.

I saw how he mirrored my expression and there was a light tingling in my stomach that caught my attention.

"The king doesn't need to know," Nick whispered.

He leaned a little towards me as if this was our own little plan, our own little secret.

"You are going to make several villages happy and you believe the king won't find out? I don't want to shatter your illusion, but I'm certain that this will be the talk of the kingdom and it will eventually reach the royal family."

"I'm certain they can understand that there was no harm in this small gesture that could mean so much to so many people." Nick smiled and his blue eyes twinkled as if all the stars were hidden in them.

"I could think of some arguments, like not to awaken the awareness of the people that such riches are being thrown away in the capital, but I would undermine the moment of happiness I attempted to create." I smiled and saw some understanding in his glance. "I will keep those arguments to myself then."

Nick stood up from his chair and offered me his arm. "Why don't we spend some time strolling through the park while the bakers get their carriages ready?" He waited until I stood up from my seat, too, and linked my arm with his.

"Why did you decide to hire me?" I waited to ask the question until we were outside, surrounded by trees and laughing children.

I felt a certain kind of jealousy. I had that sort of childhood once. I had been able to enjoy the outdoors and the small moments of happiness. But I reminded myself that my sisters could barely remember those moments and Benjamin had never experienced that kind of joy.

"Of all those people in need of saving more than I do, why did you choose me?"

"Because I don't believe in coincidences." Nick didn't look at me and instead, he stared at the horizon. "You have crossed my path, quite literally, for a reason. And I am determined to find out what that reason is. If I can make your life, and the lives of countless others, a little brighter in the process, that's even better."

"And what if the price of your kindness and longing to find out why I have entered your life is that the lives of many people will get worse?" I slowed down a little and I stared at my feet. I normally loved being surrounded by nature, flowers, and singing birds. At the moment, however, it caused nothing but an overwhelming longing I couldn't satisfy.

"I will do whatever is in my power to prevent that. If something bad happens because of anything I say or do, I will do anything I can to fix it."

"This society has been broken for so many years. One small crack can damage it beyond repair."

"And one drop of glue might be the beginning of the healing process."

I squeezed my eyes slightly and thought about it

for a moment. I wasn't sure if it was my mother's influence or simply my nature, but I couldn't share his optimistic view on life. I didn't dare to believe that this society could be fixed by a nobleman saving a girl who didn't need his rescue in the first place. I didn't dare to believe that a future where all the children had the chance to play, and no one had to be hungry, was within reach. But I enjoyed that he dared to think like that.

"If you were queen of this kingdom, what would you do?" Nick turned his face towards me, and I bit my lip while I thought about his question for a moment.

"I would send all the children to school instead of working them to death while earning less money than they deserve." I said eventually and swallowed. "I would make sure no one had to pay the crown more than they could afford." I continued while I weighed all my words carefully. "And I would try to blur the lines between the capital and the villages." I bent my head.

"I know that taking away riches to give to the poor won't create a stable kingdom, but I do believe that small changes can have a huge effect, starting with the children being able to play instead of work."

"You would make a great queen." Nick stood still as he stared at me with his eyes and mouth wide open.

"I don't think everyone here in the capital would think so. I assume they're all afraid I would take away what they consider to be rightfully theirs."

"Those few people are afraid of anything that challenges their position in this society. Those are not the people creating the future."

"But I'll never be queen and those people afraid of the change will be in charge during the rest of my life."

I let out a sigh. "I admire your hope, but I can't share it."

"Maybe I can pass some of your ideas along to the royal family, if you wish?" Nick grabbed my hand once more and squeezed it. "I can't guarantee they'll listen, but I won't know until I try, will I?" He locked his eyes with mine and I nodded, not sure what else to say.

I believed that most of his promises were probably empty. And, even if he gave it a try, I doubted the royal family and rulers in the capital would care enough to really listen to him. I was already surprised he was willing to put this much energy into my ideas to begin with.

He didn't need laws that sent children to school and still guaranteed them a plate of food in the evening. He didn't need laws to be able to see the luxuries the capital had to offer. He was born here. Maybe not with a golden spoon in his mouth, but at least with a spoon full of food in his mouth.

"I appreciate that. Telling the royal family that sending their leftovers to the villages would be the start of a better world is already a nice beginning."

"Then we will start there." Nick nodded and bent his knees slightly, even though he was many ranks above me. At least his heart was in the right place. "I assume you want to witness the delivery of the cake to Waterfield?"

It was clearly a rhetoric question, so I simply nodded.

"I will get your carriage ready then, too. Do you want to change dresses once more?" He stared at the expensive looking dress I was currently wearing.

"Yes, I want to arrive with the cake as one of them and not one of yours." My cheeks heated while I said those last words, but he seemed to understand what I meant. "After all, I'm simply your hired help and nothing more."

"You fail to acknowledge how important your presence has already become in my life."

"You have all the riches in the world, but a simple village girl has become someone of importance?"

Nick bent his head and folded his hands behind his back. "Our riches do not define us, neither does our place of birth."

Chapter Nine

Normally, I slept the entire way from the capital to Waterfield, but today, I kept my eyes on the carriages before me.

One by one, they changed direction. One of the carriages with more cake than any of the villagers had probably ever seen, had eventually gone to Firebelt. Another one had taken the path to Woodston. A third one had taken the hard road to Rockham. The fourth one was still riding in front of the carriage that was on its way to bring me home.

I was certain that everyone would appreciate the extra food, but I grew slightly more nervous the closer we got to Waterfield. I had never even seen a golden carriage before I had run into Nick and now two of those carriages rode over the damaged cobbles of the village.

Eventually, the carriages stopped in the middle of the market square and before I was able to get out of mine, the people of Waterfield have already gathered around them.

My cheeks blushed when I noticed everyone staring at me as if I was their saviour.

"There is no need to be afraid or surprised." I cleared my throat. I've never had to speak in front of so many people, but right now, I had the sudden urge to say something. "The capital just wants to surprise you all with cake."

The villagers exchanged glances, frowned, and

seemed to be frozen to the stones beneath their feet. It was as if they didn't dare to believe that the capital would grant the village commoners with such a gift.

"I promise there are no hidden meanings. It's not poisoned, and nothing is expected in return." I had to admit that I wasn't sure if this was entirely true, but if my statement were to be contradicted by higher taxes, it still wouldn't take away the joy of today. I hoped. "Could you please open the carriage and get the cake so everyone can enjoy a piece of it?" I nodded at the coachman, and he returned the nod before he did so.

The eyes of the villagers widened, and a few children almost hurt each other while trying to reach the huge cake first.

"Before I give all of you a piece of the cake…" the coachman cleared his throat and his dark voice echoed through the village, which all of a sudden fell quiet.

I found my mother in the crowd and she shook her head and crossed her arms over her chest. I didn't know what I had done wrong this time, but I knew that look all too well. Despite the fact that my mother couldn't give orders anymore, she would still try to tell me exactly why this entire situation was a problem for our family.

"I have an announcement to make." The coachman unfolded a yellow piece of paper. He coughed a few times before he straightened his back and lifted his chin.

I lifted my eyebrows and for a moment, I didn't know where to look. A part of me wanted to find a spot in the crowd, hidden and out of sight. Another part of me knew that everyone would notice if I walked away from the spot next to the coachman and his important paper.

"In a few weeks, the royal ball will be held. To show the villages that the royal ball is not just for the elite, every village is encouraged to choose two people to attend the royal ball. They will be assisted with picking out a dress or a uniform and they will be allowed to enjoy the ball in the exact same way as everyone else who is attending."

A mixture of utter shock, surprise and a slight bit of excitement was spreading like fire through the crowd. Some girls were already claiming their right to attend because they really wanted to see the capital and the royal court, while older people wondered why the royal family showed a sudden interest in the villages, since they had clearly not cared about the situation outside the capital before.

"Calm, calm…" Gareth, the representative of our village, entered the market square and lifted his hand.

He was also chief of most of the fields and workplaces and half of the villagers on the square were working for him. The other half knew all too well that this man had the ability to determine which families would survive and which ones wouldn't.

"Did you arrange this?" Gareth headed straight towards me and, for a moment, I wasn't sure if I would be better of saying yes or no.

"I might have had some influence on this, yes." I tried to get some support from the coachman, but the coachman was more focussed on guarding the cake from longing hands than the conversation. "I have a job with a nobleman, and I have told him about the circumstances in the village. He asked the royal family if it would be possible to send the cakes, that were only made for tasting and would be thrown away, to the villages where the people would be happy to enjoy them."

The farmer glanced over me, up and down, before his eyes rested for a moment under my neck. Then, all of a sudden, I felt even more uncomfortable than I already did.

"In that case, I think you should be the first candidate to attend the royal ball. You've earned it."

For a moment, I stared at him in disbelief. My heart was racing in my chest, while all the eyes on the square, including my mothers, stared at me.

Although I never liked being condemned to a life within the walls of our house, I never desired to be in the centre of attention of the outside world either.

"It is the least we can do to thank you for this wonderful gesture," he pointed at the cake while he said this.

In the crowd, I saw the girls from earlier, the ones who considered themselves suitable candidates, staring at me as if I had just taken one of their spots but was by far not important enough to do so.

If they ever visited the capital before they would know that none of the village girls would stand out in the crowd during the ball. At least not in the way they hoped. How could anyone with damaged working hands and skin dried and darkened by hot sun feel pretty among people with impeccable skin and beautiful hands?

I felt my mother praying for me to decline. In her eyes, I was already playing with fire by spending this much time in the capital with a nobleman. I wanted nothing more than to prove her wrong. I could do this. I could work for a nobleman without giving away my true nature and I could attend the ball without putting my family in mortal danger.

"Well? I assume it's not a hard question to answer? You're free to decline, but I won't offer again." Gareth crossed his arms and raised his eyebrows.

"I would love to attend the royal ball, thank you." I was surprised that my voice wasn't even trembling, but I swallowed when I heard my mother's smothered scream from the back of the crowd. "It would be my honour to be one of the two attendants from Waterfield," I continued talking, knowing that I was the only one who heard my mother's reaction.

I assumed that was a good thing.

If my mother's goal was not to stand out, then screaming in terror because her daughter accepted an invitation to the royal ball was not the best possible tactic.

"Since I believe that our crown prince and his younger brother have still not found their true loves, I propose that you are accompanied by another girl to double our chances at gaining more influence when it comes to our kingdom's politics."

I had to admit that I doubted the crown prince and his brother would ever choose a commoner from Waterfield, but it wasn't my place to take away the shimmer of hope they just got.

"Tomorrow morning, before we start our workday, I will organise the princess games to determine the second young woman that will represent Waterfield at the royal ball." The farmer turned towards me, ignoring the whispering voices of the younger girls who barely controlled their excitement, even though they didn't even know what the princes looked like. "And you will be the second judge."

"Me?" I was surprised for a moment, but then I nodded again. "Of course. I will do my very best to pick the perfect representative to accompany me."

"In that case, I would say, enjoy the cake and may the best young woman win tomorrow," Gareth barely finished his sentence before the crowd almost attacked the poor coachman.

Instead of mingling among them, I decided to use this moment to disappear and walk home. I knew all too well who and what would be waiting for me there.

Chapter Ten

"Help!"

The cry was barely audible with everyone, gathered on the market square, trying to get a piece of the delicious cake the capital had sent.

"Someone, please, help…" The screaming man grabbed my dress and forced me to stand still, even though I had not been planning on doing so. "My son…he's dying…" He almost pushed the lifeless body of a maybe eight-year-old boy in my arms.

The smell of blood was overwhelming my senses and my first instinct was to throw the child on the ground. His tiny body was barely recognizable as a body. It resembled a bundle of nerves, flesh, blood, and bones, but nothing was where it was supposed to be. My stomach hadn't growled in a long time, but it responded to this first-class dinner without hesitation.

I could only hope and pray that the father of the child didn't hear it. "What happened?"

I had seen children who had been harmed by scythes before, but not one of them had looked like this. I had to stop breathing to make being near the boy bearable, but I couldn't stop the sickness consuming me.

"I found him in the woods like this…" The father's voice was not even a whisper anymore. His lips were forming words, but he spoke without a sound. "What would do something like this?"

Even though, I could answer the question, I just

shrugged. My lungs burned because I was still holding my breath while I tried to avoid looking at the child in my arms. I had never witnessed the damage wild animals could do, that I couldn't do worse.

Maybe mother was right all this time. Maybe she's been locking us up to protect us from allegations when something like this happened. Maybe mother was right that my order for everyone to do whatever they wanted would get us in trouble.

I've heard the stories about wolves hurting, harming, and even killing people. I've heard how entire villages gathered their pitchforks and weapons. I've heard how the killer, himself, had joined the hunting party to blame some innocent animal to prevent the town from suspecting what was really happening. Not every person of my kind was good.

"I don't know." I eventually answered and it felt like a thousand needles piercing my throat.

All my muscles tensed while they fought the instinctive change my body wanted to start. I had to find a way to control myself. I had to fight the warmth glowing behind my eyes. I had to withstand the piercing pain of my teeth growing. I had to hide the sharp nails piercing the skin of the palm of my hand. And I had to make sure I wouldn't breathe more often than needed.

"What is going on here?" Gareth, the chief of this village, freed himself from the crowd.

His eyes widened when he saw the damaged body of the child and I saw him whispering a word that I haven't heard anyone in the village use since my father died.

"When did it happen?" The look on his face hardened as he took the lifeless body from me. "Where did it happen?" His lips were forming a straight line and if thoughts were lethal, my entire family, including me, would be dead right then and there.

Luckily, he didn't seem to know that one of the beasts he intended to kill was standing right in front of him.

"I have told him a thousand times that he had to stay inside after dark…" The father seemed incapable of answering the simple questions.

His eyes were red and swollen from crying and he shook his head over and over as if he tried to remind himself that this was nothing but a bad dream he would wake up from.

"I have told him that the woods are dangerous. He didn't want to listen. He believed that the stories were nothing but fairytales, designed to scare him."

I bent my head and stared at my feet. Even though I was no longer holding the dead body, I still smelled his blood and flesh when I took an occasional breath. I just didn't see a possibility to walk away from this situation, without having to answer questions I didn't want to answer or without leading them directly to their pray.

"He liked surprising my wife with flowers. He never wanted to tell us where he got them. He didn't want anyone else to steal the flowers for his mom." The father breathed in heavily between the words.

His chest was moving up and down and once in a while, he stared at his barely recognizable son. "I found him in a field with yellow flowers, not too far from the edge of the woods."

"I know that this is an unbearable tragedy. I know that you feel nothing but rage and anger right now. But we have to remain calm." Gareth spoke with a firm voice. "Those people are experiencing a moment of much needed happiness and hope. We can't ruin that moment by showing them the body of your son." He locked his gaze with the father of the child. "I promise you that his death will be avenged and that the monster that did this, will be found and killed."

A shiver rolled down my spine. I didn't hear the voice of a man who was afraid of the unknown. I heard the voice of a man who knew exactly what he was up against and how to handle it.

I wondered if Gareth had anything to do with my father and I feared that, once he realised I was my father's daughter and could be like him, I might be the next victim.

"I want to be the one killing it." The father hissed between his teeth. The tears on his cheeks dried while his sadness was replaced by anger. "That monster killed my son!"

I waited until Gareth turned to face me. "I won't tell anyone, of course. I was happy to be able to give this town something to celebrate. I will not overshadow that moment and replace the happiness with fear."

I understood wanting justice for his son, but I feared this would end with mostly innocent victims. Even if I weren't the very thing they were hunting, I wouldn't want to be a part of that.

I hoped they believed me to be just a helpless young woman, who was already struggling enough to make a living for herself.

"Just…" I made my voice tremble and I hoped I looked scared enough to mislead them. "What monster are you talking about?" I widened my eyes like I've seen humans do right before they were about to do something dangerous or scary.

"I don't want you to have nightmares, girl." Gareth smiled a little. "We will take care of the monsters while you prepare for the ball coming in just two weeks." His eyes wandered over my tender body once more. "Maybe with enough soap and expensive clothes we might be able to turn you into something attractive enough to get the attention of the royal family."

I smiled and ignored his fastening heartbeat. I knew that look in his eyes, and it wasn't impossible to guess which direction his thoughts were going.

"You were tired after a long day and went home. You have not seen this man and his son. You have not heard about the beasts terrorizing our woods." Gareth made clear that I didn't have a choice.

Even though he didn't have the same control over me as my mother had, he had the same look in his eyes.

"I was tired after a long day and went home. I have not seen this man and his son. I have not heard anything about the beasts terrorizing our woods." I swallowed after the word 'beasts' and licked my lips. I hoped Gareth would simply assume that I was afraid and was therefore not feeling very comfortable. "I will wear my prettiest smile tomorrow during the competition and I will enjoy the preparations for the royal ball to the fullest." I added a few more promises and I saw Gareth nodding happily.

"I would promise you to find and kill the beast, but I know that those beasts have been roaming our woods for as long as I can remember. So, I can't promise anything, but be careful and keep the door to your house locked at all times."

He waited until I nodded again and when I was certain he was not planning on saying anything else, I turned around.

Instead of going to my house though, I changed direction. Although I've just promised not to tell anyone about what happened tonight, I firmly believed that my family had the right to know.

I also had to assure myself that none of us has been involved in killing of an innocent child. Regardless, they might be coming for us and I had no idea how to prepare for whatever would be coming for us.

"Mom?" I knocked on the door of what had been my home until not too long ago. Normally, I just threw the door open and marched in, but somehow that felt different now that I had my own house. "Mom, I know that you're angry with me, but you have to open the door and let me in," I raised my voice and my fist hit the wood until my hand bled.

"Emily, I didn't expect you to come home ever again." Eventually, my mother opened the door.

Her lips were forming a straight line and the anger was still visible in her eyes. She was probably angry about too many things to list and even though I was curious to hear them all, I put that curiosity aside. "Don't you have more important things to do? Assisting your lord? Preparing for the royal ball?" Every word was poisoned with an emotion I couldn't name. It was a mixture of jealousy, disgust, and anger.

"I know that you seem to believe that I don't care about this family at all, but I do, and I need to speak to you and the others, before our chief discovers that father's family is still around." I crossed my arms over my chest.

I only had to order my mom to open the door for her to do so, but I didn't want to abuse my new-found powers, not unless it was absolutely necessary.

"You need to speak to us?" My mother frowned,

but she still hesitated to open the door further. "Is that an order or a demand?"

"It wasn't, but this matter is important enough to make it one if you do not voluntarily open that door without any further questions. The lives of all of us are at stake." I kept my eyes locked with my mother's and I saw the anger and disgust in her eyes fight with the worry and sorrow overcoming her.

I didn't have the intention to scare her, but by not opening the door immediately, I had no other choice. I was scared and worried. After what I told them, everyone within these walls would feel scared and worried.

"In that case, you are lucky. Your uncles and Benjamin just came back from a visit to the woods." My mother almost spit out the words and my heart skipped a beat. "It seems that you're not the only one who has inherited your father's temperament."

"They went into the woods? Tonight?" I could barely breathe, but the words were desperate screams, loud enough to be heard by the neighbours had they not been attending the feast on the market square. "I need to speak to them, right now." I took a deep breath. "I demand to speak to the entire family right now." I bent my head slightly while my mother opened the door.

She no longer had a choice.

I took that choice from her and I didn't regret it. I rushed into the house and saw my family gathered around the table. The food was on the table and Benjamin's cheeks had a colour I've never seen on him before.

"Emily!" Benjamin jumped up from his seat and wrapped his arms around my body. He had clearly not gotten my mother's message that I was a *persona non grata* in this house and that he was not supposed to still love me.

A smile spread across my face, and I pressed him a little tighter to my chest. "Benjamin, I've heard you have been to the woods today?" I tried to read his expression, tried to find out if something happened, if somehow he saw the child being attacked.

But his eyes were filled with nothing but happiness. "It was wonderful, Emily…" He sighed and his lips curled up into a smile. "We ran through the woods faster than I ever ran before and we even caught a little rabbit." He couldn't hide his excitement, despite my mother's clear judgement.

"I'm glad you had so much fun, Benjamin." I stroked his hair and then pushed him away gently. "But I do have something important to tell and I want you to be here to hear it, too. Do you think you're grown up enough for that?" I stared at him.

The news I was about to bring would destroy the new-found positive mood and I wished there was a way to warn my family without having to destroy everything Benjamin so clearly enjoyed.

"Now that I know how strong I can be? Yes." Benjamin nodded and little did he know that he was exactly proving the opposite.

He wasn't ready to hear about the cruel world outside, hunting him for what he was. He wasn't ready to be confronted with my tale of the poor boy who died in the arms of his father. He wasn't ready to lose the slight bit of innocence he still had left.

"Good, then sit down and listen carefully." I licked my lips and straightened my back.

In a way, I wished that I could simply let my mother take over again, that I could just hand her back the power I had taken, that she would solve this problem for me. But I wanted my freedom and now I had to accept the consequences of bearing the leadership, too.

"On my way from the market square to my home, I met a father with his son." I took a deep breath. I didn't know how to describe the pale white blooded skin and the bite marks all over his little body. "The boy was killed in the woods today, by someone like us." I threw the words out and saw the shocked expressions on the faces of my family members.

Benjamin's eyes watered and his tiny body was shaking.

My first instinct was to wrap my arms around him once more, to assure him that everything would be alright, but saying and doing any of those things would only give him false hope. And even though some people begged to differ, I believed that false hope was in no way better than no hope at all.

"It wasn't me!" Benjamin jumped up from his seat and he shook his head over and over while tears rolled down his cheeks. "I promise that it wasn't me and that I didn't hurt anyone!" He stared at me as if he was afraid that I wouldn't believe him.

"Benjamin…" I looked at him, but the words died on my lips. "I am not here to blame you for killing that boy. I am here to warn everyone of the villagers' reaction to this."

I bent my head and avoided his glance. I avoided everyone's glance and, in particular, my mother's. This was exactly what she was afraid of all those years, but this was not our fault. This didn't happen simply because I was in charge now.

"What did Gareth say to you?" My mother

whispered, and for the first time in all those years, her eyes were filled with pure panic and fear.

Her skin was as pale as it could get and she was clearly shivering, just like the rest of us.

"He said that he knew exactly what did this." I spoke slowly and I looked at Benjamin, realizing that he wouldn't sleep tonight without nightmares. "He said that he was going to make sure that the monster would pay the price." I took a deep breath. "I don't think he realises I'm like my father." I bent my head and stared at my bare feet. "But I do know that he will start a beast hunt."

"Do you understand now, Emily, why I was so determined to keep you and the others locked within these walls?" my mother spoke softly and a slight bit of tenderness coloured her voice. "Do you understand why I was afraid that one of those unknowing humans would see one of you? Would kill one of you?"

"What do we do now, mom?" My voice was barely a whisper.

I was carrying the weight of the leadership on my shoulders, but that didn't mean I was automatically given the knowledge and experience to solve problems like this.

Unfortunately, that was not how it worked.

"We do what we have always done." My mother tensed her muscles. "We keep an eye on each other and act like we are worried about being killed by a monster, just like everyone else." She turned her face towards me. "I hate the thought of it, but you also have to continue with everything as you planned. The competition tomorrow. The royal ball." She took a deep breath. "People notice when you let something like that slip through your fingers."

Chapter Eleven

My father taught me not to be afraid because I was stronger, faster, and smarter. He also taught me that no one could hurt me if I didn't show them any weaknesses.

I tried to hold on to this knowledge while I walked towards the village square the next morning. The streets were filled with more people than usually, and I wondered how many people willingly gave up a day of food to get a chance to spend maybe a few seconds with one of our princes.

"Ah, there is our noble saviour!" Gareth placed his strong hand on my back while he greeted me with a smile on his face.

He looked like he slept a lot better than I did, and he was a lot better at pretending that he didn't see the damaged lifeless body of that far too young boy yesterday.

"Good morning, sir." I greeted politely while I hoped he wouldn't notice the dark circles under my eyes.

I couldn't shake the fear and tension last night. I was worried about the front door not having a lock, and no matter how often I tried to remind myself that I would hear someone coming before they could get to me, I couldn't get past drifting away into a slight slumber.

"They'll figure it out…" The voice in my head was repeating that same sentence over and over. With every squeak of the floor the voice became louder and louder. Even the slightest sound made my heart race in my chest.

Eventually, I got out of bed to block the entrance with a few chairs. It didn't make me feel any safer, but at least it calmed that part of my worries. I was sure that no one would be able to get through the front door without me being alarmed.

But they didn't break into our house to kill my father either. They poisoned his food, our food, and we still didn't know how, when and where they did so. We didn't even know who did it, and they could do it again. They could try and kill me. Or my mother. Or any of my other family members, even Benjamin.

A shiver rolled down my spine when I realised that once I've eaten all the food Lord Nick had given me, I could only trust the prey I caught myself in the woods.

But to catch that food in the woods I would have to take the risk I was no longer willing to take. I always enjoyed my freedom to the fullest, but that was before I was so close to the danger.

"Are you familiar with archery?" The farmer's hand was still resting on my back, slowly sliding lower and lower. "I thought it would be enjoyable to let the bow and arrow decide which ladies are to continue to compete in the more ball and etiquette orientated tests."

Instead of disagreeing with him and following my first instinct to say that shooting arrows had nothing to do with being able to eat cake and hold a conversation, I nodded and smiled politely.

I dreamt of him last night. When I closed my eyes I saw him screaming, with a pitchfork in his hand, and all the citizens of Waterfield behind him.

"Monster! Monster! Monster!"

I shook my head and tried to forget the images and the words. I wasn't a monster. I wasn't responsible for the boy that was killed in the woods. My family didn't do it, and we were all disgusted by it as much as anyone else. But if the chief found out what I was, he wouldn't take the time to listen to my arguments.

"Ladies and gentlemen of Waterfield!" While he greeted the excited people on the market square, I tensed my muscles and curled up my fingers to make sure I didn't push his way roaming hand away with too much power.

"Today, we will choose the second girl to accompany Emily Rivers to the royal ball in the capital. Today, we will select the second competitor for the heart of a prince." His hand slid even lower and my discomfort grew with seconds.

"Since we can't have everyone participating in the ball-orientated rounds, we decided to only let the girls, who manage to hit within the middle ring of the board with only one arrow, participate." The grin on his face brightened and I shifted my weight from one leg to the other.

He didn't seem to notice, and his hand was now almost between my legs. "May the bravest and fairest of them all win!" He removed his hand to clap, and I tried to let out a relieved sigh without him noticing.

I straightened my back and did a few small steps to the side while I watched a blonde-haired girl grabbing the bow. Even if I didn't know, her features would give away that she was the farmer's daughter. I shouldn't have been surprised that he had created a contest that only his daughter could win.

I nodded at her politely.

"Don't attract any attention…" My mother wasn't

anywhere near the market square, but I heard her voice in the back of my mind. "Be polite and willing. Don't give him any reason to distrust you or to ask questions."

It was easier said than done. While his daughter's arrow landed in the exact middle of the board, I was keeping an eye on the disgusting man next to me.

My stomach already churned at the thought of his hand touching me. My entire body protested.

I wondered how many young women in vulnerable positions had been forced to endure moments like these over and over again, so they wouldn't jeopardise the little bit of money they earned that day.

"We have one candidate for the next round!" His lips curled up into a smile while he walked towards his daughter and lifted her hand up in the air. He seemed to believe what I already suspected that his daughter would be the only one capable of completing this test.

I never believed in gods. I never had any reason to.

My father was brutally taken from me. My mother became a person I didn't want to call mother any longer. My family was locked between four walls while we were created to run freely in nature. If there were any gods, they played some cruel games with the people I cared about.

I didn't know if I wanted to believe in gods who allowed such things to happen, just like I wasn't sure if I wanted to believe in gods who allowed an innocent boy to be killed in such a horrible way.

They could however make it up to me, by giving one of the other girls, or maybe even two, the unique talent to get that arrow in the absolute middle.

No prayer, no hope, no faith could make that happen after the first ten girls failed.

Most of them never held a bow before. They were struggling with the arrow, the sharp point, the string. They were cursing, screaming, crying, or suffering in silence. The few who managed to shoot the arrow, not only missed the target hopelessly, but also discovered why more trained archers usually wore arm protection.

A noble part of me doubted if this wasn't the perfect opportunity to give up my place. But I was afraid that the man next to me would use it as an excuse to go himself so he could keep an eye on his daughter.

And I was certain of one thing. He wasn't the good and considerate leader he pretended to be. He wasn't interested in Waterfield's best interests. He was only interested in his own gain, and he was using this competition to strengthen his position.

I wouldn't allow this to get any worse than it already was.

More and more girls attempted to achieve the impossible. They spend their entire lives working as hard as they could, hoping for a chance like this, a small silver lining of hope. With every failed attempt that hope was crushed into a million little pieces.

"Are there any other girls who want to try?" Gareth counted to three. "There is really no one else?"

I crossed my fingers behind my back. I prayed to each and every god and to each and every goddess, but there was nothing but absolute silence.

"I hereby declare that my daughter Lilian will accompany Emily to the royal ball." Once more, he lifted his daughter's hand up in a majestic and celebratory manner.

Lilian, however, didn't seem the slightest bit happy.

I assumed she realised that if she wasn't hated

already, she would be hated after this. In a way, I felt sorry for her. Just not as sorry as for all the other girls who had not once in their lives gotten a fair chance.

"And now, everyone back to work." Gareth was still smiling brightly while he turned his face towards me. "I will send a messenger boy to the capital to tell them that you and Lilian are ready to be picked up for the dress fitting."

I forced myself to curl my lips up, even though it was almost impossible to make it look like a smile. "I can't wait for the carriage to pick us up."

Chapter Twelve

"Is this real gold?" Lilian cocked her head while the tip of her finger reluctantly touched the window.

Ever since her father proclaimed her the second young woman to attend the royal ball, she was talking and asking questions continuously.

"How fast do you think the horses go?"

She was a few years younger than I was and it seemed that in a way she had profited more than just a little from the position her father had managed to get for himself.

"Have you lost your tongue or something?" Lilian looked up and when her eyes met mine, I couldn't help feeling a slight bit of the hate slipping away.

"No, I'm capable of talking, but I am afraid I don't know the answers." I stared at the trees passing by.

The last few times I was in the carriage, I was asleep and now, for the first time, I saw how the world slowly shifted from poverty to riches. "I think this is real gold. And I think the horses are going faster than you can run." I gave her a slight smile.

Lilian had big blue eyes and with her blonde hair, she would surely turn into a beauty once she got a pretty dress to wear. But there was a difference between looking like a princess and behaving like a princess.

If she was in any way like her father, she would never manage to become the latter. "And you? Do you think you can run faster than the horses?"

I could run faster than the horses, but that was not something she had to know. "I don't think any human can." I bent my head and realised that even though it was not a lie, it did make me slightly uncomfortable.

Her father wanted to hunt my kind. He believed that anyone who was like me or my family to be the worst monsters in the world. If only he knew that he sent his daughter to the capital sharing a carriage with one of those monsters he wanted to kill.

His daughter was in no danger from me, but I wasn't sure if he would share that point of view once he realised I could turn into a wolf.

"How are the people in the capital? Are they nice?" Lilian interrupted a short moment of silence and she placed a hand on my knee.

Her hand was colder than my skin, but if her father didn't notice the difference in my temperature, I was certain she wouldn't either.

"My father never wanted to take me to the capital with him. He said he was too busy with business meetings to show me around. But he always got me cake for my birthday, though. Is it true that the people in the capital eat cake all the time?"

"No, of course not." I shook my head and thought about Nick and all the people I met during my two days with him. "If they ate that much sugar every day, they wouldn't be able to walk anymore. They would be too heavy." I grinned and thought about Nick being as round as a ball, rolling from one restaurant to the other. "The cake is for special occasions, like the royal ball."

Lilian nodded and I noticed that she didn't look as worn out and underfed as the rest of us. Her hands weren't raw and scarred from working hard, day in, day out. Her clothes didn't look like they were on the brink of falling apart. She looked healthy. Maybe Gareth took more for himself and his family than he tried to let on.

Even though Benjamin was quite a few years younger than Lilian, he seemed so much older at times. Life has forced him to grow up too fast, just like most of the children in Waterfield. They never had the chance to be children.

Too often Benjamin was sent to bed with an empty stomach. Too often he was denied a hug or a kiss because no one had the time to hold him close. Too often he was lonely and afraid. All of it left marks on his young face. Most of the time he wore a frown on his forehead and there was a certain sadness in his eyes.

"Have you ever been to a royal ball before?"

It was hard to determine if she was seriously not aware of the fact that normally girls from Waterfield didn't visit royal balls, or if she was instructed by her father to mask her questions so she could trick me into giving away information I would never give up otherwise.

"No, but I do know that they have wonderful dresses in the capital, and I am certain that you will enjoy each and every second of this." I stared out of the window again.

The trees, cut into different shapes and figures, were a shade of green that didn't exist outside the capital. The stones beneath the wheels of the carriage were much more comfortable than the ones we rode when we left the market square. The small houses of our hometown had been replaced by the gigantic white houses covered in decorations.

"It really looks different here." Lilian followed my glance and folded her hands in her lap. The longer I had to share a carriage with her, the more she annoyed me. "Do you think that if people like us at the ball we will be allowed to live here?" She widened her eyes again while she turned her head towards me.

I opened my mouth to answer her question with a firm no, but then I thought of Nick and how willing he was to help me. I didn't dare hope for it, but I couldn't know for sure there wouldn't be more people like him. Maybe there would be someone willing to help Lilian. "I don't know."

"You don't know much, do you?" Lilian said and crossed her arms.

I raised my eyebrows while I tried to fight the disbelief coming over me.

"I'm only a simple girl from Waterfield and sometimes knowing that you don't know something is better than thinking you know something and ending up being wrong." I sounded a little bitter, but she didn't seem to notice. "I can't tell you much about the capital, but let me tell you that we are worth absolutely nothing over here."

The smile on her face faded and her lip trembled a little while she was quiet for the first time since she won the unfair competition. "Then why are they inviting us for the royal ball?" She lifted her eyebrows while she looked at me again.

I let out a loud sigh and I shrugged. I didn't have the slightest idea how Nick managed to convince the royal family to invite commoners from the villages to their annual royal ball.

"See! You don't know anything! You're boring! Father shouldn't have let you take that first spot, because you're not standing a chance with any of the princes." She rolled her eyes and lifted her chin. All the cuteness and false innocence was now turning into arrogance and I had to fight the urge to tell her that she was not going to attract the attention of wealthy people who had plenty of nicer people to choose from.

"I only started working for a nobleman a few days ago. Until then, I haven't been out of Waterfield either." I swallowed and my lips were forming a straight line while I crossed my arms over my chest, too.

I tried to like Lilian. I tried to be nice to her. I tried to forget that she was her father's daughter and had clearly gotten advantages in life. I tried not to blame her for the mistakes and injustices caused by her father.

I always thought that no villagers could become arrogant, but Lilian and her father showed me otherwise.

"You work for a nobleman?" Her jaw dropped and she suddenly moved forward and stared straight into my eyes. "How is it? What is he like? Does he like you?"

"He is my boss and so far, he's been kind and nice and I don't know whether or not he likes me."

"All those things you don't know are really getting boring." Lilian leaned back and I mirrored her movement.

I realised that not trying to answer her questions was probably a far better idea.

Chapter Thirteen

"Welcome to the capital." Nick bent his head when he helped me out of the carriage. "I had already hoped they would send you as one of the representatives of Waterfield." He grabbed my hand and lifted it to kiss my knuckles.

"And you doubted whether or not he liked you?" Lilian raised her eyebrows while she followed me, clearly annoyed that she had to get out of the carriage with the help of mere coachman.

"You really are stupid." She walked past Nick and me with her nose up in the air as if she was a royal herself.

"I see they didn't manage to find an equal match to accompany you?" Nick spoke softly while his lips formed a charming smile.

His blue eyes were glimmering in the sunlight and I only realised that I was drowning in them, when he turned his head away suddenly.

"She is the daughter of our chief, representing our village before the king." I rolled my eyes and took a deep breath. "It seems that his privileged status got to her head a little."

"A little?" Nick grinned and he shook his head. "I am certain that my brother might find her quite charming anyway." Nick looked over his shoulders to watch a handsome young man with blond hair and the same piercing blue eyes welcoming Lilian in a way closer to what she might have expected.

"I doubt that." I smiled at him and felt sorry for the younger lord. "It's not my usual habit to judge people based on their upbringing, but this shared ride with her changed my mind for this particular occasion." I cocked my head and squeezed my eyes.

Even though Lilian belonged to one of the wealthiest families in Waterfield, she was still a villager.

"And here I thought that everyone in the villages was as wonderful as you are." Nick winked while he offered me his arm. He was wearing a white suit, and I couldn't help but wonder what he would look like on his wedding day.

"There is only one me." I kept my eyes on the door of the tailor shop. Even though I've been here before, I was even more uncomfortable now than I was the first time I entered.

This time, we were here because of me and this time, the dress would be a lot more extravagant than my work dress. That also meant that my dress would be a lot more unpleasant.

"And I've managed to meet her in the woods by accident." Nick winked at me as he pushed the door open for me. "I am certain that Martha will be delighted when she discovers that one of her dresses will be worn by you."

I forced myself to smile at him, but I didn't share his enjoyment. I should have said that I didn't want to go to the ball as soon as Gareth offered me the first spot.

Or maybe I should have simply stuck to my job without trying to educate a noble on how horrible the circumstances in the villages were.

For a short moment I even regretted accepting his

job offer in the first place. After all, had I not accepted his offer, everything would have still been the same.

"I promise that you will be able to enjoy the royal ball to the fullest. No one will know which girls are from the capital and which ones are from the villages."

Nick guided me towards the comfortable couch in the middle of the room where Lilian was already sitting, a bit too close to Nick's younger brother.

"I don't believe we've met yet." Nick's brother held out his hand while he tried to free himself from Lilian's intrusion in his personal space. Now I saw him up close I noticed his eyes had two different colours, one blue and one brown. "I'm Philippe, Nicho…Nick's brother." He looked at his brother and a smile spread across his face. "I've heard more than a few stories about you."

"I hope your brother has only told you the good ones?" I frowned when I noticed Lilian's hand on Philippe's leg.

"He assured me that there were only good stories to tell." Philippe winked and I saw the smile on Lilian's face disappearing.

Abruptly, she pulled her hand back and stood up from. "You don't want to have me here, do you?"

She placed her hands on her waist, and I looked at Nick in confusion.

"What does she have that I don't?"

I took a deep breath and rolled my eyes but kept silent. Members of my family worked on the fields her father governed in name of the crown and even though I hoped to earn enough to keep them fed for a while, I didn't want to be the cause of them losing their jobs.

"I spent some time with Emily and my brother was excited to finally meet her in person, but I assure you that he's all yours for the rest of the day." Nick bent his head slightly, but I saw a certain kind of amusement reaching his eyes.

It seemed that he realised that his brother wouldn't make it to the end of the day in the company of this entitled young woman who had no manners and no consideration for others.

"What?" Philippe turned his head around, but when his eyes locked with his brother's, he shook his head. "Of course!"

He raised his eyebrows as if he and his brother had an entire conversation without saying a word. "You won't be bored." He took a deep breath and softly, probably not audible for anyone but me in the room, he added "And neither will I, I'm afraid."

I had to make sure not to grin.

In the meantime, Nick sat down next to me, even though there was barely enough space for him.

"How did they like the little surprise you brought them?" He was still smiling and for a moment, I enjoyed the fact that he had no idea of the troubles we were facing daily.

He didn't know that it had been more than just a little surprise.

"They sent me here. What do you think?" I raised my eyebrows and leaned a little towards him, away from the Lilian who seemed to have forgotten the moment of ignorance and returned to the point where she was interrupted. "They'll be talking about this for years." I placed a hand on his and noticed his skin seemed to glow a little. Was he falling ill?

"Not if we keep on giving them moments like this and not if I can convince fa…the king that things have to change in the villages." His cheeks blushed and I looked over my shoulder to the blond-haired, blue-eyed devil pretending to be an angel.

"I'm afraid it won't fix her character." I whispered the words in his ear.

Nick stood up and stretched out his hand to help me stand up, too.

"I'm certain that if we take away her father's self-proclaimed position of power, she might change her tune."

He led me away from the couch and we both acted like we were fascinated by the dresses and the overwhelming colours surrounding us.

"I am not sure about that." I shook my head.

Even though Lilian and I would never be friends and even though I disliked her attitude, I didn't want her to end up in a situation like mine.

"Most of the villagers are still poor and that is where the true problem lies." I looked at Nick. "Giving them cake and a royal ball to look forward to might brighten the mood for a while, but it won't change the daily circumstances."

"I will make sure that the king hears this and will consider any option that will actually make a true difference."

I smiled, but I had my doubts that there was something he could do. I did admire his attempts, though.

For a moment, Nick and I just stood there. My fingers couldn't resist the longing to touch the different kinds of fabric. I was surprised with how different they all were.

Some dresses were stiff and I couldn't imagine them being comfortable in any way. I doubted that any of the dresses were designed to be comfortable. But

there were also a few soft, light dresses and there was
a part of me hoping that I would find a way to convince
the designer that I longed to wear one of those.

"Excuse me, my lord, miss…" Martha cleared her
throat, asking for our attention.

Even though I was fairly certain that everyone
living in the capital led a far better life than most of the
villagers, I wondered if Martha was really wealthy or
if there was a gap in the capitol, too.

"Would you like me to present the dress you would
like miss Rivers to wear?" There was a slight glimmer
in her eyes and I could smell the excitement running
through her veins. "I am certain I still need to do some
adjustments concerning the size and measures, but it
will at least give you the first impression." She bent her
head slightly and Nick nodded at her in
encouragement.

"I am sorry that I couldn't be satisfied with a pre-
made dress, like the other companions will be." Nick
smiled. "I am grateful that you managed to get the first
impression finished for today's fitting already." He
cocked his head, the smile still on his face, but I saw
his hand grabbing one of the shelves as if he was
suddenly afraid to lose his balance.

"Nick?" I placed a hand on his shoulder. Maybe
someone else wouldn't have noticed this small moment
of discomfort, but I did. "Is everything alright?" I
whispered, making sure that Phillipe and Lilian didn't
hear us.

With shock, Nick turned his face towards me and
I saw something resembling panic in his eyes. I could
hear his heart racing.

"I'm fine. Why are you asking?" He took a few
deep breaths and then he seemed to be able to hold

himself together again. "I just had a very short night due to all the unforeseen arrangements that needed to be made for the upcoming royal ball. Nothing a good night of sleep won't be able to repair." He curled his lips up into his charming smile again. "The King might have agreed with my plan to invite quite a lot of extra people to the event, but that means we need to rearrange a few things." He winked and slowly, the glimmer reached his eyes again. "I could use a few extra hands, ears, and most of all, an extra brain for the upcoming days, if you are available?"

"I don't think I have anything better to do, my lord." I bent my knees slightly. "Apart from getting a personalised dress and refreshing my memory when it comes to manners and etiquette."

"You may consider that dress as a payment upfront." Nick turned his head towards Martha once more and with a smile on his face he asked her to get the dress she designed for me. "And if your village didn't choose you to represent them, I would invite you myself, as my personal guest of honour."

I licked my lips and attempted to look away from him but failed hopelessly. I wondered what kind of a person he would have become had he grown up in the village, had he been poor instead of rich, had he been the one needing saving instead of the one attempting to save me.

In a way, I hoped he would have still had his golden heart.

I imagined that he would have been the kind of a person who would help someone up when they fell, instead of seeing it as an opportunity to earn more by doing a part of their work. He would have been the kind of a person giving up his last piece of bread because someone else was hungrier.

I was glad that his riches had not taken that away from him. I already saw the effect of a slightly better position on Lilian. Nick was a nobleman, but he still seemed to have the ability to not look down on anyone.

I only hoped that I would be capable of doing the same now that I took over the leadership of my family without having the slightest idea of how to handle it.

"Miss? Lord? I hope that this is what you were hoping for?" Martha came back with a wonderful dress in the same shade of blue as Nick's uniform.

The skirt was created from a light material that could easily be blown by the wind and it was a slightly different shade of blue than the bodice and was wider than any skirt I had ever seen before. Just like Nick's uniform, the sleeveless bodice was covered in golden animal-shaped patterns.

"I remembered how you loved the patterns on my jacket, and I thought that maybe they could add a few to your dress, too." Nick stretched out his hand and touched the dress as if it was the most delicate thing he had ever held. "I also know how uncomfortable your red dress makes you. So, I asked her to use the lightest and softest materials she could find. I hope you will be able to enjoy the evening, despite being forced to wear a dress and not having the option to change it whenever you please."

I realised only then that I was holding my breath and when I touched the soft fabric of the bodice, I let out a sigh that was both from relief and satisfaction.

"You shouldn't have done this…" I shook my head and used my other hand to touch the wide skirt.

I already imagined myself dancing, even though I had never danced before. "Everyone will think that you and I are more than just a lord and the girl he offered a job so he could help her."

"I don't mind them believing that there is more between you and me." Nick's eyes met mine for a short moment and I heard his heartbeat prove he meant every word he said.

"I wouldn't mind if you would believe it, too." His voice was barely a whisper now and his hand gently caressed my hair.

I didn't know what to say. I didn't know how to react to his confession. There was a part of me that enjoyed the thought of being with him. He managed to make me smile, even though I had little reason to smile these days. He gave me hope when I had none.

But I also had the voice of reason in the back of my mind telling me that I shouldn't allow myself to dream of a life that would never be possible. I was just a villager. He was a nobleman.

"Would you like to try the dress on, miss?"

I shook my head and instead of answering the question I turned my head towards Nick. "I am a village girl, Nick." I grabbed his hands and frowned when I noticed that his hands were warmer than they usually were.

"I grew up with hunger, without warm water to wash myself, without a fire to keep me comfortable in the winter." I paused for a moment. "Maybe in another world and another time, maybe if I weren't born in poverty." I swallowed. "Maybe then I would have allowed myself to fall in love with you."

"It doesn't matter that you're not from the capital." Nick shook his head. "Not to me and not to anyone else. I will make sure of that." He pulled me a little closer. "Why wouldn't a village girl be able to find her place in this world? Why wouldn't I be able to find my place in hers?"

I took a deep breath and opened my mouth to speak but closed it again. Maybe if I wasn't what I was, I would have given in. "I…." I took another deep breath. "I would like to try the dress now, please?"

"Of course, the dress is yours and no matter what happens, it will always be yours."

Chapter Fourteen

I stared at my reflection in the mirror. I barely recognised myself. I still carried the scars and traces of a hard-working life, but with the pretty dress on, I looked like the version of myself my father always hoped I would become one day.

"I understand you might want to admire yourself, but I would like to enjoy the view, too." Nick cleared his throat and knocked on the door of the dressing room. "Lilian is already twirling around pretending to be a princess." Nick stopped in the middle of his sentence and, probably believing no one heard him, he murmured something about someone needing to show the spoiled brat what a true queen looked like.

I felt my cheeks blush as I took a deep breath and pushed the door open. I avoided Nick's glance, afraid his eyes were wandering over my entire body. I also avoided Lilian's glance, afraid that if looks were capable of killing, I would have long been dead already.

"How can someone make a dress as pretty as this one?" Lilian complained and Philippe shook his head and stood up. "Some people have an unfair advantage in life." She continued and Philippe curled up one corner of his mouth into a smile while he stared at his older brother.

"Why don't I get a dress like that?" Lilian crossed her arms over her chest and I rolled my eyes and sighed once more. "Why do I have to wear a dress from the store? Without golden patterns? One that doesn't even fully fit?" She raised her eyebrows a little.

"I don't have a money tree in my garden, Lilian." Philippe shrugged and all his muscles tensed while he grabbed her hands. "I'm sure that we can make the dress more fitting in time." He seemed to struggle to find the right words and sound sincere. "You will look breathtakingly beautiful at the ball." He almost seemed to choke on his last words and I felt a little sad for Lilian.

Lilian seemed to be convinced that she would end up in the capital next to one of the princes. I was afraid that if she didn't manage to show some manners when she was meeting with two lords, she would most likely not do any better with the royal family.

"Maybe I should wear something else?" I wasn't sure why I said it, but the words escaped before I could stop myself.

Maybe I was looking for an excuse to not wear a dress that matched Nick's uniform. Or maybe I was looking for a way to not attract a lot of attention.

Unlike Lilian, I didn't have an illusion that I would end up marrying a prince and living in a castle. I was only attending the ball because Nick insisted and because not attending would raise questions I was not willing to answer.

"Absolutely not!" Nick placed a hand on my shoulder. "If you don't like the dress, I will happily look for another one with you, but the fact that you look beautiful in it shouldn't be the reason for such a drastic request."

I had a lot more convincing reasons, but I couldn't list them while Lilian seemed to be dangerously close to the edge of her calm.

"I wonder at what point the people at the ball will notice that this beautiful ballgown is masquerading a poor village girl who happened to run into a lord while being lost in the woods."

"My father says I'm not allowed to go into the woods. He says it's a dangerous place." Lilian raised her eyebrows and at this point I realised how dangerously close I came to revealing my true nature to her. "He told me that people die in the woods."

I stiffened and Nick tightened his grip on my shoulder. He had quite a strong hold for a human and my sensitive skin burned under his touch.

"That's why I have taken it upon me to bring Emily home safely as soon as I found her." Nick swallowed and small pearls of sweat covered his forehead.

"Nick?" I instinctively placed my hand on his and I softened my voice when my eyes met his. "I think you're in need of some fresh air." I nodded at Philippe and looked at Martha, who's kept her distance until now. "I promise that I will not damage the dress."

I didn't wait for an answer as I grabbed Nick's hand to pull him towards the door.

"What's wrong, Nick? You seem different." I shook my head as soon as we stood outside.

Outside breeze helped the colour return to Nick's cheeks, but his body was still trembling and his muscles were still tense.

"I'm sorry, it's nothing." Nick avoided my glance. He took a few deep breaths as if the air would simply blow his worries and sorrows away. "The world is so different than I thought it to be. The thought of the danger surrounding the villages, surrounding you..." He paused for a moment and used the back of his hand to wipe the sweat from his forehead.

I was relieved that I haven't told him about the child that was killed by one of my kind, by a monster. "I didn't want to make you sick with the stories about the circumstances in the villages." I bent my head and licked my lips. "I'm sorry that I upset you."

"No!" Nick raised his voice and shook his head. "Never feel sorry about telling me the truth. Maybe the truth is not as pretty and pleasant as I hoped it would be, but it is the truth and I wouldn't want to live with the illusion for the rest of my life."

"I don't know if I would feel the same." I spoke softly and I reached for his hand, intertwining my fingers with his. I was probably trying to telling him something I wasn't sure I could express with words, but it helped and his breathing and heartbeat calmed down slowly.

"If I lived in this illusion of happiness…" I sighed. "I understand when the truth of the outside world is too much to handle." I stared at the dress I was wearing once again.

Had I lived in the capital, like my father wished for me, would I have been like him? Would I have been as gullible and unknowing as he was? Would I have been this sick and disoriented when I discovered the truth?

"You hate having to attend the ball, do you?" Nick spoke softly.

"No, I don't hate it." I shook my head. "I just feel guilty that I get to enjoy all these treats, while so many others don't even have enough to eat. I just feel guilty that I'll be having an amazing night and a lot of fun, while so many people know only work." I paused for a moment.

"But all I hear in my head is the voice of my father

telling me that he always envisioned me here and that I should enjoy it. He would say I'm allowed to enjoy myself for one night."

"I would really like you to be by my side wearing this dress." Nick pressed the palm of his hand to my cheek. "The royal ball could use someone who knows that while we're dancing and drinking and eating, there are people who would give the world to be here, too." He swallowed and I held my breath while Nick locked his glance with mine.

"I could use someone reminding me that even though I saved one girl from a horrible life, there are plenty of people who are in similar circumstances, and I can't save them all."

I smiled and instead of pushing his hand away I leaned towards it. Nick's glance was pleasant and comforting and I realised that for a moment, I stopped breathing. "Do you still want me by your side if I tell you that I've never danced in my life?" My voice was raw and my throat was dry.

"We have some time to change that. I would gladly be your teacher." Nick pulled his hand back and straightened his back. "Although, I don't know if my brother will like having to offer Lilian the same."

"He won't have a choice. I'm sure she'll so insist until he agrees." I smiled.

"I'm afraid so, yes."

Chapter Fifteen

"What will you be doing at the royal ball?" Benjamin refused to let his small hand slip out of mine and I had to admit that in a way, I enjoyed that he seemed to feel so comfortable and safe with me. "Can I come along?" He looked at me and his big, dark eyes widened.

There were so many things in life I wanted to give him and there were so many things in life that he would probably never have, but at least I was able to offer him these small moments of joy.

"I don't know what people usually do at balls, but I assume there will be dancing and surely there will be cake." I smiled at him.

The next day, Nick would send his carriage to Waterfield to pick me up for my very first dance lesson. He assured me that there was nothing to worry about and that I would probably learn the steps quite quickly, but I somehow doubted that.

I've never been good with strict rules and guidelines and I preferred moving freely, instead of following patterns someone else designed. Apart from that, I wasn't sure if I would feel comfortable with his hands touching my body for most likely the entire afternoon.

Nick confused me.

All my life, I thought that there would never be more to life that I was living. My father had the most wonderful dreams, and he never stopped talking about them, but I never believed that some day one of those dreams would come true.

The ball was still ten days away and a lot could happen in those ten days. The lifeless body of the boy, clearly attacked by one of my kind, had proven that.

"Will the royal family be there? The king and the queen? The crown prince?" Benjamin's eyes glimmered in the autumn sun and I realised how beautiful they were and how I enjoyed the reflection of the daylight in his eyes whenever he looked my way.

"Who told you about the royal family? Were your uncles telling stories again?" I stood still and curled my lips up, knowing all too well that said uncles could hear every word I said.

When I invited Benjamin for a short walk through the woods, they refused to let us leave without protection. They were afraid that we would run into one of those hunter parties that were being organised. Or that we would meet the monster who killed the boy.

I wanted to tell them that I could take care of myself and Benjamin and that I was the leader of our family, but in a way, it had felt comfortable that they were looking out for us.

I was not afraid of Lilian's father and the men he had gathered around him. I was even less afraid of the monster that was deep down just like us. But I was afraid that Benjamin's senses would overwhelm him at a certain point and that he would run out of my sight.

"Is the lord you're working for going to the royal ball, too?" Benjamin didn't seem to notice my discomfort and my slight fear.

He had a smile on his face and in the daylight, I saw how his jaws and cheeks were shaped differently than they were a couple of days ago. He was finally getting enough food to not just grow taller, as he was supposed to, but to also gain a little weight, which would make him look like father even more.

"Yes, he will be at the ball too and he expects me to be with him the entire evening." I avoided his glance and spoke as softly as I could.

My uncles wouldn't immediately tell my mother everything I told Benjamin, but I also didn't want to force them to lie for me. "I'm sure it means you will get something nice and extra to eat in return for it."

I kneeled in front of my little brother and took a deep breath before I grabbed his shoulders. "But the ball is ten days away. I thought that maybe for today you would like a small adventure on four feet?" I stopped in the middle of a meadow and Benjamin dropped his jaw when he realised what I had just told him.

"It's not good to fight your powers all the time. At some point, the powers may fight their own way out and then they might run away with you."

"Do I…" He looked around and a slight blush covered his cheeks. "Do I have to take off my clothes before we…" He didn't dare to say the words out loud and I realised that my mother taught him that.

She taught him not to be proud of what he was. Maybe she had even taught herself not to be proud of what she was, anymore.

"Yes, unless you want to rip them apart and want to run home naked." I smiled at him and to make him feel more comfortable I pulled my own dress over my head. The wind touched my naked chest and I closed my eyes for a moment to enjoy the warmth of the sun to the fullest.

Humans didn't have the slightest idea of what they

were missing by covering themselves up all the time. Nothing beat experiencing nature like it was meant to be experienced.

"Do you think mother will be angry when we come home?" Benjamin hesitated before he pulled his shirt over his head. "She told me that if someone sees us, it can be dangerous."

I opened my eyes again. I could still count all his ribs, so I swallowed while I forced myself to keep on smiling. "No, mother won't be mad at us. Mother is only worried about us." I took a deep breath and carefully weighed the words on my tongue. "Humans are sometimes afraid of things they don't know." I didn't want to make him afraid of the humans he should learn to love and protect.

Even though there had not been a war in a long time, my grandparents assured us that during those times of need even the most hateful citizens would embrace our powers. It was hard to imagine that we had once fought alongside human armies, not against them, and it was even harder to imagine that maybe in the future this could happen again.

"They don't know that we can control ourselves and that we only harm those who are trying to harm them," I spoke slowly and softly. "But that doesn't mean that you should be afraid of your powers. You should be proud of them and you should use them." I remembered how my father said the same words to me once.

"And if it's impossible for you to turn for a while, you should at least use your senses. Even though it's not always pleasant, you have to keep on telling yourself that each and every part of you is wanted and loved." I should have added what could happen if he fought parts of himself, but I deeply believed that even if my brother lost his human self for a while, he would never do anything that would harm others.

"Do your clothes hurt, too?" Benjamin took of his pants and I dropped my briefs so I was fully naked. "I don't really like wearing clothes, but no one in the village walks around naked."

I smiled a little. "If I could, I would walk around naked, too, but we're lucky." I thought about the dresses they were wearing in the capital and I thought about the uniforms with all those medals that the men wore.

"If we were born in the capital, we would have to wear even more uncomfortable clothes." I grinned. "You might think that I'm looking forward to the ball, but I am not looking forward to the dress I have to wear."

"What will your dress look like?" Benjamin also dropped his undergarments and I tensed all my muscles to get ready for our little adventure on four feet.

"I will be wearing a blue dress with patterns of all kinds of animals on it." I smiled. "I'm sure that you would love it if you could see it." I kneeled and enjoyed the feeling of dirt between my fingers while I watched Benjamin mirror my movements. "Maybe I will ask the lord if I can take the dress home."

"That would be amazing!" Benjamin stared at me with a smile on his face and with little lights in his eyes. "Will we still be able to talk if we turn?"

I nodded at him. "Yes, we can still speak if we want to. Although, I think we should try not to talk too loudly. Humans might not understand our words and might only hear sounds scaring them." I buried my feet a little deeper into the ground. "But I promise no one will harm you, no matter in which form you're walking through the woods."

"I'm not afraid when you are with me, Emily." Benjamin shook his head and I nodded at him.

"I'm really glad to hear that."

A loud howl made me straighten my back and tense my muscles. Quickly, I grabbed the dress I threw on the ground moments ago and pulled it over my head.

"Emily?" Benjamin stood up too and looked at me with eyes wide open. "Do you smell that too?" Benjamin looked afraid and his shoulders almost reached his ears.

I took a deep breath and my own body reacted to the smell, too. "Benjamin?" I kneeled in front of the youngest member of my family and I understood better than ever why our mother tried to keep us inside and away from this hard and cruel world.

"I know that the smell is disgusting, and I know that it's hard to ignore." I tried to stay calm while I kept my eyes locked with his. "I order you not to go find out what's causing the smell, I order you to get dressed right now and I order you to hold my hand until I say that you can let it go." The power raced through my veins, and I almost felt guilty when Benjamin shook his head.

His movements seemed almost mechanical while he pulled his shirt over his head and put his pants back on. He didn't show any dislike of the fabric touching his sensitive skin. Instead, he immediately walked towards me and grabbed my hand, intertwining his fingers with mine, determined to not let me go until I said he was allowed to do so.

"Emily…" My uncles appeared, wearing jeans and shirts they had been carrying on their backs. "I don't know if the boy should see this." Uncle Calvin carried the lifeless body of a girl barely older than Benjamin.

Her dress had once been white, probably before she ran into the woods and probably before whatever had managed to eat her found her there. Her skin was covered in dirt and blood and her long brown hair sticked to her forehead.

My stomach churned and if I weren't holding Benjamin's hand, I would have rushed to the bushes to get rid of my lunch. "We can't send him home alone when there is something roaming the woods killing children just like him." I tried not to tremble. I was holding the hand of my brother and I was his example. If I panicked, he would panic, too. The last thing I wanted was another wolf out of control roaming these woods.

"What happened to her…" Benjamin tightened his grip and hid half behind my back while he stared at the body uncle Calvin was carrying.

I already thought the sight was sickening, I couldn't imagine how Benjamin felt right now. It was hard to know for sure, but the girl was probably barely younger than he was.

I closed my eyes to fight the tears almost streaming down my cheeks. I wanted to protect him from stuff like this. I wanted him to love his wolf before being confronted with the dark side of being one. I also wanted him to know he was fully in control of his own wolf, before seeing what damage a wolf without control could do. I didn't want him to grow up being afraid of what he was.

"We don't know that yet, Benjamin." I locked my eyes with both my uncles, making clear that I didn't want them to tell the truth, not yet.

"We will bring the little girl to a doctor. Maybe he can tell us what happened to her." My uncles exchanged a look, and I nodded at them.

"I will get Benjamin home in a more human way. Be careful and make sure that none of the villagers sees you. They might think you are responsible for this and I don't want any of you to get hurt or worse." I tried not to panic, all too aware that Benjamin was hearing every word I was saying.

"We will see you tonight at our home, I hope?" My uncles looked at me and once more, I nodded while I tightened my grip on Benjamin's hand.

"Of course, I won't let you explain this to my mother on your own. You are all my responsibility now and even though I have no idea what to do at times and how to keep you all safe, I will try my very best not to run away." I took a deep breath as I watched my uncles running away until they were out of sight.

"Will we walk home slowly now?" Benjamin's voice was trembling and I couldn't blame him. He was only a child who has just seen the worst thing one could possibly witness.

I remembered how it felt when I saw a dead body for the first time and I wished that somehow I could take this memory away from him. But I couldn't and this image would probably give him nightmares for years to come.

"We will walk home like normal people walk home. The humans are already afraid of us and we don't want them to think that we are capable of doing anything wrong."

I froze when I noticed a familiar posture, accompanied by a familiar smell of expensive perfume, entering the clearing where Benjamin and I expected to be alone.

"And here I thought I saved you from these dangerous woods." Nick had his hands folded behind his back. Even though he was smiling, there was something different about his eyes. "My father and brother were hunting a wild animal not too far away from here." He shifted his weight from one leg to the other and a frown covered his forehead. "You really shouldn't be here, Emily."

I wondered if he saw the dead girl, too, and I also wondered if he overheard any of the words I said to my brother. I tried to remember what I said exactly and if there was anything that Nick could use to complete the puzzle of who I was and what I was. I hoped that his brain didn't comprehend anything that might have pointed towards my true nature.

"I assume that this is Benjamin I've heard so much about?" Nick kneeled in front of my little brother, who was still holding onto my hand as if it was the only thing that kept him safe right now.

I wanted to order him to let my hand go, but I realised that if I did that, I would offer the lord all the missing pieces on a silver platter.

"Yes, this is my brother Benjamin." I tried to act as normally as I could despite the circumstances and I tried to force a smile even though it was impossible for it to reach my eyes. "Benjamin? This is the lord who has been giving you all those amazing presents because I'm working for him."

"Thank you for the sandwiches and the cake, sir." Benjamin's voice was barely a whisper and my heart broke. He was looking forward to meeting the mysterious gentleman who had brightened his life with the taste of food he had never even dreamed of. Now the moment was overshadowed by the unpleasant sight he would never forget.

"You are very welcome, young man." Nick touched my brother's cheeks and pinched one of them as if Benjamin was an old friend he haven't seen in years. "I am glad to hear that you enjoyed the presents so much." He stood up and folded his hands behind his back once more.

A smile spread across his face and his glance met mine. "Although I do worry about the fact that your sister takes you into the woods, even though I already had to save her once from getting lost after dark." He winked and I squeezed my brother's hand to make sure he wouldn't say anything.

"The sun isn't even setting yet and if I'm not mistaken, we're further away from the capital than we are from the village. Maybe you are the one we should worry about, my lord. Your brother and father might think that they can go after this wild beast, but not everyone with a weapon is automatically safe." I was surprised my voice sounded a little teasing, despite my emotions being all over the place.

I had to get away from this place as soon as possible and bring Benjamin home.

"You might be pleased to hear that we were already on our way home, though." I bent my knees slightly and Nick bent his head as his way of answering.

"I assume that means I don't need to give the young lady and the young man a ride home on my horse?"

"I wouldn't want to bother the horse with the weight of all three of us." And I didn't want to bother the horse with my current mood, let alone Benjamin's.

"I will see you tomorrow then and I will roam these entire woods if you're not at home when my carriage arrives to pick you up." Nick bent his head a little more and he grabbed my hand to kiss my knuckles.

"There is no need to worry. I will be there tomorrow." I waited until Nick let go of my hand, before I turned around with Benjamin to walk away. "He's still watching. I know this is hard, but just a few more seconds, Benjamin." I spoke as softly as I could, and Benjamin squeezed my hand in answer. "You did wonderful so far, Benjamin, I'm so proud of you."

Chapter Sixteen

I held the trembling body of my younger brother to my chest. I didn't dare to look at his face, because I would see nothing but fear in his glimmering eyes.

He was looking forward to this day ever since he discovered his own powers and now it was ruined because one of his kind was leaving a trail of dead bodies in the woods. He was too young to be confronted with the remains of a child not that much older than he was, especially in the state she was in. He was also too young to wonder if he would ever be able to do so much damage.

I counted the seconds until we reached the small home of my family, the cottage that has been my house for such a long time. I would find my family probably debating whether we should flee to another place and start anew.

Even though I was not afraid of moving and starting a new life somewhere else, I was afraid that it would mean breaking all my ties with Nick.

He was too close to discovering the truth. He didn't mention the dead body, so I assumed he didn't find her before we did. But if my mother found out how close he was to discovering the truth about me, she would advise me to not take any risks.

She was right. I shouldn't take any risks and I shouldn't be playing with the lives of my family. I was our leader. I was the one responsible for our wellbeing and safety. I was the one who had to make sure that neither of us would die because of something we had played absolutely no part in.

But there was a difference between what I knew was right and what I wanted to be right. I didn't want to see Nick as a possible threat. I didn't want to be afraid of him betraying me. I really wanted to believe that the love he said he felt was truly there.

"How is he?" My mother opened the door before I lifted my hand to knock on the dark wood. Her eyes were filled with worry and somehow, I saw a glimmer of the mother she had once been, before my father was killed, before protecting our family had been more than taking care of our food and safety.

"He's in shock, I believe." I placed Benjamin in her strong arms and my hand touched his hair before I stepped back. "I wish I told my uncles to not come closer, but it was already too late."

I bent my head and stared at my feet, waiting for my mother to tell me that I was irresponsible, that I shouldn't have challenged her, that I shouldn't have taken a position I was not ready for, that I shouldn't carry this responsibility when my shoulders were not strong enough to bear it.

She didn't say anything, though. She simply climbed the stairs and I expected she would place Benjamin in one of the comfortable beds with all the pillows and blankets she could gather.

I wondered if she wanted me to wait for her here in the hallway, so we could discuss what we were going to tell the rest of the family. And we had decisions to make.

Whatever we decided, I would have to be the one to confirm it, but I wasn't sure I was the right person to do so. I didn't know if I would ever be the right person to do so.

"You do know what this means?" My mother walked down the stairs again and she placed a hand on my shoulder.

She was no longer the terrifying woman I was afraid of. In a way, she seemed to be more afraid of me now than I had ever been of her. She was most likely afraid that I would end up doing the exact opposite of what she would have done. She was probably afraid that I would do something that would get someone killed.

"I know the villagers are already on edge." I took a deep breath. "This is the second body in a short amount of time and we can only hope that whoever is responsible for those bodies, will stop whatever they're doing as soon as possible." I lifted my chin.

"What if someone is leaving bodies whenever we are around to expose us, did you consider that?" My mother spoke softly, but everyone in the living room would be able to hear us. After all, not only my mother and I were blessed with excellent hearing.

"The first body was found when you were on your way home already, away from the crowd. Now we discovered another body while you and Benjamin were preparing to turn. If the villagers can connect another body to your appearance, they might realise you are a wolf like your father. They might blame you for all the dead children."

I took a deep breath and let the words sink in. I haven't considered that possibility, and a shiver rolled down my spine. I didn't know if we had enemies in this village, just like I didn't know whether people remembered my father and why he was killed. So far, people have always been kind to me, but outside of work, I rarely spoke to anyone in town and when I did, I never talked about my dead father.

"What should I tell the others?" I looked at my mother and even though I was technically stronger than her, I felt smaller than I had ever felt.

"I would allow them to talk first." My mother squeezed my shoulder, and it was the most caring gesture she displayed in years. "Let them tell you what they are afraid of and what they think to be the best solution." She walked towards the door to the living room and carefully pushed it open.

There was nothing but absolute silence. Everyone looked up as soon as I entered the room and stared at me was with worry and fear.

They were counting on me to take that fear away, but I doubted I could do so. "We found another body in the woods." My voice was trembling a little and I shifted my weight from one leg to the other. The palms of my hands were sweating and I realised that my mother never stopped loving us.

She had simply been affected by the endless danger that seemed to be surrounding us. She knew leading a family was easier in good times than in bad times. She adapted.

"At the moment, there are two possibilities we need to consider." I took a deep breath and licked my dry lips. My muscles tensed while I locked my glance with each of them for at least a few seconds. "Maria seems to believe that someone might be attempting to reveal our true nature." My hands shook, so I folded them behind my back. "I like to believe that this might be someone like us who is desperate and screams for help." I paused for a short moment to steady my voice once more. "I want to hear your thoughts and possible solutions." I was afraid of what they would say, afraid of what they would want.

"What does your mother think?" All heads turned towards her and my mother shrugged.

She didn't want to openly challenge my leadership. "We should consider the possibility that we might have to move and find a safer place to live."

"If we moved now, I think we would attract a lot of unwanted attention." I interrupted her. "I know there is a chance that people might discover what we are, but I think we might wake the sleeping minds if we move all of a sudden, now that bodies are being found."

I tried to relax and lower my shoulders. "We don't want anyone to ask questions they haven't asked themselves yet." A plan formed in the back of my mind. "If we want to move, we have to make sure that everyone in this village understands that it has nothing to do with the bodies."

Chapter Seventeen

During the entire ride to the capital, I didn't say a word to Lilian.

Not that she seemed to mind my total silence. She managed to fill up each and every second with ongoing murmuring. She told me at least ten times that she was certain Philippe would want to marry her after the royal ball. She also added that she was not planning on promising him anything until she tried to draw attention of the princes.

I rolled my eyes. I was certain that Philippe was already looking forward to the moment the royal ball was over so he could wave at the departing carriage only to make sure to never invite Lilian to the capital again.

I was also sure that Lilian wouldn't attract the attention of the princes. She lacked manners, and princes had plenty of young women from the capital to choose from.

I let out a relieved sigh when the carriage stopped in front of a building I didn't recognise. I assumed what was where the ballroom was for the dancing lessons, and even though I had plenty of worries currently, my knees trembled a little while I stepped out of the carriage.

"Are you ready to explore your hidden dancing talents?" Nick offered me his arm.

He had a smile playing around his lips and lights dancing in his piercing blue eyes.

I didn't doubt that at the royal ball, plenty of girls wanted to dance with him, but he wouldn't ask them. He was only interested in dancing with me.

"I am not sure if I possess any hidden dancing talents." I rolled my eyes and tried to push all the thoughts overwhelming my mind to the background.

My mother was right when she spoke about us having to think about moving. I already knew how to convince the entire town that we were not fleeing. I wanted to convince everyone in Waterfield that my alliance with this nobleman became more than a simple alliance and our entire family moved to the capital and not one of the other small villages.

"I believe you are selling yourself short." Nick placed his hand on mine.

Even though he had touched me more often, I still liked how pleasantly warm his touch was.

Or maybe I've developed feelings over time that made every touch just felt like something warm, welcoming, and pleasant. "I wouldn't have too many expectations about this afternoon, my lord." I smiled though. I never had many problems with my confidence, but now my interactions with Nick gained some more importance, insecurities lingered in my mind.

"We will discover that in a matter of seconds." Nick nodded at the young woman opening the door to what I assumed was a dance school. "Thank you so much for clearing your schedule on such a short notice." He bent his head slightly and she made sure to bend even deeper, as if she was afraid to appear more important than him.

"It's absolutely no problem, my roy…" She was interrupted before she finished her sentence and I noticed that Nick seemed to make a habit of not letting people use his full title, whatever that might be.

"I appreciate it greatly, Lisa." He smiled at her and followed her through the long hallway, still gripping my hand as if he was afraid I would run away screaming.

"I doubt my piano skills are anywhere close to the qualities of the orchestra that will play at the ball..." Lisa stuttered and nervously clenched her fists.

She had perfectly clean nails and a round face with beautiful brown eyes. In the villages, she would stand out without any effort and when I looked over my shoulder, I saw jealousy on Lilian's face.

She noticed, too, that even a simple girl working for a dance school outshone both of us in beauty and grace.

I was planning on avoiding Lilian as much as possible during the royal ball. If she ended up embarrassing herself with her bad manners, I wanted no part in it.

"I will be teaching two absolute beginners today. I am sure that your talents will be perfect for the occasion." Nick nodded at her and I saw Lisa relax a little.

"I don't think there is a possibility that your piano skills could be as horrible as my dancing skills." I smiled and this time I meant it. "I never had any dancing lesson before and I've been told it's complicated, so I don't have high hopes for today." I giggled.

Nick shook his head and waited until we reached another door, this time made of glass.

When it opened in front of me, I stared in amazement when I saw the enormous ballroom with mirrors lining an entire long wall. I could see my surprised glance reflected in them. In one of the corners, there was a spotless white piano that looked as if it melted with the background wall, equally spotless white.

"In that case, I am afraid this will be for the place you will be spending the days until the ball." Nick winked at me, and I shook my head.

He had a specific sort of charm, which was emphasised by his growing feelings for me, so I questioned the intentions behind his every word and glance.

Most of all, I doubted my own intentions towards him. "Poor you and poor me." I smiled at him and he smiled back, our glances locked for a moment until we were disturbed by Lilian's ongoing chatter.

"This is a dance school?" She twirled around, not even attempting to hide her surprise and admiration.

I couldn't blame her for it

"It's even more beautiful than I imagined it to be!"

I raised my eyebrows. I imagined a lot of things, but I never even tried to imagine something like a dance school. I wouldn't know where to start.

I preferred to imagine a cosy fire burning day and night, full plates with meat and vegetables, and my brother and I running free through the woods every day.

"I'm glad you like it." Philippe sounded a bit bored, and he seemed annoyed with having to hide it.

"Is there anything else you want or need before we start?" the young woman cleared her throat, her cheeks blushing a little, while she folded her hands behind her back.

It seemed as if she was afraid of interrupting the

two noblemen and their companions.

"Would you like some water or something to eat?" Nick cocked his head slightly and tried to look at Lilian too, even though his question was directed at me.

"I had breakfast just an hour ago Nick, I'm certain I'll be fine." I didn't look over my shoulder to see what Lilian was saying.

I could hear her listing quite a few demands already and Philippe was sighing.

"Maybe we could try the beginning positions while Lilian and Philippe get something to eat?" Nick looked at me and I nodded.

I would give a lot to be able to spend the entire day without Lilian following me as a shadow, but I couldn't ask that of him.

Lilian was the second representative of Waterfield at the royal ball, regardless of whether she gained that position in an honest and honourable way.

"Straighten your back like this and make sure to always lift your chin up higher than you would normally do." Nick placed a hand carefully on my lower back and his other hand tenderly grabbed my chin to position it correctly. "After the first few lessons you might have to deal with some sore muscles." He smiled and I groaned softly.

For a while, we just danced like that. Sometimes Nick corrected my movements. Most of the time we didn't say anything at all and just enjoyed moving to the rhythm of the music.

"And here, I believed that dancing was supposed to be a fun activity." All those muscles I rarely used ached, but I most of all, I noticed how his hands were still touching me. "You should have warned me that it's actually a torturous activity."

"I can assure you that the end result will be worth all the pain and horrible moments you have to go through first." He stepped back and his eyes wandered over my body.

Although, I wouldn't call this posture comfortable, it was far from painful and far from horrible. If I considered this painful and horrible, I wouldn't have gotten through the first few years of my life, let alone the first few times my father taught me how to turn at free will, or how to stay in control.

"You look like one of those beautiful statues at the palace." Nick murmured and shook his head as if he had forgotten for a moment that even though I looked like a statue I was very real.

"For the next step you place your left hand loosely on my shoulder." He positioned my hand and I gently rested my hand on his shoulder. "I will take care of the other hand." He winked and gently put my hand in his.

I heard his heart racing and when I concentrated, I even sensed his blood rushing through his veins. He was standing surprisingly close to me and I wasn't sure if I was simply imagining it, but my skin somehow seemed even warmer than usually.

A few drops of sweat rolled down my back while he stepped a little closer and pressed his chest to mine. My first instinct was to step back, but instead, I simply held my breath and waited to start feeling a little more at ease.

"And from here, we start the dance." Nick cleared his throat and a slight blush covered his cheeks.

I had to smile. Even though he was slightly older than me, he had a sort of childlike innocence, something I already lost years ago because of the life I led and everything I lost.

"And I notice that you're still smiling. Does this mean it's not hurting as much?" his voice was light and every time he spoke, his breath touched my nose.

"Actually, learning how to dance might be one of the least painful physical activities I experienced so far." I swallowed and my cheeks heated when I noticed Nick blushing.

"I might know a few more pleasant physical activities that you might enjoy then." He looked away and avoided my glance after the last word escaped his lips and a small giggle echoed through the dance room.

"You are a nobleman, Nick." I shook my head and took a deep breath.

I tried to push away the longing to see where this could lead if I simply gave in and disregarded all the if's and when's.

"I'm a simple village girl and maybe we should stop playing with fire, because I'm afraid that we might end up burning ourselves."

"I think some wonderful things could happen if we weren't afraid of fire." Nick tightened his grip on my hand and I looked up, our eyes meeting for a short moment. "And even though you see me as part of an elite and consider me out of your reach, I've have never seen you as anything but an equal."

"I know that, Nick." I swallowed and stepped back, pulling both my hands and giving my body some room to breathe, to come back to my senses. "And I've never felt unimportant or unequal when I'm with you, but I'm sure that most of the people won't see it your way."

"I can make them." Nick looked slightly disappointed while he placed his right hand on his neck. "Had I not been a nobleman and had you not been a village girl, would things have been different between us?"

"Maybe we wouldn't have met at all." I realised that the thought of never meeting him bothered me more than the uncomfortable situation I was in now.

"Maybe we would have shared a few kisses and a few sleepless nights. Maybe we would have married each other and maybe we would have raised our own little family." I bent my head as I fought the tears burning in my eyes.

"You live here in the capital with your family and I am glad to know that there is someone with a golden heart here, someone who will listen to those who feel invisible and unseen." I paused and avoided his glance to prevent the tears from escaping my eyes and rolling down my cheeks. "But my family and I have our own problems and even though I would love to give us a fair chance, I know that there is a part of my life that I can't share with you or anyone else."

Nick dropped his arm slowly and walked towards me to place his hands on my shoulders. "I might not have known the poverty or the hunger your family has gone through, but I will never look down on you or them and I will never disregard their feelings or judge any of you in any way."

His words made me smile a little. "Some secrets are not mine to share, Nick." I whispered. "But if you care about me and my family, there is something you can do to help us." And I hoped he would.

"For reasons I can't explain, it is safer for me and my family to move to another village." I bent my head.

"Come to the capital. I will welcome you all with open arms." Nick interrupted me before I finished my sentence, and I placed a hand on his cheek.

"I don't know if that's a much safer place for us to be."

I was certain that to kill the beast, they considered responsible for the horrible killings that were happening lately, the villagers would come looking for us eventually, once they realised who we were.

"I want them to think that they can find us in the capital, but I don't want us to be here when they come."

Nick was silent for a moment. "I assume the reason behind all of this is one of those secrets that you can't reveal, not even to me?"

I shook my head. "They're mine to keep, but not mine to tell." I repeated once more, and a part of my heart started breaking.

Not that I believed being able to tell him everything would have helped in any way. I was certain that if I told him the entire truth, he would see me in a different light and his feelings towards me might change.

"What do you need me to do?" Nick tightened his grip on my shoulders, and I had to close my eyes to make sure I wouldn't end up giving in anyway.

"Everyone needs to believe we moved to the capital. After the royal ball, right before Lilian and I step back into the carriage…" One tear escaped and rolled down my cheek. "You have to make sure she hears you inviting me and my entire family to the capital." Another tear rolled down my cheek and another one and Nick used his soft thumbs to wipe them all away. "My family and I will pack all our belongings the next day and you will send a few carriages to pick us up." I gave up on fighting the tears, while Nick kept on wiping them all away as if every tear was one too many. "But instead of bringing us to the capital, you'll bring us to one of the other villages. I don't mind which one. We'll be safe there for a while."

"And if I can guarantee the safety of you and your family here in the capital, would you reconsider your plan?" Nick's voice sounded a little raw and he coughed while observing his wet thumbs.

"I don't think you can guarantee that." I shook my head, but Nick pressed the palms of his hands to my cheeks.

"I have until the end of the royal ball to convince you and I hope you will, at least, allow me to do my very best to show you that the future you just talked about, the one where we fall in love, get married and raise our own family, is within your reach."

"I don't want you to invest so much time and energy into something that might not lead to anything."

"And I would hate myself if I didn't at least try. I know you have feelings for me and I won't give up on you that easily, Emily. You believe that we don't have a chance together, but I want to prove you that we do."

Chapter Eighteen

I expected dancing to be nothing compared to what I was used to, but I had to admit that it was more tiring and more painful than I expected.

After several days, my feet were covered in blisters and every step, even the ones between my couch and my bed, felt like torture. The muscles of my shoulders and arms were still protesting, even when I tried to prepare some food.

I was used to exhaustion and hunger, but I was clearly not prepared for the impact all those unknown movements had on my body.

"Why do I get the impression that it would be better if we skipped the dancing today?" Nick offered me his hand while I stepped out of the carriage. "I can only assume that you probably feel worse than you look." He clearly hasn't looked at the mirror today. He had dark circles under his eyes and his normally glowing skin was a bit grey.

"I have to admit that I might have underestimated the dancing, but we only have four more days until the ball. I don't think we can allow ourselves to simply skip a day."

"Nonsense!" Nick raised his voice and shook his head. "I know you still feel like you have to concentrate on each and every step, but I'm sure that your muscles have added all the movements to their collective memory already."

He cocked his head slightly. "What would you say

about visiting one of the best beauty centres in the capital?" He immediately added, "Not that you need that, of course, but I've heard that it's quite relaxing."

I smiled but hesitated to answer. I had to admit that my entire body enjoyed his idea, but a little voice in the back of my mind was protesting heavily.

Each of these tasks fed my family, clothed them, and made their life more comfortable. Yet, I wasn't sure if I really wanted to tell my family that I had earned whatever they got by spending the day in a beauty farm.

"Actually, it would be a great opportunity to let people see us together. Wouldn't that make your move to the capital because of me more believable?" He smiled and blinked a few times like I had seen the girls in my village do when they were flirting.

He also made a lot of sense. It would make my whole plan more believable.

"I think, when you say it like that, I can agree," I said, once I realised it would help my plan.

Nick helped me into the carriage before he sat down next to me. I noticed the heat of his body and the pressure of his hip touching mine. In a way, it was the most comfortable and pleasant feeling I've ever had in this carriage but at the same time, I panicked a little at the thought that we would have to spend some time in such a small space.

"It's only a few minutes by carriage." Nick turned his face towards me and his blue eyes met mine.

I attempted to answer, but instead I simply nodded and turned my head away from him. While I stared at the beautifully coloured houses passing by, I asked myself how was it possible that my life changed so much in such a short time.

A few weeks ago, I was nothing but my mother's daughter, once in a while escaping the house to break the rules she had set, even though the world was dangerous for people like me, I somehow almost forgot that my father had been killed. It all seemed so long ago and the wounds were healed, even though I still sensed the scars covering my heart and soul.

Now, all those wounds were ripped open.

Not only had I managed to develop feelings for someone I shouldn't have fallen in love with, I ended up being in charge of our safety and wellbeing after challenging my mother for power.

And to make matters worse, we were confronted with a problem that could cost us all our lives.

I told my mother about my plan, about Nick being willing to help us. Now, we only had to hold on for a few more days, but one of the reasons I barely slept at night, was that I was worried the time would catch up with us.

I feared that somehow someone would figure out who we were and what we were before the royal ball is over. I was scared that my mother would knock on my door to tell me that something happened to Benjamin, or one of the others.

A few times, I imagined that if I snuck out of bed and gave into the longing of my body to turn into the form that didn't hurt, I would be able to calm my mind. All those times, my illusions were shattered by images of a barely recognizable small body in the woods, killed by a creature like me.

"Emily?" Nick placed a hand on my arm, and I shook my head to push the thoughts and worries to the background. "Is everything alright?" There was genuine worry in his eyes and even though I was now staring at him again, he did not pull his hand back.

"I'm exhausted, that's all." I shrugged, but it was a weak attempt to lie and change the subject. The frown on my forehead deepened and my already hurting muscles were a lot more tensed than they should be. "There is nothing to worry about." As if my first lie had not been enough already, I added a second one and I read in Nick's eyes that he was not believing either of them.

"Emily?" Nick said my name again, softer this time and slower, as if he wanted to make sure that it would sink in. "Do you trust me?" He swallowed and there was a glimmer of fear in his eyes. Either he was afraid that I would say no. Or maybe he was afraid that I would say yes.

"I do." Surprisingly easy the words escaped my lips and I realised that I was barely breathing. "But I've already told you that I can't tell you everything that's on my mind and I know that you can't fully trust me because of that." I bent my head and Nick's hand searched for mine.

He intertwined our fingers and I noticed that the palms of my hands were sweaty. "Is it your family not trusting me? Are they the reason you can't come and live here in the capital, with me?" The question clearly bothered him for quite some time already.

"I understand that your family is important, but what about you?" His words were filled with longing and pain and my heart broke a little more.

"They are not forbidding me to be with you, although I'm certain that if they knew I wanted to be with you, they wouldn't hesitate to do so." I took a deep breath and thought about my mother and how she already disliked when I accepted Nick's offer to work for him. "They are in danger and I know that the danger will follow us to the capital if we decide to come to live here."

"Why don't you trust that I can protect you and your family?" Nick paused and I realised that his question was not meant to be judgemental.

He was genuinely wondering why I didn't believe that he would never let anything happen to me. He had all reason to do so. After all, he wasn't aware that I was a dangerous beast and that sooner or later, a large crowd would want the heads of my family.

"Because I am fairly certain you can't." I bent my head and avoided his glance, but his hand kept on holding mine and I enjoyed the warmth and the kindness behind the gesture. "I am fairly certain that no one can."

I took a deep breath and looked out of the window when the carriage stood still in front of a big white building with huge balconies and pink curtains blowing in the wind.

The coachman opened the door of the carriage without knocking and stepped back immediately when he noticed our intertwined hands. "I'm sorry, my lord, am I interrupting?"

Nick wanted to say yes, and he wouldn't be lying, but I quickly pulled my hand and got up. "No, we were simply discussing my expectations of today."

My cheeks blushed and even the coachman couldn't miss it. I assumed that Lilian must have noticed that Nick and I disappeared. I wondered what she thought of it.

I wondered whether she told her father about everything she witnessed. I also wondered whether she suspected Nick and I were in love.

I was somehow hoping for it. I was counting on her to tell her father and the rest of the village the story I didn't want to tell, unknowingly helping me make the story about our move to the capital all the more believable.

I was almost sure that with Lilian's help, the word would spread fast.

Chapter Nineteen

"Emily Rivers?" A strong hand grabbed my shoulder as soon as I stepped out of the carriage in front of my house. "You, your family, and I need to talk."

My heart skipped a beat and I held my breath probably way longer than a normal human would have been able to do.

"The ball is tomorrow, sir. I need some decent sleep to make sure I don't look as bad as the capital citizens expect me to look." I swallowed and my eyes met those of Lilian's father.

"It won't be long, I promise." He squeezed his eyes a little and a thousand horrible thoughts went through my head.

Had he found out why my family and I were always the ones finding the dead bodies in the woods? Had he discovered that I was my father's daughter? Had he finally put all the pieces together? Had he finally linked all the stories Lilian told him about me and Nick?

"Of course, but my family doesn't live here." I looked at my front door.

I really wanted to be in my own house for a little while. Light a cosy fire, make something to eat, and go to bed early.

"I'll ask the carriage to bring us to your family's home." Lilian's father yelled the instructions at the coachman and I shook my head, whispering an excuse that wasn't mine to whisper.

"Get in." That wasn't a question either and when Gareth stretched out his hand, I placed mine reluctantly in it.

I remembered all too well where his hand roamed, the last time we were standing this close to each other, and I tensed.

He didn't try anything, though. He kept silent and I wasn't sure if that should make me feel better or worse.

If he already knew what I was, and what I was capable of, he wouldn't have come unarmed. Or maybe he would use the same kind of poison that was used to kill me father.

"Emily?" My mother threw the door of the house open before Lilian's father and I had gotten the chance to step out of the carriage. "Is everything alright? Did anything happen?" Her eyes met mine and I shrugged a little to make it clear to her that I had absolutely no idea what Gareth was doing here, but she read in my eyes that I feared the worst, just like she did.

"I want a word with you two." Gareth locked his glance with my mother's and a shiver rolled down my spine.

Benjamin was behind that door, believing that he only had to hold on for two more days, probably counting the minutes until we left our home and moved to a place where he could run freely and enjoy everything I had enjoyed for so many years, unaware how close the danger had been all that time.

"Of course, come in." My mother took a deep breath, and I almost heard the soft prayers she was whispering in the back of her mind. "Would you like something to eat? Something to drink?" She wouldn't serve anything to my family while Lilian's father was around, not before we knew whether or not he had come to kill us.

"No, I will keep it short. Emily needs to sleep well tonight." He turned his face towards me and the echo of his footsteps was almost deafening while he crossed the threshold and entered our home, our safe place, the one spot where we never had any secrets. "I just heard some concerning things from my daughter that I need to discuss."

My eyes wandered through the living room, and I nodded when I saw Benjamin sitting in my uncle Calvin's lap, holding onto his strong arms. His eyes were wide open and small pearls of sweat covered his forehead.

I wanted to say something to encourage him, to calm him down, but I couldn't find the right words, not without giving Gareth more information than he had right now.

"Benjamin…" I cleared my throat. "You look tired. Would you like going to bed early?" I spoke softly and I forced my lips to curl up into a smile. "I don't think anyone will be angry if you take one of the beds for yourself tonight while we talk downstairs."

"There is no need to send him to bed early, miss Rivers." Gareth shook his head. "I already said that I will keep it short." He turned towards me. "Lilian told me about Lord Nick and everything that's going on between the two of you."

I closed my eyes and heard my family collectively holding their breaths. If looks were able to kill, my own mother would have killed me right now.

"I didn't want to cause any problems." I made sure to shake my head quickly and avoided the stares of my family. I wanted to add excuses and possible explanations for my behaviour, but I had no idea what Gareth wanted to hear and probably not saying anything would be a far better idea than saying the wrong thing.

"I only want to make one thing clear." He squeezed his eyes. "My Lilian will marry one of the princes, preferably the crown prince." His voice was raw and deep and I realised that to him, this ball was not just a nice gesture from the royal family, but an opportunity that could change his and his daughter's life. "I hope that you don't have the illusion that just because a nobleman fell in love with you that you can try to seduce on of the princes?"

I frowned and weighted each and every word carefully on my tongue. "I never wanted to attend this ball simply to charm myself into the capital." I paused for a moment. "But I noticed how important it is to you and to your Lilian. I will not be the one to stand in her way towards the heart of the crown prince. I will even see if I can do anything to help her."

Her beauty was not in question, but Lilian would need a divine intervention if she was planning on making the crown prince fall in love with her. Not only was she less than a talented conversationalist, she lacked manners people in the capital possessed, and at times, she was just rude and unpleasant.

"I think you and I understand each other very well." He curled his lips up into a smile once more and then he nodded at my family. "I will leave you alone for now." He squeezed his eyes a little and I realised that we weren't the only ones not playing a game.

"I will lead you to the door." I took a deep breath and I stared at Benjamin before I led Lilian's father out of the living room, back to the front door. "I do hope that your daughter will succeed tomorrow."

In the living room, my family was probably having all kinds of questions and I wasn't ready to answer them yet. "She worked hard for it the last couple of weeks."

"It's a pity she misses the natural charm you seem to possess." Gareth stretched out his hand to touch my cheek. "It is easy to forget that most people with a pretty exterior are wearing a mask to hide the monster within."

He dropped his arm again and softened his voice, even though he was probably aware that my entire family would still be able to hear and understand each and every word. "You have inherited your father's chin and his soft and caring temperament." He straightened his back and lifted his chin a little.

"I do hope you will not inherit his fate, although that lies entirely in your own hands." After that last word, he opened the front door, but he turned around once more before he left the house.

"If you get me out of this village and help my daughter gain the heart of the crown prince, I won't tell the others in this town about the secret you have been hiding all this time."

With trembling hands, I closed the door behind him and fell down on the cold floor. I didn't know if he believed that my family and I had something to do with the killed children that kept appearing in the woods. But I couldn't take any risks.

He knew what we were and even though he promised to leave us alone right now, I felt the responsibility to protect my family pressing on my shoulders, but I had no idea how to protect them from whatever would be happening once Gareth discovered that even with my help, his daughter stood next to no chance with any of the nobles, let alone the crown prince.

I took a few deep breaths while I tried to swallow away all the tears I couldn't fight. I had to get back to the living room to explain my family everything, to comfort them, to assure them that I came up with a plan that would guarantee their safety. I just needed a few minutes to collect myself.

"Emily?" My mother spoke softly while she entered the narrow hallway. "I'm sorry…" She kneeled in front of me and the back of her hand touched my cheek, wiping the tears away.

"You shouldn't have to be the one to deal with all of this." She placed her hand on my shoulder and squeezed slightly. "I'm sorry that we have to hide from humans. I'm sorry that you've finally found the love I wished for you, but that you have to give it up." She pulled her hand back and for a moment, she just stared at me, her dark eyes meeting mine.

"We have to go to the living room to tell the others what we're going to do now." I tried to push myself up and my mother stretched out her hand to help me. A bit reluctantly, I placed my hand in hers and allowed her to support me.

"If only I knew what we should do right now." I sighed and tensed, my fingernails piercing the skin of my hands.

I wanted to disappear and never come back. I wanted to give into the senses, the urges, the animal inside of me that longed for a life without threats, without emotions, without all those problems I had no solutions for.

"You don't have to do this alone and you know

that." My mother grabbed my chin and forced me to look at her. "Do you love him, Emily? Have you fallen in love with Lord Nick?" her voice was firm, but without the judgement I expected and feared.

"I can't allow myself to feel anything for him, Mother." I avoided her glance and shook my head. "I can't. If I allow myself to feel anything for him, I won't be able to protect those I have to protect. Because if I allow myself to feel anything for him, I won't be able to convince him that I can't live with him in the capital, that my family won't be safe there, that even he can't protect us against the dangers and threats surrounding us. If I allowed myself to feel anything for him, I would blindly trust him with all our secrets and I would believe him when he promised to keep us all safe."

My mother didn't say anything. Instead, she wrapped her arms around me and her hand went through my hair. "Your father always believed that you would have a brighter future than we had."

A tear escaped her eye and her grip around me tightened. "I wish that he was right." She kept silent for a moment. "I wish that he was right about all those hopes and dreams he had for you."

"Our family is waiting for us." My mother stepped back and tucked a strand of hair behind my ear. "If Gareth really believes that you can help his daughter to win the heart of the crown prince, he might let us live another day so you can keep your promise." She took a deep breath and her eyes met mine again. "And you can share one last evening with the man who is everything your father and I had hoped your future husband to be." She curled her lips up into a sad smile and I mirrored her expression.

I didn't know if spending one more night with

Nick, if dancing with him for an entire evening, if being in his arms and wearing a dress matching his uniform perfectly, would make things any easier.

But I wasn't the only one who got to decide. And maybe Nick needed this last evening, this last moment, more than I did.

"I didn't give him many details, but he promised to help us," I whispered and took a deep breath. "The morning after the ball, he will send his golden carriages over, but instead of bringing us to the capital like everyone expects, he will bring us to another village where we can start a new life without anyone knowing who we are and why my father died."

"Your father would have been so proud of you." My mother took a deep breath and then turned around to lead me back into the living room.

Benjamin still sat in my uncle Calvin's lap and I saw his hands shaking a little. His lips were forming a straight line and even though he got some more colour on his cheeks the last couple of weeks, he was now pale white.

If it had been only me, maybe I would have trusted Nick, maybe I would have let him try to protect me, maybe I would have even told him all my secrets, maybe I would have even shown him what beast was lingering under the surface, what animal was close to my heart and why I liked the patterns on his uniform so much.

But it wasn't just me. It was me, my mother, my sisters, Benjamin, my uncles. I dared to believe that Nick would be able to keep me safe, but I didn't dare to allow myself to believe that he could keep my entire family safe.

"Do you really think we'll will be safe for two

more nights?" Uncle Aaron cleared his throat, but his voice was still nothing but a trembling whisper.

"We have to be." I straightened my back and uncurled my fingers. A few drops of blood rolled down the palms of my hands before the wounds closed, only needing seconds to heal completely where humans would have needed days.

"I have no doubt he's leading an entire army of angry villagers into the woods right now. Even if we managed to leave the house unseen, we would put ourselves at risk by trying to escape while every movement that's not part of their hunt is being watched closely."

I wanted to shift my weight from one leg to the other, but I also wanted to come across as much stronger than I felt right now. "I will stay with you tonight and return home tomorrow as soon as I can." I looked over my shoulder and saw my mother giving me an encouraging nod.

"We will barricade all the doors and windows and maybe we should take turns and keep watch in case Gareth thinks his daughter can win the heart of the crown prince without my help."

"What happens if she doesn't manage to win his heart?" Uncle Aaron's voice sounded a little stronger right now and his grip around Benjamin relaxed a little.

"I hope we won't have to find out because we fled this village before we were confronted with the consequences of that outcome." I took a deep breath.

"I will make sure to return home before she gets the chance to tell her father what happened." I exchanged one more look with my mother. "I won't forgive myself if anything happens to any of you and while I'm away tomorrow, I want you to keep the house completely locked." I hated to limit my family, like my mother had done all those years, but I didn't want to come home only to find the corpses of those I loved most and was supposed to protect.

"I order you all to only leave this house in case of danger and I order you all to let no one but me into this house."

My mother placed a hand on my shoulder, knowing all too well that I hated giving orders, forcing my family into something, and taking their choice away.

"I would have done and said the same thing, Emily." She was mostly assuring my family that she supported my decision, and that I did the right thing. But in the process, she was also assuring me and, even though the heavy weight pressing on my chest didn't disappear completely, I felt a little lighter.

"Emily? You should take one of the beds upstairs. Your uncles and I will make sure there is always someone awake, but you need all the sleep you can get. Tomorrow is an important day, and I don't want anything to keep you from at least enjoying it a little." She smiled, but I couldn't return it.

I would try to relax, but even though Nick would do everything he could to make me forget everything horrible in my life, I didn't think I would be able to shake this feeling, worry, and fear that I wouldn't find a home anymore when I eventually returned to Waterfield.

Chapter Twenty

"Emily?" The back of my mother's hand caressed my cheek. Her hand was warm and gentle, and I smiled, remembering how she used to wake me up like this, long ago, when I was even younger than Benjamin was now.

"It's an important day today," she spoke softly and when I opened my eyes, I saw the dark circles under my mother's eyes. She clearly didn't get enough sleep last night. "I already filled the bath with warm water."

I pushed myself up. "You know that you can take a warm bath, too?" My eyes met my mother's, and she nodded.

"But just because we were better off lately, we shouldn't grow careless with the luxuries. There might be a time of need we face again." She had so many more years of life experience. She dealt with so many problems. I just hoped that I would be able to deal with them as well as she did, someday.

She always did what was best for us, she made countless sacrifices over the years, and she put our lives before hers more times than I could count.

And I suddenly felt guilty for thinking that she had forgotten she was not just our leader, but also our mother.

"Thank you, mom." I wrapped my arms around her neck and even though the words were barely a whisper, she realised that I wasn't just thanking her for the bath and waking me up in the gentlest way possible, but for everything she had done for me during the last couple of weeks and in general.

"You're welcome, Emily." She replied and pressed me tighter to her chest.

The last time she held me like this was years ago, when we shared the edge of my father's bed, when we both heard his heartbeat stop beating in his chest, when we both felt his last breath leave his lips.

"Come, I'll wash your hair." She carefully stepped back and stretched out her hand to guide me towards the bathroom.

I could wash my own hair. I could even wash my own back, but I liked having my mother around right now. I liked pretending that I was a normal girl, like Lilian, who was about to have the most amazing evening of her entire life.

I liked pretending that the knot in my stomach was not caused by fear, but by healthy nerves because I was going meet the royal family in less than twelve hours. I liked pretending that tonight wouldn't be my final goodbye to Nick, but the first day of a new life, a new beginning.

My mother helped me take my nightgown off. Her eyes wandered over my body and her glance rested on my muscled shoulders. "If only your father could have seen how strong you have become…" She murmured while I stepped into the bathtub.

The water was pleasantly warm, and I couldn't remember the last time I was able to wash with warm water.

"Since when has your hair grown this long?" My mom shook her head, and I closed my eyes to enjoy the feeling of her hands washing my hair. "And since when have you become this beautiful?"

I grabbed a pale white cloth and gently moved it over my skin. For the first time in my life, I noticed how relaxing and nice a warm bath could be.

"I think that Gareth is right." My mother wrapped a towel around my wet hair and stepped back to look at my face while I stepped out of the tub. "If you wanted to win the heart of the crown prince, he wouldn't stand a chance." She curled her lips up into a smile. "And your father was always right, too." She took a deep breath and then she handed me another towel so I could dry myself. "Someone as smart and beautiful as you belongs in the capital, and I'm sorry that we've never been able to give you that chance."

"Mom…" I kept silent for a moment while I dried my face and my body. "Despite everything, I'm thankful that I was born into this family. Maybe this isn't the easiest life, but I'm certain that Nick wouldn't even notice, let alone love me if I wasn't the person I've become."

I bent my head and stared at my toes. "And even though Nick and I don't have the future father wished for me, I'm thankful that I had the opportunity to experience these past few weeks with him."

"I'm sure that he won't be the last handsome young man losing his heart to you, Emily." My mother handed me a small package, wrapped in pretty blue paper and a pink bowtie. "And the next time you meet someone who can makes your heart beat faster, life will be different and you will be able to share your life with him."

With trembling fingers, I opened the present. I held my breath when I noticed the undergarments, but I smiled when I found the attached letter.

"For your kindness and to make sure that even

when you decide to take my dress off, you can be seen."

"Who is it from?" My mother leaned over my shoulder to read the curly handwriting.

"It's from Martha, the woman who owns the tailor shop. She designed my dress and Nick's uniform."

I put the letter down as my hands wandered over the soft silk.

"I wish I could see you dancing in his arms." My mother placed her hands on my naked shoulders and carefully pressed a soft kiss on my forehead. "I wish I could see you in your dress."

She cocked her head and then swallowed. "Promise me that despite everything, you will try to enjoy tonight. Promise me that you will smile and laugh and promise me that you will trust me and your uncles to take care of your sisters and Benjamin." She paused for a moment and then stepped back.

"You're too young to be our leader, Emily. And if there was any way to take that responsibility back from you, I would happily do so."

"We can't stop nature, not even if we try." My voice cracked a little and I took the towel from my head. "And even though I am now the leader of our family and have to deal with all the responsibility, I'm still your daughter and you're still my mother."

"And no matter what happens, Emily, that will never change." She guided me towards a wooden chair in front of a broken mirror. "Would you like me to braid your hair today?"

"Yes, please." I smiled at my mother's reflection in the mirror. "I wouldn't want it any other way."

Chapter Twenty-One

I didn't manage to say a word during the entire ride to the capital. Partly because I wasn't sure what to talk about and partly because Lilian started speaking and didn't stop, or even notice that I didn't try to interrupt her once.

I didn't mind the lack of conversation from my side. While Lilian was wondering out loud what both princes would look like and whether one of them would grant her his first dance, I mostly tried to find a way to put my worries and sorrows as far away as possible.

"Somehow, I get the impression that you've managed to get some well-deserved sleep last night." Nick greeted me with a bright smile on his face and a slight glimmer in his eyes. He didn't wear his uniform yet, but he still looked different. "And here I thought you would be nervous about tonight."

I forced my lips into a smile and shrugged in an attempt to avoid answering his question. I didn't even have the time to worry about the royal ball, dancing, etiquette, or whether the royal family enjoyed the cake Nick and I selected for them. I had much bigger worries consuming my mind. "The circles under your eyes seem to have grown darker." I looked at him and narrowed my eyes a little. "One would almost think that you were far more nervous about tonight than I am."

Nick didn't respond but offered me his arm while he guided me towards Martha who sent me such an amazing present this morning. "That is probably because I have plenty to be worried about," he spoke softly and looked down.

The last couple of weeks, he made comments like this more often, but he never explained further and I never dared to ask.

"You are the one who has grown up here in the capital. I assume this is not your first ball?" I tried to relax my shoulders a little and I saw Martha's eyes wander over my body.

I was wearing the same dress as usual, but I nodded at her to let her know that I was wearing her present.

"No, I attended plenty of other balls before, but somehow I still believe that today I have more to lose than ever before." He turned his head towards me and a sigh escaped his lips.

"I really hoped that I was able to change your mind during the last couple of days," he paused for a moment, but I tried to avoid his glance, knowing that doing so was probably already answering his unasked question.

"And I realise that if I don't manage to change your mind in the upcoming hours, this will most likely be our last time together."

I kept silent for a moment and I looked over my shoulder to see Philippe and Lilian enter the tailor shop behind us.

Philippe had clearly not grown used to Lilian's company over time. He wore a slightly bored expression on his face and whenever he was able to look away from her, slight annoyance showed on his face, too.

Luckily for him, Lilian was not planning on winning his heart tonight and I was certain that as soon as Philippe introduced her to the crown prince and his younger brother, Lilian would lose all interest in him and would focus solely on the royal family, determined to become one of them.

Normally, I would consider it slightly rude, but I couldn't shake the impression that he would most likely be more than just a little relieved that someone else would have to endure her presence.

"In two hours, a carriage will arrive to bring us to the royal palace." Nick cleared his throat to catch my attention and I quickly turned my head to him. "The cake and all the food will be presented on a long table and as soon as all the guests have arrived, the first dance will be held and the ball will officially be opened by the King and Queen."

I nodded a little absentmindedly and took a few deep breaths. "I don't think I need two hours to get ready for the ball." I stared at my reflection in the mirror. "My mother already braided my hair and I took bath this morning." I tucked a loose strand of hair behind my ear and a slight blush coloured my cheeks.

"Your mother has done an amazing job, Emily, but we had something else in mind, and it involves makeup." Nick pressed the palm of his hand to my cheek and he forced me to look at him. "You are beautiful and you do not need any makeup in the first place, but everyone would notice the lack of it, since no woman in the capital would even contemplate attending a ball without it." He moved his hand to the back of my head and carefully pulled out the pins that were holding my hair together. "You probably won't recognise yourself, but you won't stand out for the lack of it." He pulled his hand back again and my hair fell on my shoulders.

"I only feel sorry for my mother." I spoke softly as I took the pins from him, even though I had no idea where to put them away safely and I doubted whether Martha was going to use them for my hair. "My mother wished she could see me tonight." I murmured and eventually placed the pins on the counter. "She didn't have a chance to see the beautiful dress I'll be wearing tonight and now, she won't even know how my hair looks like."

"If you'd like, I could ask one of the royal painters to draw you so your mother could get an impression?" Nick locked his glance with mine. "I might be asking the painters to draw you for me, too, since you're planning on leaving."

I swallowed, shifting my weight from one leg to the other while I felt more uncomfortable by the second. The undergarments I wore made me feel like I could barely breathe and weren't as pleasant as the ones I left at home. "I never thought anyone would ever want to draw me. I'm sure you would make my mother my really happy."

"You seem to believe that you are somehow less interesting than are," Nick spoke softly and shook his head. "I promise that once you wear your dress, your hair and face are done, no one will notice any difference between you and anyone from the capital."

"Your compliments won't change my mind, Nick." I was unsure how to respond, especially knowing that Lilian was staring at me and observing everything I said and did.

"I am not trying to change your mind with my words, Emily." Nick pressed a finger to the tip of my nose and it rested there for a short moment. "I mean them all and when you enter the ball tonight, with your arm linked with mine, I want you to remember that I said all of this to you and only you."

I frowned and for a moment, I wondered what he knew about the ball that he didn't tell me. "I will be presented as the village girl from Waterfield, won't I?" I cocked my head slightly, suddenly doubting whether he was going to try to prove to me that I belonged here by simply not telling anyone who I was.

"Yes, of course." Nick assured me, although the tone he used for these words didn't completely calm me down. "You and the other people from the villages are our guests of honour, after all."

He was not telling me the entire story, I could feel it, but I decided that asking more questions would probably only make me doubt him more, just like they would most likely increase the nervousness that already spread through my entire body.

"If we want to turn me into a girl not any less beautiful than the girls from the capital, I think we should get started." I nervously looked over my shoulder and saw how Lilian already sat down in one of the comfortable white chairs.

"It's not quite as much work as you think, but the sooner we start, the more time you have to admire your own reflection afterwards."

Martha's hands worked fast and surprisingly gently. I had no idea what she was doing exactly, but I felt she knew what she was doing.

Once she was finished, I barely recognised myself in the mirror and I held my breath while my eyes wandered over my reflection. My curled hair surrounded my face and the blush, carefully crafted by the talented girl, hid my own naturally red cheeks. The necklace around my neck sparkled in the sunlight.

I tried to convince Nick that he didn't need to give me something as expensive as jewellery, but he assured me that it was only a gift if I decided to keep it after the ball. But I already knew in that moment that I would give it back to him as soon as I could.

Maybe he would give it to another girl, someone who fit into his life better, without having to keep secrets from him.

"We do look beautiful together, don't you think?" Nick appeared next to me and placed his hands on my shoulders. The bodice of my dress and his uniform were the exact same shade of blue and the golden patterns, shaping all those animals I loved so much, seemed to face each other.

"I'm certain that you will get quite some attention tonight." He curled his lips up into a smile and I took a deep breath.

"I don't need any attention tonight." I spoke softly and placed a hand on my chest. I couldn't get used to the upper undergarments and the dress made it even harder for me to breath. "I need to make sure that Lilian somehow manages to win the heart of one of the princes and I need to make sure that my family escapes Waterfield safely."

Nick's glance caught mine through the mirror and he hesitated for a short moment. "If you'd like, I could send a few guards to Waterfield to keep an eye on your family?" he spoke softly. "I could give the order within a few minutes and they could be there within an hour." He didn't comment on the second part of my sentence.

"Are you really willing to risk your guards to protect my family?" I turned around and placed my hands on his chest. It was more of an instinct than something I thought about and the palms of my hands burned a little when they touched the stiff fabric of his uniform.

"I don't know if anything is going to happen, but if something happens, it can very well end with people dying. If you really don't mind, I'd feel comforted by the thought that they are watched over." I bent my head and concentrated on his heart beating against the palm of my hand.

"We both want to make sure that nothing bad happens to your family," Nick spoke softly as leaned a little towards me.

His forehead was warm when he pressed it to mine and I tensed, while his hands slid around my waist. "But if my guards dying to keep your family alive might convince you that I can protect them, that I can protect you, I am willing to take that risk."

I felt one of his hands moving up and a shiver rolled down my spine while he pulled me even closer towards him.

"Nick..." his name was barely a whisper on my lips, and his breath warmed the tip of my nose. "You're not making this any easier." I turned my face away from him, but my heart raced.

"Tonight, may be the very last night we share together and saying goodbye will already be hard enough..."

"When you leave the ball tonight, without a promise of coming back, I want to make sure that you can stand behind your decision. I want to be sure that I have done everything I can to convince you from choosing that path."

He carefully grabbed my chin and turned my face to his. His blue eyes met my dark ones and when he moved closer, all of my protest faded.

My lips parted a little when he pressed his lips to mine and slowly, I slid my arms around his neck. I closed my eyes and the entire world disappeared. I forgot about Lilian and Philippe, both keeping silent ever since we left the carriage. I forgot about Martha, who had given me a meaningful present. I forgot about the ball and how everyone would notice, despite my wonderful dress and make up, that I was only a simple girl from the village. I forgot about the monster roaming the woods around Waterfield, killing all those innocent children. I even forgot about the threat my family faced.

Instead, our lips melted and our tongues hesitantly touched each other, finding a slow and tender rhythm.

He tasted as perfect as he looked and his hands, softly caressing my back, made me feel safer than I felt in a very long time.

I had to step away and had to stop whatever I felt and whatever I wanted, but I didn't. I didn't walk away from the one good thing I experienced that brought me joy and happiness. I hoped that somehow, I would manage to find a way to do so later tonight.

By now, I thought that maybe Nick and I wouldn't even make it to the ball, but then Philippe coughed and cleared his throat. "Our carriages are waiting."

Slowly, I opened my eyes and for a moment, Nick and I just stared at each other before we stepped away, creating some distance between us, knowing that if we didn't do so we would spend our last night together anywhere but at the royal castle surrounded by people.

"I'm sorry." Philippe bent his head. He had his hands folded behind his back and he wore a dark blue uniform with silver accents. For the first time, the two different colours of his eyes were accentuated, and it wasn't hard to imagine that he was capable of breaking quite some hearts if he wanted to. Nick shook his head, but whatever words he tried to say didn't escape his lips. Instead, he looked at me once before he offered me his arm. "I will make this evening unforgettable." He swallowed after the last words and when I linked my arm with his, he placed his hand on my arm.

"I don't doubt you will." I looked at him once more before I caught a jealous glance Lilian gave me.

Instead of reacting, I smiled, and when I noticed the wonderful dark pink dress that was made her look prettier than I thought possible, I still hoped there was a chance she might attract one of the prices.

"How long is the ride to the castle?" My nerves slowly increased, and I shifted my weight from one leg to the other.

"Are you already counting the seconds until your grand entrance?" Nick winked and tightened his grip on my arm a little, attempting to assure me that everything would be fine.

Whatever he wanted to achieve, it didn't work as well as his kisses. I doubted that anything would ever feel as wonderful as kiss kisses.

"I doubt the entrance will be as grand and impressive as you make it to be." I still didn't believe that people would turn their heads when we entered.

"You might be surprised."

Chapter Twenty-Two

"Don't forget to look around once in a while," Nick spoke softly and squeezed my hand. He didn't say much during the ride to the castle, but in a way, we still communicated with our eyes and faces.

"I won't." I stared out of the window and noticed the countless candles lighting the path leading towards the castle on top of the hill. Even though I noticed the beauty of all those flickering flames guiding us, I wondered how many village families could be helped with the money used to pay for all of this. I let out a deep sigh and Nick squeezed me gently as if he guessed what thoughts crossed my mind.

"The future will look different for everyone, I promise," he whispered, and I turned my head to him while I squeezed my eyes a little. "Even if you disappear tonight and never come back, I will never forget that you were a part of my life, and I will never forget everything you taught me."

I gave him a slight smile and my heart beat rapidly in my chest. In the back of my mind, a little voice whispered that I should choose him, but I shook my head and concentrated on the long candle lit road in front of us.

I wondered how many people like Nick lived in the capital and how many of them would realise that the villages wouldn't have to starve if they only had a small fraction of the amount of food that would be thrown away tonight.

I wondered how many of them would realise that inviting a few extra people to attend a royal ball, wouldn't suddenly change everything.

The carriage slowed down and eventually, the horses tasked with pulling it stood completely still in front of huge golden gates.

The castle on the hill was everything I imagined a castle to be. The walls were higher than any building I ever saw in the capital, and I noticed countless guards circling the four towers, their tops hidden in the clouds. Maybe the castle was bigger than all the houses in Waterfield combined, but I didn't even dare to ask about the number of rooms.

I barely noticed Nick letting go of my hand so he could step out. I just stared at the colourful flags and banners brightening the endless grey walls. I stared at all the people wearing colourful dresses and overwhelming hair styles, on their way to the ballroom. I simply stared at the maids and servants running around to try to please as many people as possible.

"Are you ready for the most memorable evening of your life?" Nick stretched out his hand after the coachman opened the door on my side. He had a wonderful smile playing around his lips and the dancing flames were reflected in his beautiful blue eyes.

I couldn't answer his question, I couldn't say a word. Instead, I just nodded and placed my hand in his, carefully lifting my dress while I walked down the few stairs that never seemed as dangerous as they seemed now.

"This is…" I was looking for the right word, but somehow there didn't seem to be a phrase to describe all of this.

"Enchanting?" Nick waited until I stood safely on the solid ground and offered his arm. "Even though I have been to quite a few balls before, I can assure you that it's something you'll never get used to."

He nodded when a few guards bowed down in front of him before they positioned themselves to both our sides. "Although, I wish you would get the chance to give it a try," he spoke softly and after his glance met mine one more time he started walking.

I tried to see as much of the wonderful gardens as possible, but there was too much to see. I smelled the roses, blossoming at an unusual time of the year. I recognised countless animals, shaped into bushes. I heard the endless songs of the birds, living in nests built in the high trees marking the edge of the woods.

Under my feet, small stones cracked and my ankles felt a bit unstable. I wondered how many more things I would see when I got the chance to roam this garden in my different form and sighed when I realised that I would never get a chance to do so.

I was only here for tonight and when the night was over, I would never come back again.

"Careful…" Nick interrupted my calm, despite the cacophony of sounds surrounding me. ", I wouldn't want you to fall down the stairs." He tenderly tapped my hand, and I stared at the huge stairs in front of me in awe. There were so many steps that I didn't even want to think about counting them.

"We will be up there before you know it." Nick smiled at me and then we climbed the stairs, one step at a time. He walked with a certain kind of grace I never noticed before. Every time he passed someone he knew, he nodded slightly, but somehow, he seemed to know everyone.

I was probably not the only one who fell in love with his kindness, his noble heart, and his innocence. I was probably not the only one who had lost her heart to him. And even though I hated to think about another woman kissing his soft lips and drowning in his blue eyes, it was also in a way calming to know that maybe he would need time to stop missing me, just like I would need time to stop missing him, but he wouldn't have to be alone for the rest of his life. I was certain that he would find someone else.

Someone who loved him as much as I did. Someone who was right for him and entering his life at the right time.

Eventually, we stood still in front of a huge golden door. I hurt my neck while I tried to look up to see the top of it and I widened my eyes when I saw all the small patterns carefully crafted and undoubtedly telling a story that I would have loved to read if I had the time.

"I could tell you the saga of knight Robb and his noble soldiers." Nick winked, but then the door opened into an endless hallway, paved with soft red tapestry. "But that would require you to stay a little longer than one night."

I tried not to look at him and focussed on the door, wide open, at the very end of the hallway, probably leading to the throne room.

I wanted countless more nights like this with him. I wanted to hear the story of knight Robb and his noble soldiers, and I wanted to lose myself in all the other small wonders lingering around the castle and the capital. But most of all, I wanted my family to be safe.

"From what I've heard, there will be a wonderful string quartet playing tonight. I'm certain you will like them." Nick whispered.

His muscles tensed more with every step bringing us closer to the door. "And don't feel sorry for eating two or three or more pieces of cake, because we have more than enough for everyone."

I turned my head to the side, ignoring the beautiful paintings flanking us on both sides, and I saw how his lips trembled a little.

"Are you nervous?" I cocked my head and placed my free hand on his arm. "Shouldn't I be the one who is nervous tonight?" I tried to tease him a little, but now we were only a few steps away from the door and Nick's lips were forming a straight line.

"There is something I didn't tell you." He took a deep breath and avoided my glance. "I was afraid, I still am to be honest, that it would change everything between us." He bent his head slightly and he stared at his black shoes, almost reflecting his own expression.

"But tonight, I can't hide that part of me anymore." He waited in front of the door and then nodded at one of the guards. "Please, promise me that you won't be angry with me."

I squeezed my eyes and my lips parted to say something, but I was interrupted by a trumpet echoing through the ballroom, the hall and probably the enormous gardens, too.

"His Royal Highness Crown Prince Nicholas Lawrence and Miss Emily Rivers, guest of honour from Waterfield."

My eyes widened in shock and my mouth opened, but I didn't get the time to say something. I was pulled into the ballroom and all the heads turned towards us, towards me.

"I'm sorry." Nick looked at me for a brief second and then he lifted his hand to wave at all the people looking at him.

I couldn't move and all my muscles tensed while I let every moment we shared together replay in the back of my mind. I suddenly understood why he used to interrupt people who were trying to use his full title, and I suddenly realised why he could manipulate the royal family so easily.

He was not simply a lord they liked and loved, just like I liked and loved him. He was their son, he was the one who would sit on the throne one day, and he was probably the second most important person in this entire Kingdom.

In a way, I was relieved that the next man on the throne would be a man who had eyes and a heart for the poor people in the villages, and who understood that there was hunger and pain and death everywhere but in the capital. I also realised that I wore a dress tonight clearly made to go with his and that despite my longing to be invisible, everyone would see me and everyone would wonder what I did to win the heart of the crown prince.

"Is everything alright?" Nick still held my hand, and a gracious smile brightened his features.

He moved his head a little closer to mine and there was a kind of worry in his eyes that I haven't seen before.

I realised that he was not just worried about my wellbeing, but also about what impact this reveal would have on us, and how I saw him.

"I know that I shouldn't have kept this from you, but you were constantly telling me that you were a simple village girl and not worth saving, and I was certain that once you knew that I was the crown prince, you would run away from me and never come back."

I swallowed and had to admit that I wasn't sure whether I felt betrayed because he wasn't honest with me or whether I should admit that he was probably right.

Had I known that Nick, the nobleman on the horse who believed he saved me from the cold, hunger, and poverty, was the crown prince, I wouldn't have accepted his offer to work for him and I surely wouldn't have allowed him to come as close to me as he has.

"Can you please say something?" He licked his lips and I looked up.

My eyes wandered over the enormous crowd at our feet. He was the crown prince, he was the second most important person in this entire Kingdom and here he was, introducing me to all those people as the girl who had his heart.

"What do you want me to say, Nick?" I whispered and I hesitated a little while I lifted my hand carefully. I realised that I must look strange. I was the lucky woman who managed to be on the receiving end of the love of the crown prince and here I was, debating if I should run away right now or should play along for one more night before I disappeared for the rest of his life.

"I just want to hear you say that you're not mad at me and that you won't leave me before we have a chance to say goodbye." He bent his head and his dark brown curls danced during the entire movement.

He looked like a little boy who did something wrong and knew very well that he might have ruined something he tried to protect.

A part of me truly wanted to be angry with him, though. A part of me wanted to tell him that I trusted him, that I loved him and that I wasn't sure anymore if the man I got to know and the man standing before me now were one and the same.

Another part of me knew all too well that he was not the only one hiding parts of his personality. After all, I didn't tell him who I was, what I was. I was certain that once he found out why my family had to flee Waterfield, he would probably be slightly angry with me, too.

If I couldn't forgive him for not telling me that he was the crown prince, how could I ever expect him to forgive me that I kept such a big secret from him, and made him fall in love with someone he didn't entirely know?

Of course, he would never find out what I was keeping from him. He would never find out that I was not just an ordinary human and that there was another side of me, a side that scared the people so much that they wanted to kill me. But he also didn't deserve to be judged and hated for the exact same crime.

He brought me here in a dress that made pretty clear how much I meant to him, and I assumed that it also meant that his feelings for me were real, that he fell in love with me and that he would make me his queen if I would allow him to do so.

"I don't think I'm angry," I said eventually.

Lilian's glance burned my back as she entered behind me. I remembered how I promised her father to help her get attention of the crown prince, but Lilian probably already realised that she ruined any chance of marrying the second prince.

"I'm a little surprised and overwhelmed and I have absolutely no idea how to behave right now. But I don't think I'm angry."

I looked over my shoulder and caught Philippe's

glance. I was certain that Lilian was interested in him again since she found out he was a prince, but I doubted that Philippe would change his opinion regarding her rudeness and unpleasant behaviour to the point of making her his wife.

"I can assure you that you don't have any reason to be nervous." Nick curled his lips up into a smile and his shoulders relaxed a little.

"You became quite a decent dancer over the last few weeks, and you look breathtakingly beautiful." He turned towards me and his eyes met mine.

"I only hope that you might reconsider leaving me tonight." He touched my cheek with the back of his hand and my heart raced because all these people were still watching us and were witnessing all of this.

"I'm sure that after tonight, my parents and everyone in this ballroom will miss you, too. You won't just leave me behind. You will leave them behind, too. You could change the kingdom for the better. You wouldn't be just a queen. You would be their queen. A queen who knows how it feels to be one of them."

I took a deep breath and stepped back while I curled my fingers around his wrist to force him to drop his hand. I enjoyed every touch and every word and if it had just been me, I would have given in days ago, weeks ago.

"You know that if I knew for sure that my family had nothing to fear here in the capital, I would have loved to try to see what the future would bring us."

"But even though you now know that I'm the crown prince and have quite something to say in this kingdom, you still don't believe that I can protect you and your family." There was a slight bit of disappointment in his voice and the glimmer in his eyes dimmed for a short moment.

I almost felt sorry for him and wanted to lean on the tips of my toes so I could press a soft kiss on his lips. But the time Lilian's father had given me has just run out.

I wouldn't be able to help his daughter to become the next queen of this kingdom and no matter what explanation I would give him, he would use the threat, created by discovery of the lifeless bodies we found all over the woods, to kill my family.

I still didn't believe that fleeing to the capital and being guarded by the royal guard would change his mind or would be able to stop him. He already found a way past all our wolf senses once. He might be able to find a way to kill us without the guards even noticing.

I already buried my father, and I was not planning on burying anyone else.

"I'm sorry…" my voice was barely a whisper, and I tried to fight the tears on the brink of escaping, but I couldn't stop one of them rolling down my cheek.

"Even though I don't understand your decision." Nick wiped the tear away with his thumb and then placed both his hands on my shoulders. "I at least know that it hurts you as much as it hurts me." He took a deep breath.

"Don't worry too much about them or me tonight." He stepped back and then he grabbed my hand. "I want to remember you dancing and smiling and laughing." He smiled a little and nodded at me. "Are you ready to officially open this ball with me?"

I couldn't stop the smile forming on my lips. "I don't think I will ever be, so I assume we should just do it before I change my mind."

"Of course." Nick's smile brightened and he gallantly guided me towards the stairs. He offered me his arm once more and I used my free hand to lift my dress so I wouldn't step on it and stumble all the way down.

My legs were a slightly unstable while we walked down. My knees trembled a little and the palms of my hands were sweaty.

Once in a while, I turned my head towards Nick, to remind myself that he was still the same person, the gallant nobleman who thought he could save me from life and one of the very few citizens here in the capital with a golden heart.

I was insane for letting him go and for letting the chance at love slip through my fingers. No one would understand how I could refuse the chance to become a Queen. But no one would understand that I couldn't risk the lives of my family for anything I wanted and wished for myself.

"There is no need to panic." Nick stood still in the middle of the ballroom.

He stepped back and bent his head to officially great me as his dancing partner for the first dance.

"You were doing great the last couple of days, and you will do great right now." He straightened his back again and, a little nervously, I placed my hand in his.

His hand slid around my waist and pulled me into starting position. "Did I already tell you how beautiful you look tonight?"

I swallowed and avoided his glance as the music started playing. I recognised the tones and the rhythm, and I didn't need to think about any of the steps anymore.

I had to admit that the music indeed sounded a lot

better with a full orchestra. "I don't know if you did. I think I forgot everything that happened before you told me you were the crown prince." I sighed and then my eyes met his.

The reflection of the thousand candles in the endless blue was as enchanting as the rest of the ball. Despite all the overwhelming colours, all the brightness, his eyes were still brightening up the entire room. His eyes were still making my heart skip a beat and almost making me forget how to breathe.

"What would you think about tasting that cake again?" Nick stepped back and he bent his head once more as soon as the song was over.

"We have a long evening ahead of us and I wouldn't want you to dance on an empty stomach." He offered me his arm and I linked mine with his. "I also think that my father and mother would love to meet you after all the stories I told them about you." He licked his lips and I sensed his tensed muscles under my strong grip.

In the end, even the crown prince was simply a son wanting his parents to like the girl he lost his heart to. "I promise that I've only told them good things about you."

I eventually nodded and he guided me towards a long table decorated with more food than I had ever seen in my entire life. I tried not to think about all the poor people who could be fed for weeks with only what was on this table.

"I know what you are thinking right now." Nick took a deep breath, and his arm slid around my waist. "I have already asked my parents if we can bring the leftovers to the villages when the ball is over. I'm sure there will be enough left for everyone." He curled his lips up into a smile and I smiled at him.

"I think most people have never even seen half of what's on this table…" I hesitated while I reached for a strawberry. I wasn't sure if I was supposed to use my hands, but I didn't see any knives or forks and I hoped that most people were aware that I had not exactly grown up surrounded by anything like etiquette.

"You can try everything, but I hope you don't mind if I fill a plate for you." Nick leaned over the table, but before he could grab a plate, a young waiter hurried to give it to him.

"I'm sorry, Your Royal Highness, I didn't notice you and miss Rivers were already here." His cheeks blushed a little and he grabbed a second plate which he gave to me.

He bent his head and didn't allow his eyes to meet mine. "I wish you a pleasant evening and if there is anything I can do, please let me know." He bent his head even more and then stepped back into the shadows.

"I have to admit…" I swallowed and paused for a moment. The plate in my hand was warm and I realised that it was to make sure that the warm food wouldn't cool down right away. "I don't think I would ever be able to get used to conversations like this."

I hesitated and watched how Nick used his bare hands to carefully place small bits of the food on his plate. I copied the movements, although it was harder than I thought it would be to only take one piece of everything.

"I assume it's one of the reasons I kept my identity a secret from you."

Nick grabbed a few extra strawberries and a few smaller pieces of chocolate. He placed all of it on my plate and I smiled, a slight blush covering my cheeks.

"I didn't want you to avoid my glance and I didn't want you to think you had to bow for me." He took a deep breath and then searched for one of the bigger slices of cake he could find. "Around you, I could be as normal as possible." He softened his voice a little and carefully placed a big piece of cake on my plate before he took a smaller one for himself.

"Even though you kept on calling yourself only a village girl, you have always been honest with me." He paused for a moment, shifting his weight from one leg to the other. "I don't think I've ever had true friends before. You would be surprised how many people are only interested in me and my brother because we are princes."

Everyone here in the capital knew him as Crown Prince Nicholas, but he would always be Nick to me, and I believed he wouldn't mind that.

Nick hesitated for a moment, clearly waiting for me to tell him that I had everything I needed, so he could take me to meet his parents."

I looked over my shoulder and found Lilian in the crowd. I felt sorry for Philippe, who was held by her like she was planning on never letting him go again. I assumed she had accepted that second prince was better than no prince at all. "I might not be as surprised as expected to be." A deep sigh escaped, and I turned around completely.

"Yes, I think Lilian is one of them indeed." Nick turned around, too, and for a moment, we just stood there, next to each other with our plates filled and our eyes on his brother and the girl from Waterfield who believed she could marry a prince someday.

"But even here in the capital there are countless

people who long for more." Nick's eyes wandered over the crowd and once in a while, he squeezed his eyes.

He had a golden heart, but it was clear that not everyone appreciated that.

"A few times, I believed I had a true friend, someone I could count on, someone who would also like me had I been a boy from any of the villages." He took a bite of his cake and paused for a moment. "But each and every one of them ended up asking me for things even my father couldn't give them."

I kept silent for a moment, both enjoying the food on my plate and trying to imagine myself in his shoes. I had never really had friends. When I was the right age to make them, I preferred roaming the woods with my father. And after I lost my father, my mother had been too afraid of the outside world and didn't allow me to form any meaningful connection with anyone.

I imagined, though, that knowing that everyone you know was more interested in your title than your person was maybe even worse than not having any friends at all. "That must have hurt a lot. You must have been incredibly lonely. I'm sorry that I'm taking away the only true friend you ever had..." I never experienced words to be as heavy as these ones.

"At least I had the experience that true friends exist in this world, even for me." Nick tried to lighten the mood.

He placed his empty plate on the table. "Are you ready to meet my parents?"

"Every time you ask me if I'm ready, you already know that the answer is no." I put my plate aside too and I took a deep breath before I linked my arm with his again.

"Not being ready has never stopped me from doing

something, though."

Chapter Twenty-Three

I didn't realise how big the room was until we had to cross more than half of it to reach Nick's parents, our king and queen. My heart beat rapidly and suddenly my dress felt even more uncomfortable than it already was.

Even though, I was probably doing just fine, I could barely breathe. In the meantime, Nick kept on nodding at people we passed by along the way. I tried to keep my back straight and my chin high, but I was certain that everyone saw how nervous I was, sensed how out of place I was.

"We're almost there." Nick placed his hand calmingly on mine as he slowed down a little to give me the time to take a few deep breaths.

"I don't know if it helps, but I would like to tell you once more that you look beautiful tonight." He smiled a little and my lips curled up, too.

Of course, his words didn't suddenly take my nervousness away, but I had to admit that it was nice of him to try to make me feel better and more comfortable.

"Mother, Father?" Nick stood still in front of the rulers of our kingdom.

He swallowed and shifted his weight from one leg to the other, while I tried to keep my eyes down.

Nick's father was everything I imagined a king to be. His greying hair gave an impression of a wise man. He wore a uniform in a wonderful shade of blue, with the same golden animal patterns as Nick. Even without the opulent golden crown with numerous precious gems, he exuded authority and strength.

"I want you to meet Miss Emily Rivers…" Nick gave the impression that his sentence was far from finished, but he didn't continue.

"It's an honour to meet you, Your Majesty." I bowed my head and curtsied.

I was experiencing countless emotions. I never really liked our king and queen. After all, I always believed that none of them cared about the people in the villages, about the poverty and hunger, or dying children. I always thought they didn't care whether we lived or died. I always assumed that our royals and the people in the capital would only do something about the problems of the villagers if they didn't get enough supplies for their celebrations. But these two people were not just our rulers, they were also the parents of a man I loved.

"I've heard you have quite an influence on my son," the queen spoke, and I raised my head to answer but didn't dare to meet her eyes.

"Your majesty."

"Look at me, child."

Her bright blue eyes met mine and I held my breath when I noticed the golden crown on her white wavy hair. It was smaller than the king's but maybe even more opulent, with more precious gemstones.

She smiled and turned her head to the king for a moment. "We've learned of the troubles in your village from Nicholas. That is about to change. You are all part of our great kingdom, and it is time we remind you of that. Those responsible, will be punished," as she spoke, she turned her head to me and gave me a reassuring look, while the king nodded at me with a discrete smile.

"Had I been informed of the situation in the villages, I would have done something sooner. I'm sorry I never personally visited to check if everything I was told was correct." The king sounded sincere and for the first time I started to believe that things could really change in this kingdom.

"I hope that the people we invited tonight have a wonderful time." She nodded her head a little and I bowed my head to show my gratitude.

Maybe she expected me to say something, but I had no idea where to find the right words to do so.

"Our son already convinced us to send the food, left after the celebration, to the villages, but he also proposed to send some fresh food, as well. I assume that is something we can discuss later."

She suddenly grabbed my hand and I froze. "Nicholas told us that you are convinced that you are not good enough to be with him, but I hope that I can prove you wrong," her voice was soft and it was almost as if she was singing, so I relaxed a little.

I had to speak at some point, but I tried to prolong the moment for as long as possible.

I was not simply running away from her son because I was a poor girl from the village. If I could, I wouldn't have let this love slip through my fingers. If I could hold onto Nick, I would have done so. Not only that, I also had the royal promise that things in my village would change for the better. That, of course, remained to be seen, but it was a good start.

But I had a good reason to see my original plan through, though. I was doing this to save the lives of my family and even though, I would love to save the lives of countless other people in the villages too, choosing the people in the villages would mean risking the safety, and most of all freedom, of my family, of those I was truly responsible for.

We had been locked up for so many years. We had been afraid ever since my father died. All I wanted, was for them, for us, to be free. I didn't want to change cages. I wanted to find a place where no-one knows us, so we can start anew. With our wolves being an active part of our lives.

I just hoped that when I was gone, Nick would still remember everything I told him about Waterfield. I hoped that even without me, the queen would keep her word and make the lives of the villagers better, one step at a time.

"There is no need to be intimidated, my girl." the queen spoke softly once more and she squeezed my hand. "We only heard great things about your intelligence and kindness." She locked her glance with mine and I breathed in and out a few times before Nick's arm slid around my waist.

"I'm surprised that's what he told you after all my shameless complaining about the poverty in Waterfield." I swallowed and avoided Nick's glance.

"Thank you so much for welcoming me with open arms even though you don't know me. And thank you for considering the problems in my village." No matter what she thought, I was not a good partner for their son.

He was human and I wasn't. My wolf lingered beneath my skin, and I heard her almost begging me to let her out, to just leave this castle, to go to my family and to not add more pain to my already growing heartache.

The future queen being a wolf. No one would ever

accept that.

"Our son didn't have the easiest life and we're glad that he finally found someone who can help him find some calm." Her eyes darkened a little and I saw the same kind of sadness in her eyes that I've seen in my mother's when she told me that she wished she could allow me to live the happy life father always wanted me to have.

"We are happy that he is finally happy and we don't care where you come from. We promise that no one in this kingdom will judge you two just because your hearts have found each other."

Pearls of sweat covered my skin and I wanted to pull my hand back. Maybe no one in the kingdom would take me away from him now, but I would.

I would disappear tomorrow morning to a village where no one knew my family or where we came from. This was my last day as Emily Rivers and my last time spent with Nick.

I already imagined the kindness, I was facing right now, turning into rage once their son was left behind. I shifted my weight from one leg to the other and I heard Nick clearing his throat.

"With your permission to leave, I would like to show Emily around?" He linked his arm with mine again and pulled me a little closer. "She seemed fascinated by a few paintings we saw on our way here and I want to show her my favourite."

"Of course, of course," the queen spoke softly and added. "Our home is your home and you can see everything you would like to see."

"Thank you, Mother. Thank you, Father." Nick bent his head slightly and I copied his movement before he led me away.

He walked towards the closest door and one of the servants hurried to open it for us.

I didn't know if Nick noticed my discomfort, but I was thankful that he managed to get me some privacy and time to find my breath.

The hallway we entered was completely empty and for a short while, Nick and I just walked around in absolute silence. The only company were the paintings on the walls, without a doubt the ancestors who had once ruled or had been a part of the royal family.

The conversation with the queen replayed in the back of my mind and over and over I heard the same words.

"We are happy that he is finally happy."

Pearls of sweat covered my forehead and with every step, my legs seemed heavier. The more I thought about it, the more I believed that all of this was a mistake. I shouldn't have accepted the matching dress, and I shouldn't have allowed Nick to let the entire capital know that he had lost his heart to me.

I wondered when was the first time he told his family about me and whether this was another attempt to stop me from running away.

"I don't think I like this silence," Nick spoke softly as he stood still in front of a huge window.

He stared at the edge of the woods and I realised how close to the woods, my favourite place in the world, Nick actually lived.

"Can you please just say something? Anything?" He was kind and understanding, but despite that, it felt more and more like he was not simply trying to convince me to stay. He was making it almost impossible for me to leave, but if I would leave, I would never be as free as I wanted and longed to be. If only I didn't have to choose between my heart and my wolf.

I tensed and my fingers curled into a fist. I had to be careful not to cut my palms and damage the dress, but I couldn't risk Nick seeing my claws either.

I didn't remember the last time I allowed myself to run around freely, to enjoy my instincts and my extraordinary speed.

I was so focussed on the problems in the woods, on keeping Benjamin safe, on making sure that my family didn't get discovered and ended up dead.

"I don't think you want me to say what's on my mind right now." I couldn't fight the wolf and the anger at once.

I could only fight one of them and I knew which one that had to be. Maybe if I let the anger out, our goodbye wouldn't get as emotional as I feared it would be. Maybe showing him the rage that was building up inside my veins was the right way to make him let me go.

"Of course I want you to tell me what's bothering you." Nick folded his hands behind his back and turned his face towards the window.

He stared at the moon, not even half full, and the blue of his eyes reflected in the glass between him and the outside world.

"I think coming here tonight was a mistake," I tried to sound calm, even though my heart was racing. "And I feel like you think that if you announce to the kingdom that you're in love with me, I won't leave." I took a deep breath and waited for Nick to interrupt me, but he didn't say anything.

He just stared at the edge of the woods, at the trees slightly waving in the wind. He seemed younger than he ever did before.

"I told you countless times that whatever I feel and whatever you feel is not important enough to keep me here." I realised how cruel my words sounded right after they escaped my lips, but I couldn't bring myself to regret them.

"The lives of my family are at stake and no matter how we feel about each other and how wonderful you are to me, I can't risk losing them for something as uncertain and unsure as love."

"I am the crown prince…" Nick's voice sounded raw and his chest moved up and down heavily.

"I can command the entire royal guard to protect your family. We only have to convince them to come live here in the capital and no one will harm them," he hissed between his teeth and his knuckles turned whiter and whiter with every second that passed.

"I love you, Emily." He turned around and his blue eyes, now a shade darker than I remembered them, rested on my lips, forming a straight line. "I wouldn't forgive myself if I didn't try everything possible to keep you here, with me."

"Doesn't that sound selfish to you?" I tried to count to ten, tried to weigh the words before I said them, but it was as if all the emotions I had been ignoring, for the last few weeks, came out all at once.

It was anger and rage, even though I wasn't sure if I was angry with him or with the fact that we met at the worst possible time.

"But I assume that as a crown prince you're not used to not getting what you want." I swallowed. "I've wanted a lot of things in life and most of those things I couldn't get. I'm sorry that I'm taking something you really wanted away from you, but I am sure that you'll get over it.”

Nick squeezed his eyes and when his glance met mine again, something changed. He placed his hands on my shoulders and his grip tightened when he breathed out in my face.

His breath smelled like cake, like sweets, like all those amazing things I had never tasted and smelled before. But his words weren’t half as sweet as his breath.

“You have absolutely no idea what you’re talking about!” he raised his voice and I froze, all my muscles tensing at once.

“You think that everyone in the capital has an easy life, do you? You think that we have parties every day and that our entire life is nothing but an easy walk from start to finish. You think the only people having problems are the people in the villages?”

I was not afraid in my life that often, but the way his voice sounded, the raw emotion behind each word that left his blood red lips, the flames burning in his bright blue eyes, made me tremble.

“Maybe I don’t know what hunger is, and maybe I never had to sleep on the cold floor.” Nick buried his nails in my shoulders, but I tried to ignore the slight pain.

“Maybe I didn’t have to work since I was a child, and maybe I never witnessed children dying.” He breathed in through his nose and the vein in his neck was visibly beating.

“But that doesn’t mean that my life was easy and you have no right to make me feel like I have absolutely no idea what pain and suffering feel like. Maybe I don’t know what you’re going through.” He cocked his head. “But you have no idea what I’m going through either."

He abruptly let go of my shoulders and his hand went through his hair before he walked past me, his shoulder slightly brushing mine.

"Where are you going?" I turned around, but Nick didn't bother to answer.

His heavy footsteps echoed through the empty hallway faster and faster, barely giving the servant guarding the door the time to open it so he could leave.

I wanted to go after him and apologise for everything I said. I wanted to ask him about his life, and the struggles he was facing. I wanted to be the friend and lover he wished me to be. I wanted to hold his hand and assure him that everything would be alright, that his future would be brighter than his past.

But I couldn't. Even though I regretted everything I said and I wished we could share one last kiss and much more, there was also a part of me believing that this was probably for the best.

Maybe ending everything between us like this was far better than a sad goodbye after a wonderful night. Maybe his broken heart would heal sooner now I had broken it with violence and words instead of tears and empty promises.

Or maybe, I would regret for the rest of my life that this was the last conversation we ever had.

But before I actively made the decision to go after him, my legs already carried me towards the ballroom.

I could try to use my enhanced smell, but so far, Nick always hid his natural scent behind an overwhelmingly pleasant, and most likely very expensive, perfume that would, without a doubt, be worn by many other men here in the capital.

And even though I was quite familiar with the

woods, trying to look for Nick without having the slightest idea where to start could mean that I would be looking for the rest of the night without any result.

"Where is my brother?" Philippe turned around while he noticed me, standing on my own in the middle of the crowd. "Wasn't he showing you around?"

I bent my head and stared at my feet while I folded my hands in front of my stomach. had I known that my words would chase him away from the ball, I would have swallowed them.

But regrets wouldn't find Nick and bring him back, while Philippe maybe could.

"What happened?" Philippe seemed to have forgotten about Lilian, who was staring at me with fire in her eyes.

The last thing I wanted was for her to overhear anything. Her father already knew more than he should. I gestured for Philippe to step out of Lilian's hearing distance.

He followed me and leaned to hear me over the murmur of the guests.

"I thought he was using your parents to manipulate me into staying here." I stumbled over each word and my chest moved up and down while my heart hammered against my ribs. The tight dress felt like it was burning in my heated skin. "And then, all of a sudden, he yelled that I thought that he never had problems and that his life was easy and…" I realised that maybe I did think his life was easy, surely much easier than mine.

"He disappeared and I don't know where he's gone and…" All of a sudden, I thought about all those lifeless bodies we've been finding in the woods lately.

What have I done? If something happens to Nick

because of me, I would never be able to forgive myself.

I remembered his warm skin, that one time he was completely burning up, the sharp nails on my shoulder.

No, he couldn't be. He was the crown prince.

"We have to find him as soon as possible." I hissed between my teeth and the fear I already felt because the lives of my family were at stake, was now enhanced by the fear for Nick. "If he has gone to the woods…"

"He has." Philippe interrupted me and a sigh escaped his lips while Lilian placed her hand on his shoulder, clearly demanding his full attention.

"He always goes to the woods when he's angry or upset." Philippe kept his eyes locked with mine, but eventually he turned to face Lilian.

"I have something important to do. Do you think you can meet some other people while I'm gone?" He tried to keep his voice as warm and gentle as possible, but he couldn't hide the bitterness and annoyance.

My mind was going in circles and all I wanted was to find him as soon as possible. Either to save his life, or to maybe save someone else's. Meanwhile, Lilian was only getting started.

"As if there is something more important than the royal ball and dancing with your future wife." Lilian crossed her arms and there was no trace of amusement visible in her eyes.

She either believed that Philippe would marry her in the not-so-distant future, or she believed that somehow her father's privileged, and clearly stolen, position gave her the right to claim a prince.

I rolled my eyes and shifted my weight from one leg to the other. With every second that passed, the chance of something happening to Nick grew and I was not ready to find his damaged body.

I wanted to find him alive, I wanted to apologise for everything I said, I wanted to tell him that maybe we could come up with a way to be together without endangering my family, and I wanted to admit that maybe the crown prince of our kingdom could do much more to protect those I cared about than I ever could.

"My brother needs help." Philippe straightened his back and lifted his chin. He folded his hands behind his back and his glance hardened. "And I don't want to shatter your illusions, Lilian, but I'm not going to marry you." He paused for a moment, but he didn't give Lilian the chance to interrupt him.

"If you came here to find a nobleman to marry you and take you away from your village, I think you should use the rest of the evening to find him."

"Do you know who you're talking to?" Lilian shook her head and raised her voice, making it almost impossible to ignore. "I'm the daughter of the most important man in Waterfield!" she screamed and her white skin turned redder and redder making her look like a swollen strawberry.

If there wasn't a monster on the loose in the woods, and Nick's life at stake, I would have enjoyed the sight to the fullest. I was also certain that a lot of people in Waterfield would want to witness this very moment.

"Your brother falls in love with a total nobody, but I, the most important girl in Waterfield, am not good enough for you?" she sounded more desperate with each word escaping her lips.

Most noblemen and ladies around us shook their heads, whispering that people like her were the reason they stayed away from the villages as far as possible.

In any other situation, I would try to correct them, but we didn't have time for that. On top of that, Lilian was chosen to represent Waterfield.

"My brother's feelings have nothing to do with mine and I don't think you're not good enough to live in the capital. I'm simply not in love with you. I simply don't like you and now, I have to find my brother, whether you like it or not." Philippe curled his hand around my wrist and without another word, he made his way through the crowd towards the door.

"We don't have any time to lose," he hissed between his teeth when one of the many servants pushed the door of the ballroom open and Philippe walked straight towards the front door.

"Do you know how to ride a horse?" He looked over his shoulder without slowing down, and I shook my head. "In that case, you will have to learn it. We're slower if I have to take you with me on my horse. You can take Nick's. I'm sure he won't mind."

I swallowed and had to admit that I didn't dare to be that certain about it. Maybe he didn't mind me riding his horse a few hours ago, but with one conversation, I changed everything. I hoped that I could make up for it and that maybe he would forgive me in the end, but I said some pretty harsh things, and the words he yelled at me had come from a part of his soul he probably never showed to anyone else.

Philippe hurried down the marble stairs and as soon as he set foot on the green grass, separating us from the stables, he walked faster and faster until we were running.

He seemed to forget that I was wearing an uncomfortable long dress and shoes that were highly unfit to use for any physical activity apart from dancing.

He only seemed to think about his brother and

somehow it was calming that he was as worried as I was.

Chapter Twenty-Four

Not even a minute passed before we reached the stables, but it felt like it was hours later. The sun set completely and the further away we were from the castle, the more darkness surrounded us. Philippe was leading us and the light of the not even half-moon made it hard for his human eyes to see where we were going.

"You wait here. I'll get the horses." Philippe let my hand go, but he grabbed it again when the howl of a wolf echoed through the night. He tensed and stood perfectly still while he waited for the next howl.

My heart now hammered against my ribs and raced faster than ever before.

"We have to find him, Philippe..." I could barely talk and a shiver rolled down my spine. "If that wolf gets to him before we do..." I couldn't finish my sentence, because the thought of what would happen if we weren't there in time, made my stomach churn. I could taste the strawberries and the cake I had enjoyed not even an hour ago and I closed my eyes when I heard another howl, a little closer this time.

"We should be quiet," Philippe spoke softy and pressed a finger to his lips.

With his hand still firmly holding mine, he walked on the tips of his toes. Instead of entering the stables, he walked around them, and every time I heard the wolf cry, the fear inside of me grew.

What if the wolf already found him and killed him? What if that wolf would return to their human form, only to discover that they were to blame for the death of the crown prince?

All of a sudden, Philippe stood still and pressed his back against the stone wall while he used one arm to force me to mirror his movement.

"Strange…" he murmured softly. "Normally, he runs away from this castle as fast as he can." He squeezed his eyes, and his glance lingered over an unknown wolf, hiding behind one of the trees at the edge of the woods.

I haven't seen this wolf before, but the golden brown of his fur seemed to glimmer in the moonlight and every few seconds, it howled at the moon.

When the eyes of the wolf met mine, my heart skipped a beat. I haven't seen the wolf before, but I knew those bright blue eyes now staring directly into mine.

"We have to be careful," Philippe whispered and tightened his grip on my body.

"He doesn't have any control over it. I don't think he even knows what he's doing," his voice trembled a little and I wondered how often Philippe found his brother like this.

Was Nick the one? I stopped that thought as soon as I had it. Of course not. He couldn't be. Maybe he was not in control of his wolf or didn't know what his wolf was doing. But I did believe that his wolf knew just as well as Nick did, that killing children was wrong.

"I think I understand now what he meant when he said his life isn't as easy as I seemed to think it is." My chest moved up and down quickly and I curled my fingers around Philippe's arm while I allowed myself to use my inhuman strength to free myself from his embrace.

"If only he trusted me with his secret." I stepped forward and Philippe tried to reach for my arm as soon as he noticed.

"If only I trusted him with mine." I lifted my hands up and quickly removed all the pins from my hair.

I never saw a wolf out of control before, but I knew that if there was someone who could reach him and help him connect the two sides of himself, it was me.

"What do you mean?" Philippe placed a hand on my shoulder, but I didn't take the time to look at him.

I kept my eyes locked with the wolf and, once I was certain that all pins were on the ground, I kicked of my shoes.

"I need you to help me take this dress off." I tried to reach for the strings on my back and let out a soft curse when I discovered that I can't reach them.

"You need me to do what?" Philippe raised his voice a little and I saw the wolf react by stepping back and forth a few times.

"What are you going to do? Offer yourself as dinner?" Philippe hissed between his teeth now and I took a deep breath while I rolled my eyes.

Even though Philippe didn't know me as well as Nick did, I was slightly disappointed that he really believed I would take the time to undress myself only to be eaten by the beast that had taken control over Nick's mind and body.

"Of course not." I shifted my weight from one leg to the other and shook my head. "But if you're not willing to help me to undress myself, I can, of course, also shred my beautiful dress to pieces."

Less than a moment later, Philippe untied the strings on my back and eventually, the dress was loose enough to allow me to step out of it.

"And now what?" Philippe crossed his arms over his chest while he stood next to me.

He followed my glance, as if he was afraid to look at me, afraid of his eyes wandering over my naked body, covered by nothing but my undergarments.

I was just relieved that I could take it off, free myself from those human cages, and release the animal that hasn't been out for far too long.

And while Philippe seemed slightly uncomfortable about being so near to me now, I was almost completely undressed. I had grown used to being naked around other people ever since I turned into a wolf for the very first time.

Without hesitation, I removed the last pieces of clothing I wore and then I took a deep breath while I dropped my knees into the mud and buried my hands in dirt.

"What are you doing?" Philippe held a hand next to his eye to avoid looking at me and I straightened my back one more time while a sigh escaped my lips.

"Have you ever followed Nick while he was roaming these woods in wolf-form?" I cocked my head but made sure not to look away from the wolf still staring back at me.

"I tried." Philippe stiffened. "I always assumed that he was following his instincts and that those lead him to you." He removed his hand slowly and I kept silent for a moment, before I buried my hands in dirt again.

"You are probably more right than you think you are." I commanded all the bones in my body to break and slowly my hands and feet turned into lethal claws.

"The last few weeks, there have been signs of a

wild wolf near our village." I didn't explain the details.

Maybe I shouldn't trust Nick's Wolf so much, but I couldn't convince myself that my Nick, soft hearted and caring Nick, killed those children.

"Signs of a wolf controlling its human instead of the other way round." I opened my mouth while my teeth sharpened and if I wanted to say anything else I would have to do so quickly, before I didn't have the bone structure to speak.

"Do you know what wolves need to survive, especially in a cruel world where the animal part of them is judged and hated, even by themselves?"

"A pack…" Philippe swallowed and he now had his eyes completely on me. "He was looking for a pack. For your pack." He licked his lips, and I curled mine up into a slight smile.

"He was looking for an alpha." My backbone shaped into a completely different form and my ears sharpened while strong black fur covered my entire skin.

"And since few weeks ago, I am one." After the last words escaped my lips, I gave in fully to the animal not only faster, stronger and blessed with sharper senses than my human self, but also capable of communicating in a language maybe even Nick understood, no matter how deeply buried his soul currently was.

"I think this explains why my brother lost his heart to you." Philippe curled his lips up into a smile and gave a small nod, as if he were afraid I wouldn't understand his phrase anymore.

I ran towards the lost wolf, who was clearly in need of all the help he could get.

"Nick? Can you hear me?" Philippe heard nothing

but howls and cries, but I hoped his brother would understand me.

"Nick?" I repeated his name as often as possible. "Nick? What are you afraid of? Why are you hiding?" I paused for a moment and stood still when I reached him. "Nick? I can help you. Please, let me help you."

I repeated his name over and over, changing the phrases a little to see if any of them would trigger the human mind overwhelmed by the instincts and senses of the wolf containing it.

"Nick, you are such a beautiful wolf…" I cocked my head and my paws, buried in the dirty ground, carried me a little closer to him so my nose could touch his.

"Nick, you're not alone and you have never been…" My desperate howls reached out for an answer, but nothing but silence greeted me on his side and a wave of sadness came over me.

How long had Nick tried to fight his instincts and the animal inside of him, just longing to be break free? How often had Nick stared at himself in the mirror, afraid that if he looked away he wouldn't be human anymore? How often had Nick heard that the animal inside of him was a mistake, a failure of nature, something to be ashamed of, something to be afraid of, and something he could never let out? How many times had he been told that he was an abomination?

"Nick, I know that many people have probably told you that you are not allowed to love your wolf," I tried again and touched his nose with mine, softly, tenderly and without any judgement or anger.

"I want you to know that they were all wrong." I mostly repeated all the things my father once told me, the first time I turned and was afraid to lose control, to give in to the speed, the strength and the instincts guiding me to who knew where.

"This part of you that you've been fighting and hating, is one of the parts making you, you. And you are one of the most amazing people I have ever met in life. You are the first person in the world I've ever fallen in love with, and I somehow hope that you will also be the only one."

Nick lifted his head a little and in his bright blue eyes, I saw a glimpse of recognition. Even though his consciousness was buried deeply, it was still there and the small glimmer in his eyes was enough to encourage me to continue, to find more things I could say to him, to convince him that his wolf needed him as much as he needed the wolf.

"If only I knew that you and I were the same, that you were facing the same problems my family and I are facing, that you were a lost wolf in need of an alpha." I tried not to think about the words too much.

I tried to find them inside of me, in my heart, left there by my family and all the people who always assured me that I was perfect the way I was, that I was beautiful the way I was, that I was worthy the way I was.

I remembered countless moments of doubts, countless of times I was afraid they were wrong, that I was a monster, but right now, when I saw Nick standing in front of me, with his golden-brown fur and his piercing blue eyes, I realised none of us could ever be a monster.

"Emily?" His voice was nothing but a weak whisper, but a certain kind of relief spread through my entire body.

"I don't know what is happening to me..." He lost

all confidence, all the natural charm he carried wherever he went. He was wearing a mask just as I did.

"You don't need to worry about any of this, Nick." I stepped a little closer and my head touched his.

"There are many more people like you and I can assure you that we're all beautiful and amazing." I pressed my head to his side and he did the same to me.

His heart was beating loudly in his chest, faster than it should and even though he was now present to guide and control his wolf, he was not yet embracing his other side and couldn't shake the slight fear of the beast lingering beneath his skin.

"We are faster than most other living creatures. We are stronger than our human counterparts and we have all the heightened senses allowing us to notice sounds, and smells, and movements before human eyes and ears and noses do." I still moved my head, caressing his side and making sure he knew that he was not alone, that I was really here, that I was not just a voice inside his head.

"If the humans let us, we would be the perfect protectors and guards." I talked and talked, and I heard my father's voice in every phrase I howled at the man clearly fighting with a part of him that he hasn't been able to control.

"You don't think we're monsters? You don't think we are dangerous and should be contained? You don't think we should do everything we can to not let the wolf inside escape?" Nick hesitated for a moment, but then he pressed his nose to my side, and I enjoyed his touch even more now that I finally allowed all my senses to respond.

"Your wolf is not a monster and has never been," I spoke softly and carefully I stepped back so my eyes could meet his again.

"Just like my wolf has never been a monster and all those people telling you that you have to fight the wolf and not let it out, they only forced your wolf to break free now and then."

"What did I do?" Nick looked at me and his eyes reflected fear and worry. "Please, can you tell me what I did?" A slight cry echoed through his words and I bent my head, knowing that all my attempts to make him love the wolf could be undone when he heard about the dead children.

I wanted to be sure that his wolf didn't do it. There had to be another explanation for him being around whenever a murdered child was found, and I had to find it.

"Nick, I want you to know that my family and I understand why your wolf needs to break free once in a while." I hesitated.

I dreaded the moment of telling him about the dead children.

"What did I do, Emily, please?" Nick pushed his nose against mine and I lifted my head again.

"I don't believe you did anything, Nick." I didn't want to lie to him. We were past that.

Lying to him now would break the trust we built, but I was afraid of what would happen if he couldn't be as certain as I was that he was not the one to blame.

"We found two dead children near our village, but I don't think it was your wolf's doing. It couldn't have been you." I paused for a moment and made sure to use my head to comfort and touch him a few more times. I just couldn't hide the slide tremble in my voice.

"I will teach you how to control your wolf and make it a part of you, and I can assure you that from this day on your wolf will never do something without you knowing about it."

"Dead children?" Nick shivered. His paws trembled. "Did my wolf kill them?"

I used my entire body to assure him I was still there, and not going anywhere. Not today. Not tomorrow. Never. "I don't think so. I truly believe it wasn't you."

"But what if it was me?"

I was losing him. "Nick." I pressed my entire flank to his. "I truly believe it wasn't you."

"But you can't prove it." Nick shook his head. "If it was me…"

"We will worry about this later." I had to rebuild our connection. "We will use every resource possible to figure out who did this. If it was you, we will think about what to do next. But that wolf you have hated for so long is still a part of you and has always been a part of you. I truly believe you are incapable of murdering children. I truly believe your wolf is incapable of killing children, too."

I wasn't sure if he believed me, but he calmed down a little.

"Your wolf is good, Nick. You are good. Please believe that you are good."

"Can you promise me that you won't leave me anymore?" pain coloured his voice and his howls were more desperate than before.

"I would never leave a wolf in need of an alpha, Nick." His heartbeat slowed down a little and my muscles relaxed a little, too.

"The hatred and fear my family and I are running from are the same hatred and fear you are facing, and we know that none of us will survive this on our own."

I stood perfectly still now.

"I am certain that my family doesn't want you to be alone and I know they will welcome you with open arms into our pack, into our family."

"I'm probably mistaken, but that almost sounds like a marriage proposal." He teasingly pushed my nose again and I pushed back.

Welcome back, Nick.

"Let's return to our human forms, shall we? Before you manage to twist more of my words to please your lovely ego." I stepped back and created a safe distance between us.

"I never got the chance to teach Benjamin everything about being a wolf, but now I get the opportunity to make up for it by tutoring you." I paused for a moment. "Rule number one is that you can't fight the urge to change forever. The wolf needs to be free once a while. The human needs to be free once a while, too." I buried my claws a little deeper in the dirt and stretched my back one last time.

"So now that your wolf is satiated, you can turn back into a human."

"I appreciate you telling me all that, but can you also explain how exactly I turn from wolf back into a human?" Nick cocked his head a little and I locked my eyes with his.

"That lesson might be a little too complicated to start with, but for now I will help you change." I paused for a moment.

"I order you to return to your human form, Nicholas Lawrence."

Chapter Twenty-Five

The cold evening wind touched my naked skin, but even if my natural body warmth hadn't kept me from shivering, I wouldn't have dared to move. I kept my eyes on the wolf in front of me, his bones breaking, his fangs and fur disappearing. His blue eyes remained the same, even though his entire body changed into his human form, the form I knew and already loved before knowing there was a wolf hidden inside of it.

Even though he was slightly older than I was, he had so many things to learn because no one had ever taken the time to teach him. He didn't have someone who kept on reminding him that he was perfect and beautiful as a human and as a wolf. He didn't have someone taking him to the woods to practice the change back and forth over and over until he could do it within seconds.

He only had this self-hatred enhanced by everyone around him either being afraid of the beast he could turn into, or afraid of what the people of his future kingdom would think of his hidden side.

I smiled when his eyes wandered over my naked body before he noticed that his own bare skin was covered in dirt, too. I smiled even brighter when his cheeks slightly blushed because I didn't even attempt to cover any parts of me.

"You really believe I didn't kill those children?" he spoke softly, afraid that his whisper would be carried by the wind and heard by his brother, who still didn't dare to move.

"It's not my fault you are dealing with all the hate and anger?" His bright blue eyes met my dark ones, and I made sure not to look away and avoid his glance.

"We don't know for sure, yet. But I really believe you didn't do it. Your wolf might have taken over control and might have followed his instincts, but your wolf is still a part of you, and you would never kill those children." I believed my words were true and hoped looking into the issue wouldn't lead to a discovery Nick wouldn't be able to live with.

"Will the people in the village believe I didn't do it?" Nick hesitated, as if he didn't know for sure what to believe right now. It would take time to trust his wolf.

"The people in the village would blame any wolf they can find." I stretched out my hand and my palm touched his glowing cheek.

"I can't blame them for wanting to protect their children and I can't blame them for being afraid of us and the damage we can cause," I spoke slowly and took a deep breath while my chest moved up and down way quicker than normally.

"But I really can't believe you did this, either." I curled my lips up a little and my hand wandered over his face and neck.

"You never learned how to love a vital part of yourself and that vital part of you has therefore overwhelmed you, but it's still a part of you. It's still you." I paused for a moment. "Everything is going to be different now." I thought about my mother, who wished so much for me to get the future, she and father always dreamed of for me. "We owe it to the people in your village to find whoever killed those children and to bring them to justice." Nick moved a little closer towards me and he curled his fingers around my wrist to make sure I wouldn't pull my hand back.

I took a deep breath. "We will."

"And I owe it to your family to clear your name." He tucked a strand of hair behind my ear.

I shook my head. "Even without those murdered children, they would have discovered sooner or later what we are. They don't need proof we are the killers. They already believe we are monsters and once they hear about our wolf side, they will attempt to kill us anyway." Just like they did to my father, so many years ago that I could barely remember how his voice sounded, how he smelled and how he moved.

"Gareth told me yesterday that he already knew about my family, and he'll follow through on his threats now that I failed to secure Lilian the marriage with the crown prince."

Nick's wonderful chuckle sounded like music to my ears and with his lips curled up into a smile, he shook his head. "I don't think I can imagine myself with Lilian, not even when I try very hard." He guided my hand over his body until it was positioned right above his heart, firmly beating against his ribs.

"I think her father might be a lot less interested in a future alliance between you and his daughter once he finds out that you are the very thing he is trying to protect everyone from." I shifted my weight a little and swallowed before I let out another deep sigh.

"It will take many years to change the general opinion on humans turning into wolves, whether or not they are dangerous, and whether or not they should be hunted and killed."

"Does this mean that I will spend the rest of my

life on the run with you?" Nick cocked his head slightly and while he closed his eyes, he leaned towards me. "Because although that idea doesn't sound too tempting, there is also a part of me that might like that idea more than just a little." His lips touched mine and I smiled into the brief and tender kiss.

"I think I could make an entire family disappear into the anonymity of an unknown village." I curled my arms around his neck and my chest touched his. "But I'm afraid that even I can't make a crown prince disappear in his own kingdom." My mouth covered his and then I closed my eyes to enjoy his body warmth and tender touch to the fullest.

"Emily? Nicholas?" Philippe cleared his throat and when my eyes flashed open, I saw him standing closer with his head turned away from us. "I don't know if people are looking for us, but I don't think they should find you two like this." He carried two bundles of clothes in his arms.

"I would give a lot to be able to wear my own loose dress instead of the wonderful ballgown you had made for me." I winked while I stood up and tried to get the dirt of me as well as I could. "How do you not hate wearing all those tight-fitting clothes?" I reached for my undergarments and took a deep breath, trying to find the willpower to put them on again.

"If I remember correctly, I already told you that sometimes the things you can't buy with money are the things we long for the most." Nick clearly got dressed fast in the middle of the woods and I remembered our short meeting right after my uncles found another body.

Could I really be certain that he hadn't been the one killing them? I was relieved he at least had not seen the damaged and lifeless body we carried back to the village that day, to the devastated and broken parents wanting nothing but justice.

"My parents weren't exactly understanding when it came to my dislike towards my uniforms and my longing for midnight runs in the woods." He paused for a moment while I stepped back into my dress and asked Philippe silently to retie the strings on my back.

"I assume you actually weren't in danger when I found you in the woods?"

I curled my lips up into a smile and cocked my head while I tried not to complain too much since Philippe clearly didn't understand how much I hated the tight clothes I was forced to wear today, and all the other days I spent in the capital with Nick.

"When the people in the villages speak about the dangers in the woods, they are talking about creatures like us. Unless your brother was carrying his hunting weapons, I was always perfectly safe." I groaned while Philippe pulled the strings once more. "And I could have been home a lot faster had you had not insisted on making sure I would get there without getting hurt or harmed." I rolled my eyes when Philippe stepped back and admired his work even though I could barely breathe. "I don't know if you have gotten the chance to explore it yet, but we can outrun horses easily."

"I am certain my wolf knows it, but I'm afraid I personally haven't gotten the chance to find out yet." Nick cocked his head slightly while he pressed a quick kiss on my nose. "But I assume you will make sure that I experience it for myself in the very near future."

"I will open this wonderful new world for you, Nick." I slid my arms around his waist and without taking my eyes of him I stepped into my shoes. "You have no idea how many unforgettable experiences are waiting for you, because despite what humans think about us, there are quite a few activities being way more pleasant with enhanced senses." I winked and I pressed my lips on his to prove my point.

"Like eating strawberry cake?" Nick whispered as he gently tucked a strand of my long loose black hair behind my ear. "I am afraid that we can't recreate your hair style."

A giggle escaped my lips and my hands went through his hair. "I am certain it won't be that hard to make people believe that we found a perfect way to make up after our heated conversation." I stepped back and smiled when I noticed his hair being as much of a mess as mine.

"Just like I think not that many people will doubt that Philippe is now scarred for life because he was forced to witness it."

Chapter Twenty-Six

Even though barely an hour passed since Nick and I argued, that one hour contained an entire lifetime. Everything seemed different now that I knew his secret and he was aware of mine, everything seemed still the same but without all the walls and problems standing between us, keeping us apart.

I was no longer simply a village girl and he was no longer a nobleman having everything his heart could possibly desire. We were both not entirely human. We both carried this animal within us, both capable of protecting and damaging the realm.

"I think my mother will be extremely happy when she hears what you've done for me and what you will do for me in future." Nick tightened his grip on my arm and his lips curled up into a smile while he stood still for a moment before entering the ballroom again.

"Ever since the first time my second nature revealed itself, they didn't know what to do." He paused for a moment and squeezed his eyes. "And somehow, they seemed to believe that maybe I was cursed, that maybe I was the only person in our entire Kingdom dealing with this."

"If my family and I had known that the crown prince was struggling with his second nature, we would have offered to help, but after what happened to my father, we couldn't risk exposing ourselves." I swallowed and bent my head, wondered how everything between us would have been had we met under different circumstances.

"What happened to your father?" Nick spoke softly and he looked over his shoulder to make sure the hallway was empty of other people. "You do realise that my family and I were always responsible for your lives, and we would never allow something to happen to him simply because he was who he was, what he was."

"We were never able to prove anything. My father was completely healthy one day and then close to dying the next. Someone might have poisoned our food or his food only, but we threw everything away right after he got ill, to make sure that no one else died at the hands of the cowards who didn't even dare to come close enough to swing a sword." I couldn't shake the feeling that Lilian's father might had something to do with it.

And I didn't doubt that I would have had my claws out to slit his throat before he would have even gotten the chance to finish his confession. "We acted like it was a tragical accident and we made sure that no one saw a wolf anywhere near Waterfield again. We wanted everyone to think that only my father was capable of changing, that we escaped his faith because he married a human woman, and his wolf didn't manifest in his children."

Nick looked over his shoulder, his eyes resting on his younger brother for a few seconds before his glance met mine.

"If both parents are wolves, all the children are wolves too. However, you're not the first wolf born from two humans." I paused for a moment and my eyes lingered over Nick's face, his blushing cheeks, his red lips, the veins, visibly beating in his neck, his heart almost following the same rhythm as mine.

"Maybe your brother will one day have wolf children too." I curled my lips up into a smile, knowing that at least Philippe's child would never face the self-doubt and self-hatred Nick dealt with ever since he was a child.

"If we ever decide to start a family, we know for sure that our family will not just be a normal family, but our own little pack of wonderful creatures capable of making this world a far better place if we teach them how to use their talents."

"A wedding proposal and an implication that you want to start your own wolf pack with me, all at once?" Nick smiled at me and gently tucked a loose strand of hair behind my ear. "For someone who was talking about the impossibility of a shared future for a very long time, you clearly went through a radical change of mind."

"I am glad that despite everything you went through, you didn't lose your sense of humour." I leaned a little towards him and my hands touched his neck softly. "I hope you know that if I could have married you, I would have done so, even before I discovered that you and I shared the same secret."

"And here I thought that there was at least one person in the world who loved me more as a wolf than she would ever love me as a human." Nick took a deep breath before he stepped back, realizing we postponed entering the ballroom for far too long already.

"Your wolf was always a part of you, even when I didn't know it was there." I placed my hand on his chest, right above his heart. "I fell in love with you because of who you are, because of what you are, because of all the things I knew and felt."

"If you two keep on exchanging love poems, I'm

going inside to find Lilian. Let's see if she has calmed down a little by now." Philippe rolled his eyes while he walked past us, but I could see a smile lingering on his lips. He winked before he disappeared into the ballroom filled with people.

"How sickening are we if your brother voluntarily seeks out Lilian's company? Especially since he told her, right before we left that he didn't like her and that she shouldn't have any illusion of marrying him?" I squeezed my eyes a little and then I shook my head.

"He actually found the courage to tell her that?" Nick raised his eyebrows. "I admit I already doubted that he had it in him." Nick kissed my lips once more before he offered me his arm. "Ever since I forced him to keep her company, he was complaining about her rudeness and lack of manners, but one has to admit that Lilian does possess a certain determination that maybe even matches yours."

"Are you trying to offend me or attempting to compliment me?" I cocked my head as we entered, and my eyes wandered over the crowd. "Do you have any idea how much determination it required to keep holding on to the plan to leave you tonight after the ball?"

"Your plan to leave me annoyed me a lot more than Lilian ever has."

"Lilian is gone." The smile on my face disappeared when Philip appeared in front of us.

"After our fight, she asked for a carriage to bring her back to the village." His lips formed a straight line and I realised he heard and understood more of the conversations, Nick and I had, than I thought.

"They tried to keep her here, telling her I would come back, but she insisted and said that this ball was one huge disappointment anyway." He paused for a moment. "She just wanted to see her father and wanted to tell him that the wolf girl stole her crown prince."

My eyes widened and I opened my mouth to say something, but the words just didn't want to come out. My heart hammered and my blood raced through my veins, thinking how we should have anticipated this. "My family…" I could barely breathe, and my entire face drained of colour. "Once Lilian reaches her father and tells him what happened, he will go after my family." My hands and knees shook, so Nick tightened his grip around my waist.

"I have to get to them first. I turned around and left the ballroom without looking over my shoulders to see if Nick and Philippe were coming after me.

"Emily!" Nick placed a hand on my shoulder and forced me to slow down, even though the precious seconds ticked away much faster than I could handle. "Will you please allow us to help you?" He forced me to turn around and his bright blue eyes met mine.

"We can give you one of our personal carriages. Those horses are faster than the ones Lilian is traveling with." Nick scratched the back of his neck and nervously shifted his weight from one leg to the other. "Or I could saddle my horse and bring you to Waterfield myself?"

I smiled with sadness and shook my head. "Nick, I don't know how much time we spent in the woods, but I can't reach the village in time if I travel by carriage or horse." I stretched out my hand and touched his glowing cheek. "I will travel by foot in the only form that allows me to outrun everything else."

"You don't have to do this on your own, Emily." Every time he said my name, my heart skipped a beat, but every heartbeat meant that I was losing time I didn't have. "I will come with you."

"No…" I sounded a lot firmer than I meant to, but I shook my head and stepped back. "I have to do this alone, but if you want to help me there is something you can do."

Once I quickly I gave them instructions, my feet carried me down the marble stairs.

Halfway the grass field I've already kicked off my shoes and when I was out of sight of any prying eyes, I allowed my body to change and shred my dress into small pieces.

I hoped Philippe or Nick would find them before anyone else could, but I had no time to worry about that right now. There were too many lives at stake, and I was the only one who could save them.

Chapter Twenty-Seven

Once my shift was completed, I gave into my instincts fully. The green trees forming the forest were one big blur while my paws carried me further away from the castle and closer towards the border of Waterfield.

The guilt was weighing on me. I felt it was my fault they were in danger. I was the one consistently refusing to follow my mother's rules to stay inside hidden. And the attacks on the children began when I became the leader. It is possible that I attracted the killer as well, and not just Nick.

Or maybe I wasn't the one to blame. Maybe I was the one who decided that it was the perfect moment to take over and carry all the responsibility for my family on my shoulders, and now I had to prove that I was ready for it."

I slowed down when I saw the lights of the houses of Waterfield. I tried to use my enhanced hearing to find out if something was going on in the village, if I could hear the sounds of screaming people or howls of my family.

But I heard nothing, and I hoped it was a good sign. I managed to cross the woods in time before Lilian's carriage. I had a fair chance of getting my family away from here safely.

I decided to not think of the possibility that silence could also mean I was already too late. I tried not to lose myself to my fear.

I had to remember to be careful either way. If I got caught before I reached my family, I wouldn't be able to save anyone tonight. I also wouldn't be able to save Nick from himself. And I wouldn't be able to find the other wolf to ensure the safety of so many children in the village.

The lack of street lanterns was working in my advantage. The moon brightened the roads just enough to create shadows around houses, which made me seem like a ghost, as long as I made sure to stay close to the walls keeping me hidden from prying eyes.

I looked up when I heard footsteps and screaming. They weren't too close yet, but they were a lot closer than I wanted them to be. As quickly as I could, I ran to the house I once shared with my family.

Even though I could hear the voices and the drumming of the footsteps clearly now, they had not reached our house yet. But with each footstep, the time to get my family to safety was running out.

I quickly returned to my human form and knocked urgently until my mother opened the door, her eyes wide open when she realised I was naked.

"What happened?" her voice trembled.

She looked around before she closed the door behind me. She probably heard the stamping feet and angry shouts as clearly as I did.

We rushed to the living room.

"We don't have time for an explanation." I shook my head as I noticed that Benjamin was not there. "Where is Benjamin? We must leave the house immediately! I believe that Gareth gathered the entire town, and the mob is rushing towards our house."

My mother's eyes widened, and she rushed upstairs.

I looked at the rest of my family. "Change now and run towards the castle, as fast as you can! Help is waiting at the back of it. Don't look back until you're safely there."

My uncles and sisters nodded and did as I ordered. I tried to ignore the fear in their eyes, as well as the fear building inside of me.

"Maria! Benjamin! Hurry, we have to run, now!" I heard the mob approaching our street.

It felt like eternity, but I finally saw my mother coming down carrying an almost awake Benjamin in her arms.

"Benjamin, we're going to the castle, but we're going to run, and I need you to keep on running until we get there, no matter how tired you are, no matter how afraid you are, no matter what happens. Some bad people will be chasing us. Do you understand that?" I locked my eyes with his and he nodded.

"If I stop running, will they kill me?" his voice was small and his fear was breaking my heart.

"I will do everything I can to make sure they don't."

The sound of the footsteps and voices was coming closer. They could turn around the corner and rush at our door at any moment.

My mother and I exchanged looks knowing that our time just ran out.

"Quickly, use the window in the back and catch up with the others. They are running towards the castle. I'll be right behind you." This was our last chance to escape.

I could see the lynch mob in the glow of the flames they were carrying. I could now understand the words they were yelling.

"Kill the monsters! They killed our children! Now we kill them!" I was just climbing out of the window when Lilian's father broke down the door and saw me outside.

"Look! They're trying to escape! Grab them!" Gareth yelled.

I didn't see any of the others near me, and I hoped they reached a safe distance, but I didn't want to lead the mob towards them, so I stared at the mob that broke into the house.

I knew I shouldn't linger too long within the borders of the village, but I wanted to make sure my family is far enough.

I should flee as soon as possible to find shelter in the darkness and shadows, but the drumming of their feet, the flickering of their flames and their deafening accusations made it difficult for me to focus and decide which way to run.

"Let's kill the monsters!" Gareth raised his voice. His eyes focussed on me and a shiver rolled down my spine while the torch he held lit his face.

I took a few steps back while Gareth threw the torch behind and climbed outside the window. The rest of the mob left the house, and I assumed would be around the house in no time.

I saw the fire quickly spread through our living room. Everything we left behind would be nothing but ash in a couple of minutes. The table, the couch, the mattresses on the floor. And once the living room was devoured, the flames would take the rest of the house.

I held my breath, waiting for the mob to come closer, to throw more weapons. Maybe I would not be able to keep my promise to Nick to return to him, but I found comfort in the thought that I had saved the rest of my family.

"Emily…" My mother appeared next to me and made sure to brush my leg gently. "You have to leave. Now!" her words resonated in my mind, while I observed the mob shrink a little in fear at the sight of a big wolf.

I shook my head. "I'm the alpha now. I have to protect them."

"Yes, you are the leader now." My mother pushed herself in front of me. "And as a leader it's your task to survive and to lead them. It's my job as a mother to protect you."

I realised what she was doing. She was sacrificing herself for me, trying to save me before anyone saw me shifting.

"Mom…" my voice was barely a whisper.

"Run, Emily! Do your job and let me do mine."

She turned towards the mob. I heard her growling. I saw her lowering her head and getting ready for whatever battle was waiting for her. But I still hesitated.

"Run now, Emily, before they kill us both!" resonated in my mind, so I fought my instincts and ran.

I ran despite the sounds I heard behind me. I ran when the growls of my mother became howls. I ran when the howls of my mother became whimpers. I ran when the smoke in the air became thicker, when the most disgusting smell ever filled my nose. I ran as fast as I could to outrun the people in my human form.

They didn't care that the wolf they were killing was a mother. They didn't they care that the wolf they were killing was inhabited by a human soul. And they didn't they care that they had no proof that they were murdering a monster.

When I reached the edge of the woods, all I wanted to do was curl up and cry, but I shifted instead. I wanted to scream, and yell, and shout, but I couldn't do any of that before the rest of my family was safely inside the castle.

Without slowing down, I noticed a pair of eyes staring at me and I sighed relieved when I found a tiny wolf.

"Follow me and try to not leave too many trails." I made sure to keep my instruction as short as possible while I ran.

The footsteps behind me sounded further and further away, but it wouldn't be long before they reached the forest.

I decided to change direction. I followed my instincts while I took paths I never ran before. I used the moon as a guide to make sure I ran in the right direction and eventually, I found the path leading directly to the stables.

I looked over my shoulder a few times, even though the mob was too far behind by now.

"Are we almost there?" My eyes met Benjamin's.

Instead of howling the answer, I nodded my head slightly before I sped up.

I sensed how tired he was, and I just hoped he didn't see or hear what happened to our mother. I only heard her horrific end, and I would never forget the sounds.

Fortunately, I could already see the lights of the stables in the distance and a relieved sigh escaped me when I saw the two silhouettes carrying bundles of clothes.

Once I reached Nick, I turned into my human form.

All the hard work to make me pretty had been for

nothing. Dirt covered my hands and feet, and my hair was nothing but a mess with twigs and leaves.

Before I could say anything, Nick draped a comfortable cape around my shoulders. His hands trembled a little while he tied the ribbon on the front to cover my nakedness as quickly as possible.

"You have no idea how relieved I am that you made it back to me safely." He spoke softly and placed his hands on my shoulders. "Your uncles and sisters are inside. Where is your mother?"

A few tears rolled down my cheeks. "They killed my mother." My entire body shook. I could barely keep myself up. "They killed her." Nick carried me inside, while Philippe took care of Benjamin.

In a way, I still couldn't believe it. Once in a while, I looked over my shoulder, somehow hoping to see her running towards us. Of course she didn't come. She stayed, so we could get away.

"It could have been all of them. If I were moments later, it would have been all of them…" I could barely talk.

Now I was back at the castle, at a place where I hoped to be safe for at least a night, the energy left my body and all the emotions I tried to fight during my run to the village and back overwhelmed me.

"Benjamin was asleep…" I only told half of the story, but I couldn't find the words nor the courage to tell the full story, to describe the images that kept replaying in the back of my mind.

"But everyone else is here now, aren't they?" Nick wrapped his arms around me and whispered, knowing probably all too well that the wolves could hear us.

"I promise that we will look after them, that my guards will look after them and that anyone who tries to harm them, or you, will not live to tell the story." He tightened his grip a little and I buried my face in his neck while I tried to remind myself that I had to keep breathing.

"Nick and his brother will help us, Benjamin," I whispered. "They have food and clothes and warm beds for us to sleep in." I paused for a moment. "I know a lot has happened tonight. But we are safe here, I promise."

"The angry men won't find us here?" Benjamin looked at me, tears glistening in his eyes.

I couldn't promise him Gareth and the people from our village wouldn't find us here. Even if they didn't know where we hid, they would probably come to the castle to get help.

"I don't know, but if they find us here there are a lot of good men who will protect us."

Chapter Twenty-Eight

Telling my family that my mother was killed by the angry mob, was one of the worst things I ever had to do.

I would never forget the look on Uncle Calvin's face. He and his older sister will never fight again over something trivial, only to laugh about it later. Luckily, Uncle Aaron was there to comfort him.

Nora had taken the news even harder. She had screamed, and cried, and cursed. I wanted to comfort her, but the moment I tried to come close, she threw pillows at my head until I left her room.

Eventually, I also told Charlotte. She replied with silence, before she grabbed her sketchbook and started drawing. For a moment I just sat next to her, until she assured me that she was fine and that I should try to get some sleep too.

Lastly, I walked into Benjamin's room. Benjamin looked peaceful. His head rested on a comfortable pillow and the sheets.

I wished the world was a better place. I wished I could give him a life where he didn't need to be afraid, where he didn't need to hide, where he didn't need to run away in the middle of the night. I wished he still had a mother to take care of him.

He was no longer a baby we could coddle. We could no longer tell him that the world was a nice and safe place. He saw death now and would fear it for the rest of his life.

Nick waited for me when I left Benjamin's room.

"This is your room for the night." Nick opened the door next to Benjamin's, to a room as big as our entire house. Paintings covered the walls, and a huge, comfortable-looking bed waited for me.

A part of me wanted to fall down on the bed and sleep until all of this was over. Another part of me realised that, apart from my mother, my entire family was safe inside the palace.

All of a sudden, everything that happened in the last few of hours caught up with me. Discovering that Nick was a lone wolf. Running faster than the wind to my hometown to warn my family. The masses with the burning torches and terrible screaming. My mother.

Especially my mother. The way she stood there, bravely. The way she forced me to leave her. The way her howls became whimpers. I hoped we could go back at some point to recover her body, or what was left of it.

All of my energy was gone. I stood in the middle of the room, a couple of paces from the bed, and yet, I couldn't bring myself to move. I tried to focus on Nick's heartbeat, I tried to count my own breathing, but with every breath I heard my mother's whimpers again. I saw the mass with the torches again. And I remembered that I lost her tonight.

"Do you want to talk about it?" Nick spoke softly as he wrapped his arms around me. His head rested on my shoulder and for a moment, I closed my eyes while his warm breath touched my neck.

"Do you want to tell me what happened?" his voice was barely a whisper and his arms, crossed over my chest, wrapped me a little tighter to his warm body. "She must have been a hero."

I stopped breathing and needed a few seconds to let the last words sink in. "They killed her…" The moment the words escaped my lips every part of me broke down.

My heart shattered into a thousand little pieces. My knees trembled and my entire body shook, the weight on my shoulders and the pressure on my chest crushing me.

"And because of her, you and your family escaped the same fate." Nick rocked me in his arms, whispering soothing words into my ears. "All she wanted was to give you and your family a chance to live a long and happy life."

I could barely breathe. Moving my chest up and down was overwhelmingly painful and every time I filled my lungs with air, it was as if an invisible force wanted to prevent me from doing so. My heart hammered against my ribs and every muscle in my body tensed until I couldn't fight it any longer, until a scream escaped my lips and the tears rolled down my cheeks.

"I will send the guards to find her body as soon as possible." Nick turned me around so I could bury my face into his shirt. "So, you and your family can say goodbye to her." He rocked me back and forth and his hands rubbed my back in a calm and tender rhythm.

"I don't know if I want to see what they've done to her…" I shook my head and hoped that Nick wouldn't mind that my tears would ruin his beautiful clothes. "I want to remember her like the strong and powerful woman she was." I sniffed in between words and my shoulders shuddered while the wolf inside of me howled and cried for attention.

I couldn't give in to the wolf right now. I couldn't

allow the wolf to grieve and roam around freely. It would be far too risky to let my wolf roam outside with an angry mob on the hunt for blood. Escaping my human emotions by giving in to the animalistic longings of my wolf would only cause more problems I couldn't solve.

"I just want to lie down and sleep, but I don't know if I can bring myself to move without shifting." I didn't have energy to look up, but Nick understood, and in a silent answer, his arm slid under my knees while he lifted me and carry me to bed.

"It's okay to be sad and to grieve, Emily." Nick caressed my hair as he walked to the bed and lay me down. "And I will be there to help you, to remind you that your mother did what every mother does for her children. She protected you until her very last breath."

He curled up next to me and embraced me once more. His arms were like a warm, safe cocoon, and for a little while, it felt like nothing could harm me as long as he held me.

I didn't know how long I cried, just like I didn't know how long Nick held me, rocking me in his arms and saying all the sweet things he could think of.

At a certain moment, I had no tears left in my body and my sniffing faded. My breathing calmed down and the weight from my shoulders lifted slowly.

I opened my eyes to look at the paintings covering the walls and the ceiling. We were surrounded by trees, animals, waterfalls, and candles gave the entire room a special glow.

"It's beautiful..." I could barely talk, but I stretched out my hand as if I could touch the ceiling and the images above me, as if I had to prove to myself that the nature surrounding me wasn't real.

Nick smiled when he saw my glance wandering over the decorations. "I thought you might like this room." He tightened his grip around me and for a moment, and stayed silent for a while, allowing me to notice all the small details, before he turned to look at me.

"You are beautiful, even right now, even with red and swollen eyes, even with your cheeks covered in tears." The back of Nick's hand wandered over my face, over my neck and then he pressed his forehead to mine.

"I never lost someone I cared about, let alone the way you did, but I want you to know that I am so thankful and honoured that you are my alpha."

"I don't know if I'll be able to be much of an alpha for a while…" I whispered and took a few deep breaths while I discovered new animals, hidden between the leaves or behind the bushes.

"I promised not to die, but I nearly broke that promise today." I didn't know whether I wanted to sit up or lie like this forever. "I'm sorry."

"The only thing that matters is that you are here now." Nick closed his eyes and his nose brushed mine. "The only one in this room who needs to apologise is me." His lips lingered above mine for a moment. "I'm sorry. I know it won't bring your mother back, but I am truly sorry," he whispered, his breath warming my lips, his arms making me feel more at home more than I ever felt.

"I'm sorry my father and I let it come this far. I'm sorry we didn't notice things were not well in the villages. I'm sorry we never realised there were more wolves who needed our protection. I promise, will spend the rest of my life looking for ways to make it up to you."

"Nick..." I stretched out my hand and my palm wandered over his stubbled chin. "My mother wouldn't want you to feel guilty for the rest of your life." I swallowed and closed my eyes, too. "But she did want us to change the world. She gave her life for me and my family because she believed there was a way to make this world a better place." I pressed my lips to his and strangely enough, there was a certain comfort in his soft and tender kiss.

"Who knows how many other people like us are out there, hiding, terrified that someone will come after them, afraid to be proud of their nature."

"We will find them all and we will let them know that they are under the official protection of the crown." Nick whispered and his hands wandered over my shoulders and arms.

He kissed me again and again and again until we couldn't keep our eyes open any longer. I fell into a restless sleep, knowing there would be a lot to do tomorrow.

I had to comfort Benjamin. I had to be there for the rest of my family. I had to come up with a plan to deal with the masses still looking for more wolves to kill. I had to talk to the King about the villages and why none of his help and money reached the people who needed it most.

I wouldn't have to do all this alone, but I was still the alpha, no matter how broken and damaged I was.

Chapter Twenty-Nine

"Your majesty?" A firm knock on the door by one of the guards woke us the next morning. "Your father requests a meeting with you."

He didn't attempt to open the door, but there was urgency in his voice. "There has been an uprising in one of the villages and we've received messages that the inhabitants of Waterfield are heading towards the castle to speak to the King and Queen."

Despite my lack of sleep and the lightness in my head, I sat up in immediately and noticed I was still dressed in the clothes I wore last night.

"Why couldn't this night last forever..." I whispered and wished I had time to clean up and change clothes. "Everyone knows that you and I became quite close during the last few weeks." I hesitated and stared at him. "They must know that you have been the one providing us shelter."

"Emily..." Nick pushed himself up and leaned on his elbows. "The sun is barely up. I don't believe they dared to travel during the night. We still have time to come up with a plan."

"They want blood. They want to be certain that nothing like this will ever happen again. They want all the wolves they know about killed and they'll probably also ask for all the heads of future wolves on a silver platter." I buried my face in my hands. "They won't be satisfied with promises to find the actual murderer and having them face justice." I shook my head and took a few deep breaths. "Two of the children were killed and the rest have been poisoned by Gareth's lies."

"I won't allow anyone to harm you or your family. We will explain everything to my father and I'm certain he will help us come up with a solution to satisfy everyone." Nick crawled towards me and placed both hands on my shoulders.

I closed my eyes and tried not to play a thousand scenarios in the back of my mind. Not one of them ended with me and my family being allowed to live a calm and peaceful life. Not one of them ended with Nick and me side by side making this kingdom a better place. Not one of them ended with happiness.

I had to find a way to protect my family, to protect Nick, and all the other wolves in the kingdom. I just couldn't figure out how we could satisfy an angry irrational mob. I buried my hands in my hair and closed my eyes.

"Why do you act like you carry the weight of the entire world on your own?" My longing to have you by my side might be selfish, but I didn't plan on making it a one-way promise." He pressed soft kisses to my cheeks and my neck. "Your promise not to leave me alone also means that I promise not to leave you alone."

"Your Highness? Miss Rivers??"

Nick and I exchanged a glance before I hurried to wipe my tears away.

"The King is still waiting."

I waited until Nick got up and then we walked towards the door. "We're ready."

I could only hope to the kind would have a plan that would end with as few calamities as possible.

The king looked tired. He had dark circles under his eyes and his hair looked as if he didn't bother to brush it this morning. His clothes were just as wrinkled as ours. Maybe he hadn't even seen his bed last night.

When I stared at him, I realised how much Nick looked like him.

"Good morning, as you both know, we have a matter of urgency to discuss." If he noticed, he didn't mention our messy clothes or physical appearances.

"I don't think we can postpone the inevitable any longer. We need to discuss a plan before the people from the village arrive."

I folded my hands behind my back. "I'm the leader of my family, but only since recently, and I'm afraid that I don't possess the experience and knowledge my mother did." I stared at the marble floor beneath my feet. "I am not sure how I can contribute to the solution of this kind of problems yet. I'm sorry. I wish I could be of more help."

"Emily…" Nick whispered and wrapped an arm around me. His fingers combed my hair and for a moment he whispered hushing words in my ear until my heartbeat steadied.

"Do you think I never doubted myself?" The king stood up from his chair and placed his hands on his desk.

"But here I am. No crown prince is given much choice in the matter. When the time comes, we all have to accept our responsibilities. Much like yourself at this moment" He shook his head and smiled. "There is no rule book for us. All we can do is try to do our best for the people we are responsible for, as they are counting on us." He straightened his back.

"And it's best we start doing that immediately. We have no time for doubts and useless discussions."

"I don't know what to do right now, your

majesty…" I shook my head and my chest hurt. "I don't know how I can keep everyone I care about alive."

The silence was deafening and my eyes wandered through the king's study. His walls were also covered in paintings, but where my bedroom was decorated with animals, his study was covered in paintings of the king's predecessors. All of them were men. All of them shared features with the king and Nick. But they all looked serious and slightly intimidating.

"That is something we cannot decide until they arrive and state their grievances." the King interrupted my silence. "We don't know much yet." He sat down again. "But for now, we can strengthen our defences and be ready to protect the capital, should they decide to behave as they did last night."

We had an inkling of what their grievances might be. And I could only hope they would not behave as the crazed mob.

"And I have a few questions about the man that represents your village, the chief of Waterfield." He pointed at the open books on his desk.

"I've been reviewing the decrees and taxes with my advisors all night. We've been calculating and recalculating and it seems that large sums of taxes owed to the kingdom have gone missing."

I couldn't imagine how he felt right now. All this time, he was certain he took care of his people in the best possible way. And then it came to light that one of his appointed officials was misappropriating taxes and impoverishing the village he was in charge of.

"What if the people won't listen? What if they come as the same angry mob, we faced yesterday, and attack the capital?"

The king bent his head. I didn't know what was going through his mind, but I didn't like the way he avoided my glance.

"I understand that you and your family want to help, but for now, it might be better if you stayed out of sight. Perhaps, we might be able to reason with them if we can refocus on the living conditions in the village."

I shook my head. "But this is my responsibility, too. This is all happening because of me and my family."

"It is not," the king spoke softly. "You may be an alpha and, if I understand correctly, that makes you the leader of your pack, but I am the ruler of this kingdom. If the people in my kingdom are so discontent that they are willing to take matters into their own hands, it is solely my responsibility. And if they decide to cause an uprising, I'm afraid, I will be forced to respond in kind."

I swallowed.

"I know that we did not treat our son the way we should have," his voice cracked.

"I want him to become king and you to become his queen so that together, you can change this kingdom and leave it a far better place than you found it." He paused for a moment. "I want people like my son to grow up without having to hide, without having to be afraid."

I shared his dreams and yet, I feared we wouldn't see them come true. No one knew the extent of damage Gareth's hatred and lies have caused already.

And yet, I wanted to believe that the king would find a solution. I wanted to believe that the future he pictured, with Nick as his successor and me supporting him, would come true one day.

"What is the most common reason for wolves to lose control and become dangerous?"

The answer was not complicated, but would people accept it, was.

"A wolf will never cross a line his human is unwilling to cross." I thought about the murdered kids, and what kind of a person would do such a thing.

"However, to become one with the wolf, it's important to learn how to control it, and not to lose your human self."

The king furrowed his eyebrows. "So, what we need, is a place where young wolves can learn to control themselves, while they're also raised to be decent human beings."

I nodded.

"Done." The king slammed his hand on his armrest. "We will establish an academy for wolf children. A place where it is safe for them to learn and make mistakes away from society."

I tried to picture it. A building, much like the castle I visited now, with hidden nooks, paintings, and a huge library filled with books. A forest where the wolves could play and burry their paws in the mud and dirt. Trees to hide behind and holes to sleep in when being a wolf felt more comfortable than being a human.

I smiled. I didn't know if the promise to educate wolves would calm the mob, but it was a promise I appreciated.

"And once the wolves graduate, we will find them functions where their heightened senses and power are considered assets."

I wondered what Benjamin wanted to be if he could choose a future far brighter than any future he probably pictured so far. I imagined myself running around in wolf form, catching poachers, and thieves, and other criminals. I imagined myself showing the world that we were far from dangerous. Instead, we were excellent protectors and would keep this kingdom safe.

"We will also have to assure them that the person responsible for the killed children is found, captured, and judged."

Nick cleared his throat. He kept his hands folded behind his back, serious expression on his face, much like those I've seen in the paintings. He gave an impression of a king to be.

"That will be our priority, of course." The king nodded.

"But it's not something that will comfort the people now," I could barely hide the tremble in my voice.

What if we couldn't calm down the mob? What if things escalated and the Royal Guard was forced to use violence to prevent the uprising?

"Your majesty?"

We all looked up when a flustered man entered the throne room.

"The guards say the people have entered the gardens."

We were out of time. They were here and all I could hope for was for our plan to work.

"Make sure the Guard is armed and ready as instructed last night." The king stood up. "Emily, I assume you and your family want to know what is happening. Can I trust you and your family to stay out of sight or do I need to have the Guard accompany you to make sure you do? We don't want further

escalation.”
     As if that were even possible.

Chapter Thirty

I tried to focus on my breathing and the heartbeats of my family surrounding me.

"I don't know what will happen now, but I hope that this kingdom will be a safer place when I return." I was happy to know that my family would be inside, guarded by Nick's most trusted people.

"I'm scared…" My little brother's hand firmly held mine and he pressed his head to my side.

He trembled. He already lost his mother to these people. Of course, he was afraid of the rest of us getting hurt too.

I was mostly afraid of him getting hurt somehow. "It's okay, Benjamin." I whispered and fought my own nerves and fear.

Last night, I allowed myself to feel all the hurt and pain, but right now I had to be the leader. Until this was solved, until my family was safe, until all those angry people were far away from me, I had to be strong.

"Whatever happens, I, and those guards you see, will protect you." I didn't want to lie to him, didn't want to give him any false hope. I therefore couldn't promise him that he would be fine, and nothing would happen to him.

"I won't be far away. I promise." I nodded to uncle Clavin. Benjamin's hand let mine go as soon as his uncle's arms held him.

I left the room and watched a guard close the door.

"The balcony is this way, miss." The guard walked

away and I followed him.

With every step the heartbeats of my family sounded fainter and fainter. The yelling and the cursing from the mob outside became louder and louder.

As promised, I stayed out of sight. But even though the crowd couldn't see me, I could hear and see them.

I tried to find familiar faces, but apart from Gareth and Lilian, it was difficult to recognise anyone else. There were so many people in front of the palace. And it seemed not only from Waterfield, but also from elsewhere.

The marble balcony trembled with the stomping. The people carried torches and improvised weapons. Their clothes were covered in mud and dirt as if they marched all night. Mostly they were men, with few women among them.

The royal guard was positioned in front of the palace with their weapons raised, blocking the angry mob from coming closer. There were so many more of them than I had imagined. I could only hope there wouldn't be reason for them to act. A lot of the villagers would probably not survive that.

The people seemed to understand that. They slowed gradually before they came to a stop and their yelling became quieted somewhat.

"Citizens of my kingdom," the king's voice thundered over the crowd and the last of the screams of the crowd died down.

"What is the meaning of this? How dare you come to the palace armed? What is so important that you are willing to risk your lives? I want one of you to step forward and speak, now!"

Even I shuddered, but Gareth took a step forward. Two strong men protected his sides. Lilian wasn't too far behind him, holding a torch and still wearing the dress she wore to the royal ball the previous night.

I also recognised a few of the young women who competed for the invitation to the ball and some I worked with in the past. They all frowned and the flames of the torches reflected in their eyes. I could hear their hearts beat faster and faster and I almost wanted to cover my ears to soften the cacophony overwhelming me.

"We're here for the wolves. Wolves killed our children and that needs to end now!" Gareth spoke firmly and the crowd yelled in agreement.

Nick stood next to his father and once in a while, he glanced my way as if he wanted to be sure I was still there.

"I heard the disturbing stories about the fates of your children. Why haven't you come here sooner instead of taking matters in your own hands?" The King didn't hesitate.

"I mentioned the wolves to you before." Gareth shook his head and shrugged. "Nothing was done, so we're solving the issue ourselves. We know they are hiding in the palace, and we want them brought before us for judgement."

The crowd behind him cheered.

"Is that so? You all decided to threaten the crown? Instead of respecting the laws and seeking justice according to those? How many of you are willing to lay down your lives for this? My guards are ready to oblige," the king spoke with determination and the crowd started murmuring.

"And you, chief of Waterfield, will address the crown as it is appropriate."

"Your highness..." Gareth spoke slowly as if he

suddenly understood that he doesn't have the upper hand. "The laws are made for humans. Not for monsters. Those wolves are wild and dangerous animals and they should be hunted and killed. It is only a matter of time before they kill again." The crowd murmured in agreement.

"It is not your place to decide who does or does not deserve to live. You have already taken matters in your hands last night and some of you will be punished for it," the king spoke with such authority that it awakened hope inside me. Hope for better future.

"The wolves are as much a part of this kingdom as the rest of you, and I will not tolerate any persecutions unsanctioned by the court." The King straightened his back. "I will personally make sure they are protected, taught and given opportunity to run free. They will be a part of a special guard of the kingdom."

The silence was deafening.

"I will not tolerate wolf hunting, and the culprits will be brought to justice. They are our allies not our enemies.

The silence persisted. it seemed as though everyone needed some time to understand what the king implied.

"Our children were murdered by a wolf and you want them to be a part of our society?" Gareth shook his head in disbelief and the crowd yelled in disagreement.

"And your children are still in danger because your mob killed the wrong wolf last night. Not to mention, I've been receiving reports recently that your children are dying in the fields working. Why is no one coming forth with that? Is that something that you all accepted?" the king changed the focus and the murmurs of the crowd became louder.

"Gareth Tiller, you are accused of deceiving the crown, stealing from the kingdom, exploiting the villagers of Waterfield and causing the death of multiple children and adults."

The silence after that statement was deafening.

"What?" Lilian shrieked, but after one look from her father she clamped her mouth shut.

"Me?" Gareth pointed at himself.

"I would never hurt the people of Waterfield." He straightened his back.

"Arrest him." The king nodded at his guards and a few of them stepped forward.

Within a few steps they reached him.

"Drop your weapons."

Gareth shook his head. "I did nothing wrong!"

His eyes searched for someone to help him, but everyone around him had worked on those fields. They knew children died. If the king really didn't know about them, they all knew who was truly to blame.

"Drop your weapons!" the guard yelled louder and Gareth finally dropped his axe.

Two other guards grabbed Gareth's arms and pulled him in front of the king.

On his knees, he looked less confident and less intimidating.

"Gareth Tiller," the king didn't just address Gareth, but the entire crowd, too. "Answer these questions honestly or stay silent."

"No! Father!" Lilian found her voice again, but a guard grabbed her around the waist before she could come any closer.

Attracting attention was probably the worst thing she could do for her father. Everyone now looked at her. Everyone saw how healthy she looked, how unblemished her skin was. Everyone remembered how her dresses always looked prettier than theirs.

"Did children, and adults, die in your fields?" The king ignored Lilian's interruption.

Gareth shook his head. "Yes, but that wasn't..." He couldn't finish his sentence.

My hatred increased, but I was terrified of what would come next.

"Did you report those deaths to me?"

Gareth bent his head. "No."

The crowd gasped.

After every death Gareth had assured them that the king would hear of it, that he would beg the king to lower his demands. We all thought the king didn't care.

We were all wrong. The king did care. Gareth didn't.

"Gareth Tiller," the king continued and the crowd quieted once more.

"Did you withhold goods that were meant for the crown?"

Gareth shook his head. "There simply wasn't enough, your highness."

The king straightened his back and looked at the crowd.

"Did you report to me that Waterfield has issues fulfilling its quota?" Gareth bent his head once more. "No, your highness."

Murmuring of the crowd became louder.

It shouldn't have come as a surprise anymore and yet it was clear that the villagers only started to realise how deep Gareth's betrayal went.

"A few last questions."

I held my breath. Listening to the crowd, I realised

that I wasn't the only one.

"Are there families in Waterfield dying from hunger?"

Gareth lost his balance.

We all knew the answer.

"Yes, your highness."

"Did you report those deaths to me?"

"No."

I exhaled.

"Gareth Tiller. I hereby declare you guilty of deceiving the crown, neglecting your duties as the chief of Waterfield, and causing the deaths of multiple children and adults."

Gareth struggled against the guards to get on his feet. "This can't be happening! You can't do this! Children were killed! You were supposed to listen to us and kill those wolves!" He gestured to the palace.

Luckily, my family was safely inside and didn't have to hear this.

"Do you have more crimes to confess, Gareth?" The king raised his eyebrows.

"No, of course not..." Gareth's voice trembled. "A wolf killed those children." His heartbeat gave him away, but although I could hear that, and maybe Nick could too, the king couldn't use that as proof.

Gareth killed those children. In his blind hatred for us, for wolves, he was prepared to do anything, even killing children. He accused us, wolves, of being monsters. Meanwhile he was the true monster.

"It looked like a wolf killed them." Gareth tried to pull himself together. "The wolves are dangerous."

The king gestured for Nick to step forward. Although I had assured Nick that he couldn't have been the murderer, his relief was clearly visible. He really didn't do it. Gareth had. "Crown prince Nicholas, my son and your future king, is one of those wolves." The king looked proud.

"He has been the one telling me about the poverty in Waterfield. He heard about the children dying in the burning sun, from being overworked, from lack of food. He is the one begging me to do something about it."

I nodded at Nick encouragingly. We knew that sooner or later, his people would learn that he was a wolf, like me and my family, like probably others in the kingdom.

"My son is a good person and always has been." The king let his glance wander over the crowd.

"Does he deserve to die simply because he can turn into a wolf?"

People started whispering and exchanging glances.

"Has anyone ever seen a wolf kill a person?" The king challenged anyone to come forward, but no one did.

"We won't accuse people of crimes because of what they are." He looked at his son. "We judge people based on their actions. My son will make a great king one day. With the help of his wolf and his pack."

Gareth stared at the king and the crown prince. His jaw dropped and he tried to stand up, but the guards pushed him down. "You can't prove anything."

"What have the wolves ever done to you, Gareth Tiller?"

Gareth didn't say anything.

"Why do you hate the wolves so much, Gareth Tiller?"

Once more he kept silent.

"We should ask his daughter." Nick looked at

Lilian, still held by two guards.

Tears streamed down her face. Was she crying because of the punishment waiting for her father? Or was she crying because she would lose her position and luxuries?

"Lilian Tiller." The king waited until the guards forced Lilian to kneel next to her father.

"Did you know children were dying on your father's fields?"

Lilian cried even harder. Of course she knew. Everyone knew.

"Yes." Her voice sounded small and breakable.

"Did you know children were dying of hunger in Waterfield?"

"Yes." She sniffed. Her entire body trembled and instead of keeping her down, the guards had to keep her up.

"Did you know your father murdered children so he could blame the wolves and get them killed?"

"Yes."

I blinked and stared at Nick. He gave me a small nod.

She confessed in front of many witnesses.

Lilian seemed to realise what she just did. "No! I mean no!" Her eyes widened and she looked at her father.

But the damage was already done. She confessed. Her own sins and his.

The crowd, angry and willing to face the guards not that long ago, stared at the two of them. Gareth has been telling them that the wolves and the king were to blame for everything.

Now everyone knew, he was the only one to blame. It was, however, not up to them to pass judgement. It was up to the king.

"Gareth and Lilian Tiller," the king cleared his throat. "For your crimes, you will both be sentenced to death. Because of the seriousness of your crimes, your punishment will be carried out immediately."

Guards stepped forward to bind their hands behind their back. Other guards stepped forward with chopping blocks. I was glad Benjamin was inside. No matter how much these two hurt the villagers, he didn't have to see the punishment being carried out.

"Any last words?" The king looked at Lilian and her father.

"A wolf becoming king will be the end of this kingdom, mark my words." Gareth hissed. "One day you will all think of me and wished I had succeeded."

He laid his head on the chopping block.

I didn't know what the future would bring. Gareth was wrong, though. Nick becoming the king of this kingdom would be the best thing that ever happened to it.

"Father!" Lilian sniffed.

"I'm sorry. I'm so sorry. Please, forgive me." Lilian refused to follow her father's example, but a guard pushed her down.

She shouldn't have begged him for forgiveness. She should have begged us.

A few seconds later two swords came down and their heads were of. Although it was a far from a pretty sight, I was relieved. Not only because Gareth was gone, but also because everyone knew that the wolves were not to blame for the deaths of the children.

With those two gone and the king's promises for better governance, maybe wolves and humans could live together peacefully now.

The king let the silence linger for a moment, before he spoke once more, "One more murder needs to be addressed today.

I felt tears welling in my eyes. My mother's.

"Yesterday, a wolf was brutally killed. There was no trial. There was no judgement. There was only execution." The king paused.

Although Lilian and Gareth died only minutes ago, they had a public trial. An even fairer trial than they deserved.

"If those involved in her murder step forward now, they will not be sentenced to death. If no one confesses, I will start an investigation and will be less lenient."

For a moment, nothing happened and then, six men dropped their weapons and stepped forward with their arms raised.

"You all confess to the murder of Maria Rivers, incited by Gareth Tiller?"

All six men nodded their heads.

"I sentence you all to prison for one year. After that, you will serve the crown for five more years in whatever way we see fit."

I could cry because the king kept his promises. Cry because those who had killed my mother would not just walk away and continue their lives as if nothing happened.

I was a leader now, though. I allowed myself only a few tears and then I straightened my back and did what my mother did, presented a strong and confident leader.

Nick had just been announced as a wolf to a crowd of people taught to hate us. This time, I wanted to be the one comforting him.

"Citizens of this kingdom," the king addressed the

crowd again.

"Hatred and greed have never led to a better world and future. Hatred and greed made Gareth blind for the needs of Waterfield and even led him to murder innocent children. Hatred led to the loss of an innocent wolf, who left a child behind."

I smiled and Nick smiled at me.

"We will welcome those with kind hearts, whether human or wolf."
I'm sure the wolves will do awesome things for our kingdom if we let them."

We would no longer have to hide. We could use our speed and strength.

"If we let them, they can help our farmers plough their fields. They can carry sick children to a doctor. They can chase thieves and other criminals. They can rescue our loved ones from dire situations like a fire. Maybe they can even make the difference in our army if we trust them to fight for us."

More and more weapons were dropped and the guards stepped back, looking a little less threatening.

"Go home. I will send my son Philippe and a contingent of guards to Waterfield to put things in order until a new representative can be designated. Together, we will build a fairer and more beautiful future for our kingdom. For the humans and the wolves."

Chapter Thirty-One

The moment Philippe and his guards left, and the gardens surrounding the palace were calm and empty again, I returned to my family.

We knew that things wouldn't change overnight. Changes never happened overnight. And yet, it was the first time we dared to believe in a better future. For us, for the people in Waterfield, for the people in the other villages, and for everyone else in the kingdom.

I hoped that in the upcoming weeks, months, and years, more and more wolves would feel comfortable to come forward. I hoped that the king revealing that the crown prince was a wolf, would gain some trust.

I would do everything I could to find other wolves, too. I wanted the school, the king had talked about, to work. Not only for wolves, but also for humans.

Children needed a safe place. A place where they could learn and play. Not a place where they had to assume adult responsibilities and work adult jobs.

Luckily, Cookie, the famous cook in charge of the palace kitchen, had taken Benjamin under her wings. She heard how many dishes he never even heard about and was determined to rectify that immediately. It wouldn't take away the pain, but it would hopefully distract him for the rest of the afternoon.

Nora and Charlotte tried to distract themselves. Nora by getting lost in the royal library, searching for romance novels, and Charlotte made herself comfortable in a broad windowsill with a sketchbook.

I let them be. I knew it was their way of dealing with emotions.

Just like Uncle Calvin dealt with his emotions in the typically Rivers' way. As soon as the king appeared, he started talking about all the ideas he had for the school. Along with Uncle Aaron, he disappeared into the king's study and were only disturbed by maids bringing in lunch and tea.

"What do you need right now?" Nick wrapped his arms around me while I stared at the forest behind the palace.

"What I always needed and wanted." I placed my hand on his.

"Want to come with me to let our wolves free for a while?"

Nick kissed my cheek as an answer.

Less than half an hour later we were outside running through the woods.

Around me, small animals tried to get away from me and hide in holes and bushes, afraid I would see them as my next meal. After everything that happened here in the woods, I couldn't blame them for being afraid of me.

I couldn't blame them for being afraid of my extraordinary speed and strength, my long fangs and sharp claws, and the astute human mind that was in control.

"You have a lot of experience dealing with heavy days like this one." Nick's wolf was, at times, a little disoriented when trying to follow me, but he was determined to keep up.

"Well, I believe that I made a mistake of underestimating the challenges you faced." I slowed down and waited for him to catch up.

Even though we were running through the land surrounding the palace, I saw nothing but grass and trees for as far as I could look. In a way it was comforting to know that no one was near, that no one could see us, that no one could harm us. In a way it also felt kind of lonely.

In Waterfield there was always a light burning, there was always a drunkard stumbling home from the tavern, there was always a couple sneaking away to steal a few kisses.

Here, nothing reminded us of the chaos of the day, of the trial, of my mother's murder. The grass was waving calmly in the autumn breeze. The trees were dancing to the rhythm of the wind. As if nothing changed and as if the price we paid for the change weren't too high.

"And I might have underestimated yours." He ran next to me. He was a little out of breath, so I decided to stop running and sit down. He sat down next to me.

"It's easy to judge someone you don't know." I stared at the wolf, the prince who was no longer a stranger.

"It's easy to think that you know what their life looks like." I took a deep breath and even though I was the strongest wolf in my entire family, I was young and inexperienced. "It's easy to believe that they are not carrying any weight on their shoulders."

During the short moment of silence, Nick placed his head on his paws.

"My mother fainted the first time I turned into a wolf." He closed his eyes as if he relived the memory. "Her scream didn't just physically hurt me, it also broke my heart in a thousand pieces." He took a deep breath.

"I know that my mother loves me unconditionally, but ever since she met my wolf, I sensed that she was afraid of me, afraid of what might happen."

"And you thought that if you never turned again, her fear would fade, and she would forget that the wolf inside you existed." I lay down next to him.

"You didn't know that by doing so, you were denying a part of yourself to exist." I stared at the wolf next to me. He was beautiful. In time, his wolf would be as magnificent and royal as Nick himself.

"I didn't know anything and, despite everything you've told me already, I think I still don't know anything." He looked at me and his nose touched mine.

"You probably know more than you think you do." I opened my mouth and playfully snapped at him.

"You probably noticed that you could hear conversations no one else can hear." I remembered how Gareth's heartbeat had given him away.

"And I assume you're wearing that strong perfume of yours to mask the smells of the world around you." I sniffed while he nodded.

"And even though you're probably used to it, you noticed that, no matter how expensive and wonderful the fabric is, clothes and sheets never seem to be as comfortable on your skin."

"I thought that was simply a weird trait I had." Nick jumped up again and I followed.

"I'm sorry I made you wear those dresses with corsets." Nick bent his head and almost kneeled down in front of me.

"How can I not forgive you? You have been wearing those stiff uniforms your entire life. I feel sorry for you."

Nick looked up again and after one small nod, I

started running again.

"You know that our troubles will never be truly over, don't you?" I looked over my shoulder while I ran towards the palace.

"You know that, once in a while, there will be people thinking that we are monsters and shouldn't be allowed to exist, let alone rule?" I watched Nick following me. He was learning fast.

"Maybe one day, they might even try to dethrone you or your children or grandchildren, simply because we are what we are." I stopped at the stables.

I changed into my human form and commanded Nick to do the same. It would take a while before he was able to change on his own. It didn't matter. I liked him as a human and I liked him as a wolf.

I would never leave him again.

I wrapped my arms around him. Now I knew that Nick felt pleasantly warm because he was a wolf like me, I felt the constant need to touch him.

"I am a proud member of your pack now." Nick leaned down and pressed his lips to mine.

"And if that means that we will have to show the world time and time again that we are good, I will happily do so."

We let each other go and dressed ourselves. The times the staff of this palace had to rush towards their crown prince with clothes was over.

"I have you now." Nick offered me his arm and I laid my hand in the crook of his elbow.

"And as long as we're together, we will be able to deal with whatever comes our way."

Chapter Thirty-Two

Not that long ago, I was afraid there wouldn't be a future for me and my family. Now I knew there was.

Philippe said that the people in Waterfield were doing better already after a few days of him and his guards looking after them.

There were a few promising candidates to become Waterfield's next representative. But this time, the crown would keep a closer eye on them and every other representative.

My sisters started talking about returning to Waterfield. Nora mostly because she already missed the carpenter's son. Charlotte because she felt a palace was too big for her.

But first, we wanted to give my mother the goodbye she deserved.

"Are you sure you want me to be there with you?" Nick placed a hand on my shoulder and his eyes met mine through the mirror. "If you want this to be a private affair with you and your family, I understand." His simple white shirt barely hid his well-trained torso, moving up and down while protecting his rapidly beating heart.

"I don't just want you to be there."

I wore a simple white dress that didn't even reach my knees. The straps on my shoulders have already irritated my skin a little, but I wouldn't have to wear the dress for long anyway.

"I need you to be there." I took a few deep breaths

and brushed my loose hair one last time. "I'm not sure if you noticed, but I can be quite selfish at times, too." I curled my lips into a slight smile and Nick buried his face in my neck, leaving a trace of small and tender kisses from my jaw to my collarbone.

Nick looked up again and slowly I turned around so my dark eyes could drown into his blue ones. "Not all of us can be selfless heroes and I will even admit that I am somehow relieved you have not inherited all your mother's personality traits." He tucked a strand of hair behind my ear and then the palm of his hand rested on my cheek.

"I hope you will never feel the need to sacrifice yourself for the safety and happiness of the rest of your pack and family."

I bent my head and lifted my hand to touch his neck. "My father would have liked you." I spoke softly and then looked up again so my glance could meet his once more. "You are everything he imagined his son in law to be. You are everything he imagined the crown prince one day to be."

"Did he ever imagine that his son in law and the crown prince would be the same person, and a wolf shifter too?" Nick leaned towards me, his eyes half closed, and his lips slightly parted.

"Maybe you are even better than anything he could have imagined." I leaned on the tips of my toes so I could press a soft kiss on his lips.

"I think we should go. The rest of my family probably already awaits us." I stepped back and a sigh escaped my lips.

During the last couple of days, more and more memories came back. I remembered the pile of dirt, covering the body of the man I loved so much. I remembered my mother's kind words and most of all, I remembered how she didn't cry, how her voice didn't tremble, how she straightened her back and lifted her chin even though she just lost the love of her life in a cruel and unfair way.

Nick linked his arm with mine, like he did so often before. "I'm sure they're together now, watching over you and they are probably incredibly proud of you." He nodded when the servant in front of the door opened it.

My family already waited for us in the hallway, all dressed in spotless white simple garments. Benjamin held the hands of my uncles.

He was crying often, at random moments. Especially now that he realised what truly happened to our mother and what could have happened to all of us. He would need time and even then, I doubted if the wounds would fully heal.

Benjamin already grew up without a father and he was far too young to lose his mother, too. Life was never fair to him, but I hoped that Gareth's trial was not in vain and that his freedom started now.

No one disturbed us while we walked through the castle in absolute silence, holding onto each other, our heads bent, our eyes staring at our bare feet sinking into the blood-red tapestry.

No one giggled while we crossed the gigantic field between the palace and the stables, not even when the grass tickled our toes. No one complained about the overwhelming smell and the almost deafening neighing of the horses when we walked to the edge of the woods.

My mom once told me that she wanted to be buried next to my father, but my father was buried in the woods surrounding Waterfield. I couldn't be sure that it was safe to leave her remains there.

But that also felt too far away from the castle, from where I would live for the rest of my life. Maybe it was selfish, but it felt right to bury her in the woods surrounding the castle, in a spot I could see from my bedroom window.

We held still next to the pile of dirt, barely reaching my ankles. Nick positioned himself next to me, so his side could touch mine, while the others made sure to surround the grave.

In a couple of years, there wouldn't be anything left of her, apart from her bones. In a couple of years, no one would notice anymore that her body was so badly damaged.

"Not only did my mother guide us through the hardest period of our lives…" I took a deep breath and cleared my throat, but my voice wasn't as steady as my mother's had been during my father's wake.

"She has also given her life to protect us and to give us a chance to fight for our future." I took a deep breath. "We are here to honour her courage and thank her for everything she gave us, in her life and by her death."

There was a short moment of silence. Benjamin sniffed while the tears rolled down his cheeks and uncle Aaron placed a hand on his shoulder, trying everything he could to comfort the boy, even though there was nothing that could fill the hole in his heart, even though there was nothing that could heal his wounds.

"We are born of dust and to dust we shall return." My hands trembled while I lifted my dress, moving it over my head and dropping it in the dirt behind me. I kneeled down and buried my hands in the ground before I allowed the wolf inside of me to break free.

A loud howl escaped and soon, my mother's grave was not just surrounded by her family anymore, but her pack as well. I howled once more and turned my head to the side when a wolf with bright blue eyes pressed his body against mine, not planning on stepping aside until we returned to our human forms.

One ray of sunshine managed to break through the leaves shielding us from its burning heat.

I curled my lips into a smile and once more, I howled, cried at the universe that brought us everything we longed for, but also asked the highest price for it.

Then I kept silent, giving my family the time to mourn my mother in their own way, with their own howls, with their own cries, with all those words that meant anything and everything at once.

Benjamin's howls and cries cut me to the bone. He wasn't even born yet when we buried my father, so for him, this was the first time losing a parent, losing someone so close to him. He was far too young.

"Maria Rivers was the leader we needed and loved." I paused for a moment and shifted my weight a little. "Maria Rivers kept us safe for many years. Now it's my turn to follow in her footsteps. It's my turn to keep you all safe and it's my turn to keep any other wolf in the kingdom safe." I bent my head and howled once more. "May we carry her love in our human hearts and may we carry her spirit in the souls of our wolves." I closed my eyes and when I opened them again, my paws were once again feet and hands.

One by one, each member of my family stood up to put their clothes on in absolute silence. One by one, they turned around and walked away. Benjamin stayed close to my uncles, while Nora and Charlotte tried to comfort each other.

I stayed at the grave. I wasn't ready to leave yet and the wolf next to me, unable to return to his human self without my help, curled up to my side. My head rested on his and I took a deep breath.

"My mother would have enjoyed being a grandmother. One day I will tell her all about the kingdom my children could grow up in. Because of her. Because she sacrificed herself to save my life."

Nick licked my face.

"I hope they will never know a life without the freedom I so desperately wanted and fought for."

Epilogue

"Do you think your father is still happy with his grandchildren?" I stared at the royal garden, or what was left of it, and shook my head in disbelief.

"I already feel sorry for the teachers and matrons having to deal with them at the academy in a few years. I wonder if they are really not capable of controlling themselves or if they are simply using it as an excuse to destroy everything they please." I curled my lips up into a slight smile and cocked my head when I noticed two little wolves hiding behind one of the bushes they didn't ruin, well aware that I saw what they've done.

"Concerning the fact that both you and I never did anything like this, I am inclined to say the latter." Nick's head rested on my shoulder while he carefully draped his arms around me.

I allowed a small giggle to escape my lips and with renewed courage the little wolves crossed the gigantic grass field before they turned back into their human little selves.

"I want them to enjoy their freedom for as long as it lasts and as long as they stick to destroying the gardens, I am willing to accept the consequences."

"Their freedom will last forever, Emily." Nick spoke softly as he rocked me in his arms.

"Everyone in the kingdom now knows that there are no guards more loyal than those with the wolf genes." He tightened his grip around me a little and he gently kissed my neck. "And everyone knows that there are no better protectors than wolves with the capacity to think like humans.”

“Are you angry, mom?” Maria looked at me with her bright blue eyes wide open and her thumb in her mouth.

She looked so innocent, but her looks would only fool those who never met me. She not only inherited my black hair, but also my stubbornness.

“I promise it wasn’t on purpose!” she raised her voice, as if she were trying hard to convince us. “Nicky and I were playing, and we forgot that we weren’t humans but wolves!”

I raised my eyebrows and tried my very best to not let the amusement show on my face. “You simply forgot that you were wolves?” I repeated, knowing very well that Maria was aware how unlikely that sounded.

“You didn’t notice you were running around on four paws instead of on two feet?” I raised my eyebrows and made sure that my lips formed a straight line instead of the smile threatening to show on my face. “Just like you didn’t notice that your conversations sounded like howls instead of words?”

The seven-year-old nodded her head firmly, as if she was truly convinced that she would be able to make me believe what she was telling me.

“I may be your mother, Maria, but that doesn’t mean I’m a fool.” I curled my lips up into a smile and stared at her and her younger brother standing next to her.

Nicky learned quite early that if he kept quiet when he did something he was not allowed to do, Maria would not only come up with a story, but would also take the blame.

"We will discuss your punishment later. I think the two of you first need a bath, because I don't believe that your grandparents like to welcome you at their dinner table like this." I freed myself from Nick's embrace and placed a firm hand on their necks to guide them towards the door.

"They simply don't know what it's like to be a wolf," Maria protested, almost making me push her to move her forward.

She grew stronger each day, just like she increased her attempts to test my limits with each year she grew older. One day, she would be the leader of the family, the alpha of our pack, but I hoped that the day wouldn't come before she understood the consequences and was ready to carry the responsibility.

I wanted her to be a child for as long as possible. I wanted her to be my little girl for as long as possible. And I wanted her to be the little know-it-all I loved from the moment I felt her growing inside of me.

I bit my lip to prevent myself from laughing and instead took a deep breath. "There are quite some things in their lives you don't understand either, young lady." I guided them through the hallways, but not one of the servants stared at the little beasts covered in dirt from head to toe.

They got used to the sight over the last few years. And they probably didn't forget how Nick and I looked after our so-called lessons in the woods either.

"Shall I take care of the little ones from here, your royal highness?" Without allowing me to answer the question, the young maid grabbed the hands of my children and waited until the other servant opened the door to the bathroom.

"And how did you two end up so dirty this time?"

She fully concentrated on my little prince and princess, and I shook my head while hearing Maria repeating the same excuses, she tried to serve me.

None of the servants ever believed her stories, of course, but somehow, they couldn't bring themselves to tell her that. One look in the bright blue eyes she inherited from her father was enough to make everyone forget why they were angry with her in the first place.

"I don't think he will ever admit it, but I believe my father forgives them everything just because they are so adorable, and they know it," Nick leaned against the doorframe and spoke my thoughts out loud.

His dark brown curls covered his eyes slightly and he had his lips curled up into a playful smile. "They could even destroy the throne room, and he wouldn't be angry with them."

"I can assure you, that as soon as they break things inside the castle, I will be the one getting angry." I raised my eyebrows and curled my arms around his neck.

Even after all these years, I could still drown in his eyes, in those beautiful blue eyes always staring at me as if I was the most precious treasure in the entire palace. "Even freedom does have its limits."

"I'm certain they are both unaware of that, yet." Nick kissed me and his hands rubbed my back. "One day, we will tell them about your mother, about your life in the village, and about my life here in the castle," Nick spoke softly. "One day, we will tell them what price we paid for their freedom and the price your mother paid so that they could play freely, without being afraid that someone might harm them. That without your mother, we wouldn't have our own little family."

My nose brushed his and I curled my lips up into a bright smile. "There is something I need to tell you." I stepped back and grabbed his hand to place it on my stomach.

"I don't think our family is complete, yet. I hope you'd like to expand our little pack?" The lights flickered in my eyes, and I giggled when he stared at his hand, only a few inches away from his third child.

It was too early to hear the heartbeat yet, but he would certainly be the one to pick up our little one's first sounds with his sharp ears.

"You know very well that I welcome each and every little one of our wolves into this world with all the love in my heart." He pressed his lips to mine.

"I can't wait to tell your father that there will be another little destroyer coming soon," I murmured before I closed my eyes and pressed my body as closely to his as humanly possible.

"Maybe we should promise him that we will teach this one some manners," Nick said as he held me tighter.

"Let's not make promises we can't keep."

Acknowledgements

This is it! This is my official debut novel! I've been writing all my life, but there's a difference between writing to entertain yourself, and your friends, and publishing a book.

Firstly, I really want to thank the entire team of Butterdragons Publishing. I wrote a story, but it's thanks to you that it became a real book. Thank you so much for believing in me and my stories.

I also really want to thank my two writing buddies.
Inês, you were the first one to assure me that this story was worth it. You didn't even like romances and yet you cheered for Emily and Nick. Thank you for always being there for me.
Sharon, sometimes we end up chatting more than writing during our writing nights, but there is no one better to brainstorm with. Quite a lot of rewrites for this story have been done while Skyping with you and it did make the story, and all my future stories, better. I can't wait to see one of your books being published too!

Quite a few years ago, I promised the girls of the RHFF that I would thank them if I ever published a book. You were the very first ones actually reading my writing AND telling me to write more. You made me believe that I could truly be a published author one day. Without your encouragement, there wouldn't be a book today.

I want to thank all the authors I met during the last couple of years. Jen Minkman, your workshops made me look at my writing in a different way and made my stories a lot more lifelike. Leigh Bardugo, when I started my first NaNoWriMo you gave me the best writing advice ever: FINISH THAT FIRST DRAFT! Victoria Larque, you inspired me to finally take the leap to become an author and your stories will always be among my favourites.

I also want to thank my close friends, especially Marjolein and Bjintse, and family, especially my mom, dad and brother Erik. I've had a rough couple of years but look at me now! I could do this, because you were always there to support me. Your love is truly unconditional, and you allow me to be me, with all my quirks, with my huge collection of books, with all those story ideas floating through my head. Thank you so much for always being there for me and for making even me believe in me.

And I want to thank you, dear Reader. You gave this debut author a chance and I will be forever thankful for that. I hope you enjoyed this story as much as I enjoyed writing it!

About Annette van Geloof

Annette van Geloof writes romantic fantasy because she deeply believes that everyone deserves a happy ending and a little bit of magic in their life. Even though no life is without challenges and hurdles to overcome, she finds a way to put smiles on her readers' faces.

Annette was born in a beautiful, picturesque town in the Netherlands, but like so many of her peers, she left her hometown to pursue her education to become a music therapist, which she succeeded. However, life had other plans, and she pursued a career in a financial world instead. Nevertheless, books remain her biggest love and every spare moment she has, she reads or writes her own stories. Unless she is exploring the world on her bicycle, that is – she is Dutch after all.

Other BDP books by Annette van Geloof

Guardian Angel